檸檬樹出版

檸檬樹出版

實用英語
會話大全
— mini book —

靈活運用英語必備的 4,500 句會話

王琪 編著

檸檬樹

作者序

本書為 2005~2008 年間暢銷書《生活會話萬用手冊》增修版，經典重現，絕對值得擁有！

學習任何一種語言，最有成就感的，莫過於能夠開口和外國人交談或溝通。所以，一旦具備基本的單字、文法、句型能力，大家最迫切想要加強的，應該是「會話能力」吧。

不過，「學習」是一回事，「活用」是另一回事。碰上真正需要說英文的時候，你的腦中可有話題線索？心中可有敢開口的膽識？

回想一下你曾經接觸的英語會話課程，應該都是老師問一個問題，學生回答相對應的答案；並反覆不斷地進行「一問、一答；一問、一答」的練習。但是，生活中的真實對話，通常不會如此制式與僵化。

在真實的對話中，自己可能是「主動發言、發問的人」，也可能是「被動接話、反問的人」。而且，在第一次的「一問、一答」之後，接下來的，可能是更多的「一問、一答」，或是「回應、再回應、反問、…」等等。對話過程總是豐富多元，並充滿互動性，這才是最自然而真實的會話實境。

因此我認為，想要確實提升英語對話能力，除了最基本的——能夠正確運用單字、句型，最重要的，則是擁有「開啟話題、延續話題」的能力。

在本書中，我特別安排「左頁‧右頁」互相對應，宛如模擬對話過程中，不同的角色扮演。

安排同一個主題，同時學習「表達句」（我⋯。）及「發問句」（你⋯？），藉此熟練與他人互動時，言談間一來一往的英語交談元素。當有機會面對各種場合，才能展現「有話說、敢開口」的能量。

全書包含 8 大類實用會話：
■自我介紹　■日常生活　■喜怒哀樂　■想法主張
■表達善意　■出國旅遊　■職場英語　■聊天話題

全書收錄 4,500 句貼近生活的實用表達。寫作時，我經常反覆思考著「這時候，還有哪些可能的對話？」希望能夠提供最完整、實用、趣味的內容，期望大家在自學時，能夠感受到「內容的互動性」，用英語體驗「一來一往的交談樂趣」。

本書特色

本書教你『用英語聊不停』的『聰明接話術』！
左頁：學習【用英語表達自己】
右頁：學習【用英語詢問對方，讓話題持續】
內容涵蓋 8 大領域，158 主題，4,500 句會話
從生活到職場、從個人到出國
適用於「聊天開場、接話、提問、附和」
堪稱足以應付任何狀況的「英語攀談語句庫」！

■ 8 大領域：交談不冷場的互動式英語溝通

1 類：【左頁】自我介紹　　【右頁】我想認識你
2 類：【左頁】我的日常生活　【右頁】你的日常生活
3 類：【左頁】我的喜怒哀樂　【右頁】你的喜怒哀樂
4 類：【左頁】我的想法/主張　【右頁】你的想法/主張
5 類：【左頁】表達善意　　　【右頁】回應對方的善意
6 類：【左頁】出國旅遊　　　【右頁】聽懂外國人說什麼
7 類：【左頁】辦公室英語　　【右頁】和同事&客戶溝通
8 類：【左頁】開啟聊天話題　【右頁】如何讓話題持續

■ 左頁：開啟話題的【豐富線索】

※【我的名字】（*可參考P 30）：

與主題相關的第一人稱表達句，從「我……」開始，
展開交談、開啟話題。

〔我名叫…〕My name is…

〔你可以叫我…〕You can call me…

〔家人暱稱我…〕My family calls me…

〔我的名字的涵意是…〕My name means…

〔我的名字是爺爺取的〕

My name was given to me by my grandfather.

〔我的名字是算命來的〕

My name was chosen by a fortune teller.

■右頁：延續話題的【聰明提問、臨場附和】

※【你的名字？】（*可參考 P 31）：

與左頁呼應，可表達「詢問、回應、了解、關心」，
進一步延續話題。

〔你叫什麼名字？〕What is your name?

〔我該怎麼稱呼你？〕What should I call you?

〔你的名字是誰取的？〕Who gave you your name?

〔你的名字真好聽。〕Your name sounds nice.

〔請問你的名字怎麼拼？〕

May I ask how to spell your name?

〔你的名字有特殊涵意嗎？〕

Does your name have any special meaning?

■ 內容超具體：幫你準備好可接話的步驟和內容

逐句條列會話句，方便找到「想說的、最適合說的那一句」；並能自由安排「交談步驟、話題推衍」。

※左頁：【自己談減肥】

〔談方法〕減肥的方法太多了。
〔談影響〕身體一胖穿衣服就不好看。
〔談困難〕減肥要有意志力才能成功。
〔談陷阱〕很多減肥廣告都誇大不實。

※右頁：【詢問對方對於減肥的看法】、
　　　　【表達附和意見與關心】

〔問原因〕你又不胖，幹麼減肥？
〔問成果〕你成功瘦了幾公斤？
〔問方法〕哪一種減肥方法最有效？
〔關心提醒〕減肥可別傷了健康。

■ 滿足：字典查詢不到的「中文想法，英文怎麼說？」

學英文時，我們總想知道：「這句話，英文該怎麼說？」可是字典無法具體查詢到答案，也未必有老師可以詢問。本書特別大量收錄這一類的說法。例如：

〔你是『舞林高手』嗎？〕
Are you an [expert dancer] ?

〔最近有什麼『好事』發生？〕
Has [anything positive] happened lately?

〔我們家『三代同堂』。〕
My family has [three generations living together] .

〔同事覺得我是『開心果』。〕
My colleagues think that I am a [funny person] .

〔我幾乎每個月都『透支』。〕
I [overdraw my account] nearly every month.

〔家庭和事業很難『兼顧』。〕
It's really difficult to [look after both] family and career.

〔我想『我們各做各的』好了。〕
I think that we should [each do our own jobs] .

■ 達成：自己有話說，聽完對方說，也有能力加碼問！

※左右頁都有「關鍵字框」提示表達要點，交談時不
　缺乏聊天線索，使用英語不詞窮！
※善用「發問句」就能開啟新話題，讓交談持續！
※善用「回應句」銜接對方發言，持續互動不冷場！

本書使用說明

左頁 vs. 右頁
相同話題,不同立場的會話表達!

左頁	右頁
開啟話題的 【豐富線索】	延續話題的 【聰明提問、臨場附和】

---

004 我的家。

❶ 我住在台北市。
　I live in Taipei City.
❷ 我家總共 4 個人。
　There are four people in my family.
❸ 我是單親家庭長大的。
　I grew up in a single-parent family.
❹ 我是獨生子。
　I am the only son in my family.
❺ 我們家人感情很好。
　My family is close.
❻ 我排行老大。
　I am the oldest child in my family.
❼ 我住公寓。
　I live in an apartment.
❽ 我們家三代同堂。
　My family has three generations living together.
❾ 我貸款買房子。
　I bought a house with a loan.
❿ 我跟父母同住。
　I live with my parents.
⓫ 我和妹妹共用房間。
　I share a room with my sister.
⓬ 我一個人租房子住。
　I rent a house and live alone.
⓭ 我們家是雙薪家庭。
　Our family is a double-income household.
⓮ 我 3 年前搬到這裡。
　I moved here three years ago.
⓯ 我家樓下是 7-11。
　Downstairs from my house is a 7-11.

004 你的家?

❶ 你有兄弟姊妹嗎?
　Do you have any brothers or sisters?
❷ 你們家有 幾個人 ?
　How many people are in your family?
❸ 你跟家人 感情好 嗎?
　Do you get along well with your family?
❹ 你 住哪裡 ?
　Where do you live?
❺ 你 一個人住 嗎?
　Do you live alone?
❻ 你的房子是買的嗎?
　Did you buy your house?
❼ 你租房子嗎?
　Do you rent a house?
❽ 你的家是單親家庭嗎?
　Did you come from a single-parent family?
❾ 你住的地方 有多大 ?
　How big is the place you live in?
❿ 你住 公寓 嗎? 還是 大廈 ?
　Do you live in an apartment or a large building?
⓫ 你跟家人 住一起 嗎?
　Do you live with your family?
⓬ 你從小住在這裡嗎?
　Have you lived here since you were young?
⓭ 你喜歡住郊區,還是住市區?
　Do you like to live in the suburbs or the city?
⓮ 你 搬過家 嗎?
　Have you ever moved house?
⓯ 你有自己的房間嗎?
　Do you have your own room?

左右頁都有〔關鍵字框〕提示表達要點,
交談時不缺乏聊天線索,
說英語不詞窮!

本書使用說明

附贈超好用「檢測學習成效遮色片」，
驗證是否牢記句子，確實提昇英語能力！

只要取出隨書附贈的【檢測學習成效遮色片】
蓋在頁面上，英文句子就會隱形消失，
看著中文要知道「這句話，英文怎麼說」，
便於檢測「這個句子你記住了沒？」！

※本書相關書籍另有：《實用英語會話大全》（軟精裝，
1MP3），「檢測學習成效遮色片」亦適用！

英語時態用法說明 1
【現在簡單式】和會話的關係

使用型態：（1）be 動詞現在式（2）一般動詞現在式

（1）描述＆詢問：經常如此的事

■ 我們隨時有專人為您服務。（主題 137）

Our expert staff ⌈ is ⌉ always at your service.

＊「隨時有專員為您服務」屬於「經常如此的事」。

■ 我沒有一份工作做得長久。（主題 069）

I ⌈ don't keep ⌉ jobs for very long.

＊「從沒有工作做得久」屬於「經常如此的事」。

■ 你常買名牌嗎？（主題 143）

⌈ Do ⌉ you buy name-brand items often?

＊「常買名牌嗎」屬於詢問「經常…嗎」。

（2）描述＆詢問：目前的狀態

■ 我的父親已經退休。（主題 046）

My father ⌈ is ⌉ retired.

＊「已經退休」屬於「目前的狀態」。

■ 你記得他大概什麼時候打的嗎？（主題 132）

⌈ Do ⌉ you remember when he called?

＊「你記得…嗎」（你目前記得…嗎）屬於詢問「目前
　的狀態…嗎」。

英語時態用法說明 2
【過去簡單式】和會話的關係

使用型態：（1）be 動詞過去式 （2）一般動詞過去式

（1）描述＆詢問：發生在過去的事

■ 我和我先生是同班同學。（主題 009）

My husband and I ⬜were⬜ classmates in school.

* 老公「以前是同班同學」，屬於「發生在過去的事」。

■ 我今天中午吃很少。（主題 040）

I ⬜had⬜ a small lunch.

*「稍早前的午餐」屬於「發生在過去的事」。

■ 我想你不是故意的。（主題 081）

I am sure you ⬜didn't mean⬜ it.

* 意指「我想你之前的…、當時的…、並不是故意的」，
「之前的…」或「當時的…」屬於「發生在過去的事」。

■ 你的老闆白手起家嗎？（主題 050）

⬜Did⬜ your boss start his own business?

*「老闆以前白手起家嗎」，詢問「發生在過去的事」。

（2）描述＆詢問：過去經常如此的事

■ 我整天以淚洗面。（主題 060）

I ⬜cried⬜ all day.

*「整天、頻繁地傷心流淚」，屬於「過去某時點經常
如此的事」。

【現在完成式】和會話的關係

使用型態： 助動詞 have / has ＋ 動詞過去分詞

（1）描述＆詢問：過去某時點發生某事，且結果持續
　　　到現在，或結果對現在仍有影響

■ 工作中我學到很多東西。（主題 021）

I have learned a lot from my work.

＊「從工作中學到很多」（過去某時點發生的事），「且
結果對現在仍有影響」（當時讓我學到很多，直到現
在這些能力都對我有影響）。

（2）描述＆詢問：過去持續到現在的事

■ 我一直都很健康。（主題 033）

I have always been very healthy.

＊「過去到現在都健康」屬於「過去持續到現在的事」。

■ 你從小住在這裡？（主題 004）

Have you lived here since you were young?

＊「從小到現在都…嗎」詢問「過去持續至今都…嗎」。

（3）描述＆詢問：過去到現在發生過、經歷過的事

■ 久仰大名。（主題 133）

I've heard a lot about you.

＊「以前」（過去的時點）到「現在」這一段時間，曾
經聽過你的大名。

英語時態用法說明 4

【現在完成進行式】和會話的關係

使用型態： 助動詞 have / has ＋ been ＋ 動詞-ing 型態

（1）描述＆詢問：從過去開始、且直到現在仍持續中

■ 我來公司五年了。（主題 020）

I have been working with this company for five years.

*「五年前開始」（從過去開始）在這間公司上班，直到現在仍在這間公司。

■ 我和男朋友交往五年。（主題 048）

My boyfriend and I have been dating each other for five years.

*「五年前開始」（從過去開始）交往，直到現在仍持續交往中。

（2）描述＆詢問：現階段持續發生的事

■ 最近看起來氣色很好喔！（主題 055）

You've been looking good these days!

*「最近看來氣色很好」指「現階段、最近這一段時間，氣色都持續很好」。

■ 最近睡得好嗎？（主題 152）

Have you been sleeping well lately?

*「最近…嗎」意即詢問對方「現階段、最近這一段時間，都持續…嗎」。

【現在進行式】和會話的關係

使用型態： be 動詞現在式 ＋ 動詞-ing 型態

（1）描述＆詢問：說話當下正在做的事

■ 我在想這麼做是不是比較好？（主題 075）

I am considering whether this is a better way to do it.

＊「說話當下正在想…」屬於「說話當下正在做的事」。

（2）描述＆詢問：現階段發生的事

■ 我努力減少臉上細紋。（主題 026）

I am trying to reduce my facial wrinkles.

＊「現階段正在努力於…」屬於「現階段發生的事」。

（3）描述＆詢問：現階段逐漸變化的事

■ 我的女友越來越任性。（主題 067）

My girlfriend is getting more and more wild.

＊「以前不是這樣」，但「現階段卻變成…」。

（4）描述＆詢問：現階段經常發生、且令人厭惡的事

■ 你總是給我惹麻煩。（主題 083）

You are always making trouble for me.

＊「現階段經常…，且令人感到厭惡」。

（5）描述＆詢問：已排定時程的個人未來計畫

■ 我今年年底要結婚。（主題 009）

I am getting married toward the end of this year.

＊ 我「已排定年底要結婚」的未來計畫。

【過去進行式】和會話的關係

使用型態： | be 動詞過去式 | ＋ | 動詞-ing 型態 |

描述＆詢問：過去的當下正在做的事

■ 買的時候就已經說了「貨出概不退換」。（主題 120）

When you | were buying | it, we told you that it couldn't be returned.

*「當你在買的時候，我說…」指「過去的當下你正在買，我說…」。

■ 吉米有說找我什麼事嗎？（主題 132）

Did Jimmy say why he | was calling | me?

*「吉米找我的時候」（過去的當下）「他是否正在說…嗎」（詢問當下正在做的事）。

【未來簡單式①】和會話的關係

使用型態： 助動詞 will ＋ 動詞原形

（1）描述＆詢問：在未來將發生的事

■ 我的父母親希望我趕快結婚。（主題 046）

My parents hope that I will get married soon.

＊「目前」還沒結婚，父母親希望「未來我將趕快結婚」。

（2）描述＆詢問：有意願做的事

■ 我一定會報答你。（主題 079）

I will definitely pay you back.

＊「我一定會…」表示「我有意願…」。

（3）描述＆詢問：根據直覺預測未來發生的事

■ 你這樣會累出病來的。（主題 072）

You will wear yourself out and get sick.

＊ 根據自己的經驗或直覺預測，未來可能會累出病來。

（4）描述＆詢問：某人經常性的習慣

■ 有時候我到便利商店買午餐。（主題 038）

Sometimes I will go to the convenience store to buy lunch.

＊ 可以用「現在簡單式」表示「經常如此的事」。但如果「有時候到…買午餐」是「某人經常性的習慣」，則適合使用「未來簡單式」。

英語時態用法說明 8

【未來簡單式②】和會話的關係

使用型態：| be 動詞 | + | going to | + | 動詞原形 |

（1）描述＆詢問：未排時程、但預定要做的事

■ 我很多同事最近要離職。（主題 051）
Many of my colleagues | are going to quit |.
* 沒有排定時程，但「很多同事預定要離職」。

■ 我老了一定會去拉皮。（主題 146）
| I'm going to tighten | my skin when I get older.
* 沒有排定時程，但「老了要去拉皮」。

■ 接下來幾天是你負責接待我嗎？（主題 136）
| Are | you | going to be | my guide for the next few days?
* 沒有排定時程，詢問「接下來幾天你預定要做…嗎」。

（2）描述＆詢問：根據現況預測未來發生的事

■ 再說下去我就要睡著了。（主題 064）
| I'm going to fall | asleep if you keep talking.
* 根據「現況」（目前我正在聽你說話的狀況）預
  測，如果你繼續說下去，未來我將會睡著。

目錄 Contents

2 我的日常生活 vs. 你的日常生活

主題	左頁	右頁

3　我的喜怒哀樂 vs. 你的喜怒哀樂

主題	左頁	右頁

4 我的想法／主張 vs. 你的想法／主張

001 我的名字。

❶ 我叫 凱蘿・陳。
My name is Carol Chen.

❷ 我姓 林。
My last name is Lin.

❸ 你可以叫我湯姆。
You can call me Tom.

❹ 家人暱稱我為「糖果」。
My family calls me Candy.

❺ 朋友都叫我「小貓」。
All my friends call me Kitty.

❻ 我沒有 英文名字 。
I don't have an English name.

❼ 我的英文名字是老師取的。
My English name was given to me by my teacher.

❽ 同事習慣叫我的英文名字—詹姆斯。
My colleagues usually call me by my English name—James.

❾ 我不喜歡我的 綽號 。
I don't like my nickname.

❿ 我的名字常 被唸錯 。
People often pronounce my name wrong.

⓫ 有一個朋友和我同名。
One of my friends has the same name as me.

⓬ 我的名字是 爺爺取的 。
My name was given to me by my grandfather.

⓭ 我的名字是 算命來的 。
My name was chosen by a fortune teller.

⓮ 我的名字的涵意是「勇敢」。
My name means "brave."

001 你的名字？

❶ 你 貴姓 ？
What is your last name?

❷ 你叫什麼名字？
What is your name?

❸ 我該 怎麼稱呼 你？
What should I call you?

❹ 請問你的名字 怎麼拼 ？
May I ask how to spell your name?

❺ 你 有綽號 嗎？
Do you have a nickname?

❻ 你有英文名字嗎？
Do you have an English name?

❼ 我可以叫你吉米嗎？
Can I call you Jimmy?

❽ 請問你是 林先生嗎？
Are you Mr. Lin?

❾ 你的家人怎麼叫你？
What does your family call you?

❿ 你的名字是 誰取的 ？
Who gave you your name?

⓫ 你的名字有特殊涵意嗎？
Does your name have any special meaning?

⓬ 你喜歡你的名字嗎？
Do you like your name?

⓭ 你想 改名字 嗎？
Do you want to change your name?

⓮ 大家都會唸你的名字嗎？
Is everyone able to pronounce your name?

⓯ 你的名字 真好聽 。
Your name sounds nice.

002 我的年齡。

❶ 我 今年 25 歲。
I am twenty-five years old this year.

❷ 我 未滿 18 歲。
I am not yet eighteen years old.

❸ 我快 50 歲了。
I am almost fifty years old.

❹ 我 30 多歲。
I am thirty-something years old.

❺ 我 屬羊 。
I was born in the Year of the Goat.

❻ 我 剛過 40 歲的生日。
I just had my fortieth birthday.

❼ 我生於 1980 年。
I was born in 1980.

❽ 我同事都 比我年輕 。
All my colleagues are younger than me.

❾ 我和你同年。
I was born the same year as you.

❿ 我跟我妹妹相差 10 歲。
There is a ten-year age difference between my
younger sister and me.

⓫ 我比我哥哥 小 3 歲 。
I am three years younger than my older brother.

⓬ 我早過了 適婚年齡 。
I have already passed the age for marrying.

⓭ 我 年紀不小 了。
I am not young anymore.

⓮ 我看起來比實際年齡年輕。
I look younger than my actual age.

002 你的年齡？

❶ 你 幾歲 ？
How old are you?

❷ 你滿 20 歲了嗎？
Are you twenty years old yet?

❸ 你應該 快 30 歲 了吧？
You'll be in your thirties soon, right?

❹ 你的 生日 是哪一天？
When is your birthday?

❺ 你是 哪一年出生 的？
What year were you born?

❻ 你的 生肖 是什麼？
What year were you born in?

❼ 你們兩個誰的年齡比較大？
Which of the two of you is older?

❽ 你跟你弟弟相 差幾歲 ？
How much younger than you is your brother?

❾ 你姊姊比你大幾歲？
How much older than you is your sister?

❿ 你可以考駕照了嗎？
Are you old enough to take the driver's license exam?

⓫ 我們的 年紀差不多 。
We are about the same age.

⓬ 你聽誰的歌長大的？
Whose songs did you listen to while growing up?

⓭ 你看起來總是這麼年輕。
You always look so young.

⓮ 你的身材 保養得真好 ！
You are in really good shape.

⓯ 你跟我姊姊 同年 。
You and my older sister were born in the same year.

003 我的家鄉。

❶ 我是 台灣人 。
I am Taiwanese.

❷ 我是高雄人。
I am a Kaohsiung native.

❸ 我來自 台灣的中部 。
I come from central Taiwan.

❹ 我在台灣東部出生。
I was born in eastern Taiwan.

❺ 我非常愛我的家鄉。
I love my hometown very much.

❻ 我的 童年 在家鄉度過。
I spent my childhood in my hometown.

❼ 家鄉永遠是我 最眷戀 的地方。
I will always be most attached to my hometown.

❽ 我 10 歲就離開家鄉。
I left my hometown when I was ten.

❾ 我從小就 離鄉背井 。
I have been living away from my hometown ever since I was young.

❿ 我對家鄉沒什麼印象了。
I don't have much of an impression of my hometown.

⓫ 我常回家鄉 探望父母 。
I often go back to my hometown to visit my parents.

⓬ 我的家鄉是繁榮的大城市。
My hometown is a prosperous city.

⓭ 我的家鄉盛產稻米。
My hometown is rich in rice.

⓮ 我的家鄉非常美麗。
My hometown is beautiful.

003 你的家鄉？

❶ 你的家鄉 在哪裡 ？
Where is your hometown?

❷ 你來自哪裡？
Where are you from?

❸ 你在 哪裡出生 ？
Where were you born?

❹ 要不要聊聊你的家鄉？
Do you want to talk about your hometown?

❺ 你 想念 家鄉嗎？
Do you miss your hometown?

❻ 你的家鄉有什麼 特產 ？
What is the signature product of your hometown?

❼ 你的家鄉以什麼 聞名 ？
What is your hometown famous for?

❽ 你的家鄉近來有什麼改變嗎？
Has your hometown experienced any changes recently?

❾ 你 幾歲離開 家鄉的？
How old were you when you left your hometown?

❿ 你想回家鄉看看嗎？
Would you like to visit your hometown?

⓫ 你 幾年沒回 家鄉了？
How long has it been since you last returned to
your hometown?

⓬ 你常回家鄉嗎？
Do you return to your hometown often?

⓭ 你打算 返鄉定居 嗎？
Do you plan to return to and settle down in your
hometown?

⓮ 家鄉還有親人嗎？
Do you have any relatives left in your hometown?

004 我的家。

❶ 我住在台北市。
I live in Taipei City.

❷ 我家總共 4 個人。
There are four people in my family.

❸ 我是 單親家庭 的孩子。
I grew up in a single-parent family.

❹ 我是 獨生子 。
I am the only son in my family.

❺ 我們家人感情很好。
My family is close.

❻ 我排行 老大 。
I am the oldest child in my family.

❼ 我住公寓。
I live in an apartment.

❽ 我們家 三代同堂 。
My family has three generations living together.

❾ 我 貸款 買房子。
I bought a house with a loan.

❿ 我跟父母 同住 。
I live with my parents.

⓫ 我和妹妹共用房間。
I share a room with my sister.

⓬ 我一個人 租房子 住。
I rent a house and live alone.

⓭ 我們家是 雙薪家庭 。
Our family is a double-income household.

⓮ 我 3 年前搬到這裡。
I moved here three years ago.

⓯ 我家樓下是 7-11 。
Downstairs from my house is a 7-11.

004 你的家？

❶ 你有兄弟姊妹嗎？

Do you have any brothers or sisters?

❷ 你們家有 幾個人 ？

How many people are in your family?

❸ 你和家人 感情好 嗎？

Do you get along well with your family?

❹ 你 住哪裡 ？

Where do you live?

❺ 你 一個人住 嗎？

Do you live alone?

❻ 你的房子是買的嗎？

Did you buy your house?

❼ 你租房子嗎？

Do you rent a house?

❽ 你們家是單親家庭嗎？

Do you come from a single-parent family?

❾ 你住的地方 有多大 ？

How big is the place you live in?

❿ 你住 公寓 嗎？還是 大廈 ？

Do you live in an apartment or a large building?

⓫ 你跟家人 住一起 嗎？

Do you live with your family?

⓬ 你從小住在這裡嗎？

Have you lived here since you were young?

⓭ 你喜歡住郊區？還是住市區？

Do you like to live in the suburbs or the city?

⓮ 你 搬過家 嗎？

Have you ever moved house?

⓯ 你有自己的房間嗎？

Do you have your own room?

005 我的個性。

❶ 我活潑 外向 。
I am a lively and outgoing person.

❷ 我害羞 內向 。
I am a shy and introverted person.

❸ 我話不多。
I'm not a talkative person.

❹ 我喜歡 交朋友 。
I like to make friends.

❺ 我很有 正義感 。
I have a strong sense of justice.

❻ 我勇於接受挑戰。
I have the courage to take on a challenge.

❼ 我喜歡幫助別人。
I like to help others.

❽ 我天性 樂觀 。
I am naturally optimistic.

❾ 我個性隨和。
I have an easygoing personality.

❿ 我 脾氣很好 。
I have a good temper.

⓫ 我害怕孤獨。
I am afraid of loneliness.

⓬ 我幽默 愛搞笑 。
I am funny and like to joke around.

⓭ 我容易緊張。
I get nervous easily.

⓮ 我有一點 固執 。
I am a bit of a stubborn person.

⓯ 我是急性子。
I am a rash person.

005 你的個性？

❶ 你一向這麼樂觀嗎？
Have you always been this optimistic?

❷ 你 容易緊張 嗎？
Do you get nervous easily?

❸ 你總是這麼沈默嗎？
Have you always been such a silent person?

❹ 你說話都是 這麼直接 嗎？
Do you always speak this directly?

❺ 你從小就這麼內向嗎？
Have you been this introverted since childhood?

❻ 你喜歡結交朋友嗎？
Do you like to make friends?

❼ 你 擅長交際 嗎？
Do you have good communication skills?

❽ 你 勇於 發表意見嗎？
Do you have the courage to express your opinions?

❾ 你是 急性子 嗎？
Are you an impatient person?

❿ 你覺得自己固執嗎？
Do you think that you are stubborn?

⓫ 你喜歡嘗試 新事物 嗎？
Do you like to try new things?

⓬ 你的個性 隨和 嗎？
Do you have an easygoing personality?

⓭ 你害怕 面對壓力 嗎？
Are you afraid of facing pressure?

⓮ 會議中你經常發言嗎？
Do you usually speak up in meetings?

⓯ 你習慣獨處嗎？
Are you used to being alone?

006 我的興趣。

❶ 我的興趣是 聽音樂 。
My hobby is listening to music.

❷ 我的興趣是看 各種展覽 。
My interest is attending various exhibitions.

❸ 我很喜歡出國旅行。
I really like to travel abroad.

❹ 我習慣每天 散步 。
Taking a walk is my daily habit.

❺ 我習慣假日去戶外走走。
I usually go out during the holidays.

❻ 我 習慣 睡前看書。
I have the habit of reading before bed.

❼ 我常常 跟朋友 看電影。
I often go to the movies with my friends.

❽ 我常常跟家人去爬山。
I frequently go hiking with my family.

❾ 我超愛 講手機 。
I love talking on my cell phone.

❿ 我喜歡跟人聊天。
I like to chat with others.

⓫ 我最近 迷上 網路遊戲。
Lately I've gotten into online gaming.

⓬ 品嚐美食是我的嗜好之一。
Enjoying gourmet food is one of my hobbies.

⓭ 我 最大的嗜好 是釣魚。
Fishing is my biggest hobby.

⓮ 我很愛看電視。
I love watching TV.

⓯ 我超愛打電動。
I love playing video games.

006 你的興趣？

1 你有什麼嗜好嗎？
What is your hobby?

2 你常 看電影 嗎？
Do you go to the movies frequently?

3 你有看書的習慣嗎？
Do you read regularly?

4 你常 出國旅行 嗎？
Do you travel abroad often?

5 你 偏愛 哪一類型的電影？
What kind of movies do you prefer?

6 你喜歡看哪一類的書？
What kind of books do you read?

7 你喜歡看表演嗎？
Do you like to watch performances?

8 你的 嗜好真昂貴 。
Your hobby is very expensive.

9 你喜歡聽哪一種音樂？
What kind of music do you like?

10 你常聽音樂嗎？
Do you listen to music very often?

11 我想你應該有很多 CD 。
I bet you own a lot of CDs.

12 你喜歡看電視嗎？
Do you like to watch TV?

13 你常看哪些 電視節目 ？
What kind of TV shows do you usually watch?

14 你習慣 上網聊天 嗎？
Do you have the habit of chatting online?

15 你的嗜好該不會就是 吃東西 吧？
Eating wouldn't be your only hobby, would it?

007 我的專長。

❶ 我 精通 四國語言。
I am fluent in four languages.

❷ 我的英語 能力很強 。
My English is quite good.

❸ 我很會跳舞。
I am good at dancing.

❹ 所有運動都 難不倒我 。
There is no sport too difficult for me.

❺ 我跑得很快。
I can run very fast.

❻ 我彈得一手好鋼琴。
I am good at playing the piano.

❼ 我有救生員 執照 。
I have a lifeguard license.

❽ 我是電腦 高手 。
I am a computer expert.

❾ 我游自由式。
I swim freestyle.

❿ 我是一個好廚師。
I am a good cook.

⓫ 大家都說我唱歌 很好聽 。
Everyone says that I am a good singer.

⓬ 我 擅長 做各式糕點。
I am good at making various cakes and desserts.

⓭ 我會開車。
I can drive a car.

⓮ 我是空手道黑帶。
I have a black belt in karate.

⓯ 我對畫畫 很拿手 。
I am good at painting.

007 你的專長？

1 你的 拿手科目 是什麼？
Which is your best subject?

2 你 最擅長 什麼？
What do you excel in?

3 你會說 幾種語言 ？
How many languages do you speak?

4 你會說英文嗎？
Do you speak English?

5 你精通電腦嗎？
Are you good with computers?

6 你 會演奏什麼 樂器？
What musical instruments can you play?

7 你會游泳嗎？
Do you know how to swim?

8 你 幾歲開始 學鋼琴？
When did you begin learning to play the piano?

9 你會做菜嗎？
Can you cook?

10 你的 拿手菜 是什麼？
What is your best homemade dish?

11 你是 KTV 高手嗎？
Are you a KTV master?

12 你擅長運動嗎？
Are you good at sports?

13 你是 舞林高手 嗎？
Are you an expert dancer?

14 你會開車嗎？
Can you drive a car?

15 你是 說話高手 嗎？
Are you a good speaker?

008 我在別人眼中。

1 同事覺得我是 開心果 。
My colleagues think that I am a funny person.

2 朋友喜歡 找我訴苦 。
My friends like to talk about their problems with me.

3 老闆誇我 幹勁十足 。
My boss speaks highly of my energetic performance.

4 主管說我很細心。
My manager says that I am very careful with details.

5 父母親覺得我太 孩子氣 。
My parents think that I am too childish.

6 老闆誇我做事認真。
My boss speaks highly of my earnest attitude toward work.

7 男朋友覺得我太依賴。
My boyfriend thinks that I am too dependent.

8 長輩讚美我 聰明伶俐 。
Older people praise my cleverness.

9 大家都說我很有耐性。
Everyone says that I am a patient person.

10 有人說我是 溫室裡的花朵 。
Some people say that I am a sheltered person.

11 有人覺得我太嚴肅。
Some people think that I am too serious.

12 朋友要我別太 情緒化 。
My friends tell me not to be overly emotional.

13 大家都說我是 小迷糊 。
Everyone says that I am a muddle-headed person.

14 大家都說我脾氣好。
Everyone says that I have a good temper.

15 我是父母眼中的乖孩子。
According to my parents, I am a well-behaved child.

008 你在別人眼中？

1 有人說你情緒化嗎？
Does anyone think that you are moody?

2 你的朋友 怎麼形容 你？
How do your friends describe you?

3 朋友覺得 你善變嗎？
Do your friends feel that you are a fickle person?

4 有人說你很固執嗎？
Does anyone say that you are stubborn?

5 我想你應該讓 老師傷透腦筋 。
I bet you give your teachers a lot of trouble.

6 老師對你的成績滿意嗎？
Is your teacher satisfied with your performance at school?

7 主管滿意 你的表現嗎？
Is your manager pleased with your performance?

8 孩子 嫌你囉唆 嗎？
Does your child think you are a nag?

9 有人說你太沈默嗎？
Does anyone say that you are too quiet?

10 男朋友覺得你體貼嗎？
Does your boyfriend think you're considerate?

11 父母親一定 以你為榮 。
Your parents must be very proud of you.

12 你一定是個好爸爸。
You must be a good father.

13 你一定是個 賢妻良母 。
You must be an excellent wife and a loving mother.

14 朋友常找你訴苦嗎？
Do your friends usually complain to you about things?

15 客戶一定很 滿意 你的服務。
Your clients are probably very satisfied with your service.

009 我已婚／未婚。

❶ 我 單身 。
I am single.

❷ 我完全 不想結婚 。
I really don't want to get married.

❸ 我前年結婚。
I got married two years ago.

❹ 我上個月 訂婚 。
I got engaged last month.

❺ 我今年年底要結婚。
I am getting married toward the end of this year.

❻ 我結婚十年了。
I've been married for 10 years already.

❼ 我的婚姻很幸福。
I have a happy marriage.

❽ 我是個家庭主婦。
I am a housewife.

❾ 我和我先生是同班同學。
My husband and I were classmates in school.

❿ 我是 奉子成婚 。
I got married because I was pregnant.

⓫ 我結婚不到 半年就懷孕 。
I became pregnant less than six months after marriage.

⓬ 這是我的 第二段婚姻 。
This is my second marriage.

⓭ 我 離婚 好幾年了。
I've been divorced for quite a few years.

⓮ 我跟婆婆 關係很糟 。
I have a bad relationship with my mother-in-law.

⓯ 我後悔結婚。
I regret getting married.

009 你已婚／未婚？

❶ 你不想結婚嗎？
Wouldn't you like to get married?

❷ 你結婚了嗎？
Are you married?

❸ 你考慮 相親 嗎？
Have you considered a matchmaker?

❹ 你什麼時候要結婚？
When will you get married?

❺ 你先生如何向你 求婚 的？
How did your husband propose to you?

❻ 你 結婚幾年 了？
How many years have you been married?

❼ 你的 新婚生活 如何？
How's your life as a newlywed going?

❽ 你後悔結婚嗎？
Do you regret getting married?

❾ 你和你太太 怎麼認識 的？
How did you meet your wife?

❿ 你何時要訂婚？
When will you get engaged?

⓫ 你打算 幾年後生 小孩？
How many years until you have a child?

⓬ 你想要生幾個小孩？
How many children would you like to have?

⓭ 你跟 公婆相處 得如何？
How are you getting along with your in-laws?

⓮ 你為什麼離婚？
Why did you divorce?

⓯ 你想 再婚 嗎？
Would you like to get married again?

010 我的身高。

1 我的身高 160 公分。
  I am 160 centimeters tall.

2 我很久沒 量身高 了。
  I haven't measured my height in a long time.

3 我很滿意自己的身高。
  I am fine with my height.

4 我的 身高中等 。
  I am of average height.

5 我的身高遺傳自父親。
  I inherited my father's height.

6 我跟你 一樣高 。
  I am just as tall as you.

7 我 比姊姊矮 3 公分。
  I am three centimeters shorter than my elder sister.

8 我 比弟弟高 5 公分。
  I am five centimeters taller than my younger brother.

9 我是 矮個子 。
  I am a short person.

10 我羨慕比我高的人。
  I envy people who are taller than me.

11 我是我們家 最高的 。
  I am the tallest one in my family.

12 我的身高只有 145 公分。
  I am only 145 centimeters tall.

13 我的身高 超過 190 公分 。
  My height is over 190 centimeters.

14 我上國中後才突然長高。
  I suddenly grew taller after starting junior high.

15 我是我們班最矮的。
  I am the shortest one in my class.

010 你的身高？

❶ 你的 身高多少 ？
How tall are you?

❷ 你覺得自己夠高嗎？
Do you think you are tall enough?

❸ 你希望 再長高 一點嗎？
Do you wish you were taller than you are now?

❹ 你的家人都像你這麼高嗎？
Is everyone in your family as tall as you?

❺ 你跟他 誰比較高 ？
Who is the taller, you or him?

❻ 你跟我弟弟一樣高。
You are as tall as my younger brother.

❼ 你跟你哥哥身高 相差多少 ？
What is the difference in height between you and your elder brother?

❽ 你又長高了。
You've grown taller again.

❾ 你看起來比你爸爸高。
You look taller than your father.

❿ 你不瞭解 矮個子的痛苦 。
You cannot understand the pain of being a short person.

⓫ 你的身高真令人嫉妒！
Your height makes people jealous!

⓬ 你的身高 適合打籃球 。
Your height is perfect for playing basketball.

⓭ 你的女朋友 好嬌小 。
Your girlfriend is so petite.

⓮ 你的身高可以去 當模特兒 。
You could be a model with your height.

011 我的身材。

❶ 我的體重 48 公斤。
My weight is 48 kilograms.

❷ 我的體重不到 60 公斤。
My weight is not quite 60 kilos.

❸ 我是 胖子 。
I am a fat person.

❹ 我很 苗條 。
I am very slim.

❺ 我羨慕 吃不胖 的人。
I envy those who eat a lot but don't get fat.

❻ 我是 中等身材 。
I have an average figure.

❼ 我比我哥哥重 10 公斤。
I am 10 kilos heavier than my elder brother.

❽ 我比我妹妹瘦。
I am thinner than my young sister.

❾ 我的 胸圍 34 吋。
My chest measurement is 34-inches.

❿ 我的手臂 肉肉的 。
My arms are fleshy.

⓫ 我的 大腿太粗 。
My thighs are too big.

⓬ 我靠 運動維持 身材。
I exercise to maintain my figure.

⓭ 我覺得自己很胖。
I think I am fat.

⓮ 我覺得自己太瘦。
I think that I am too skinny.

⓯ 我最近胖了。
I've gained some weight recently.

011 你的身材？

❶ 你的 體重多少 ？
What is your weight?

❷ 你希望自己多重？
How much is your ideal weight?

❸ 你是不是 又胖了 ？
Did you get fat again?

❹ 你 如何保持 身材？
How do you keep your shape?

❺ 你怎麼瘦到 皮包骨 ？
How did you become just skin and bones?

❻ 你為什麼 想減肥 ？
Why do you want to lose weight?

❼ 你胖了幾公斤？
How many kilograms did you gain?

❽ 你應該不到 40 公斤。
You probably don't even weigh 40 kilograms.

❾ 你知道她的 三圍 嗎？
Do you know her measurements?

❿ 我想他至少有 90 公斤。
I think that he weighs at least 90 kilograms.

⓫ 你看起來完全 沒有贅肉 。
You look like you have no fat on your body.

⓬ 我真羨慕你的好身材。
I am jealous of your good figure.

⓭ 你的 身材真好 ！
What a great figure you have!

⓮ 十年來，你的身材絲毫未變。
Your figure hasn't changed a bit in the past ten years.

⓯ 減肥已經成為全民運動。
Weight loss is a popular exercise.

012 我的皮膚。

1 我變白了。
I've become fair-skinned.

2 我的皮膚 白皙 。
I have fair skin.

3 我很 容易曬黑 。
My skin tans easily.

4 我曬黑了。
I've got a tan.

5 我的膚質很好。
My skin is very good.

6 我的臉色蒼白。
My face looks pale.

7 我的膚質 不容易上妝 。
My skin does not take to makeup easily.

8 我是 油性 肌膚。
I have oily skin.

9 我的皮膚很光滑。
My skin is very smooth.

10 我是 混合性 肌膚。
I have a combination of skin types.

11 我的皮膚容易過敏。
My skin is easily irritated.

12 我有 黑眼圈 。
I have bags under my eyes.

13 我的皮膚很有光澤。
My skin shines.

14 我容易 長痘痘 。
I break out in pimples very easily.

15 我一熬夜就 臉色暗沈 。
My skin darkens if I stay up late at night.

012 你的皮膚？

❶ 你怎麼都 曬不黑 ？
How come you don't tan?

❷ 你希望肌膚白皙嗎？
Do you want your skin to be whiter?

❸ 你打算曬成古銅色嗎？
Do you want to have a bronze-colored skin tone?

❹ 你的皮膚 容易過敏 嗎？
Do you have sensitive skin?

❺ 你不怕曬黑嗎？
Aren't you afraid of getting too tan?

❻ 你怎麼長 這麼多痘痘 ？
How come you have so many pimples?

❼ 你的皮膚 白裡透紅 。
Your skin looks very healthy with a touch of rose.

❽ 你打算進行 雷射除斑 嗎？
Do you intend to have laser therapy to get rid of your spots?

❾ 你的皮膚越來越好了。
Your skin is getting better and better.

❿ 你變白了。
Your skin is whiter.

⓫ 你完全 沒有皺紋 。
You don't have any wrinkles.

⓬ 你 曬黑 了。
You've gotten a suntan.

⓭ 你的臉色很蒼白。
Your face looks very pale.

⓮ 你得好好保養皮膚。
You should take good care of your skin.

⓯ 你的 痘痘變少 了。
Your acne is getting better.

013 我的臉蛋。

❶ 我的臉圓圓的。
I have a round face.

❷ 我的 臉很大 。
My face is big.

❸ 我的臉比手掌還小。
My face is smaller than my palm.

❹ 我的臉型 像爸爸 。
My face is shaped like my father's.

❺ 我是娃娃臉。
I have a baby face.

❻ 我的 面貌姣好 。
I have a good-looking face.

❼ 我的 長相普通 。
I am an ordinary-looking person.

❽ 我的額頭很高。
I have a high forehead.

❾ 我的 臉頰肉肉的 。
My cheeks are chubby.

❿ 我有雙下巴。
I have a double chin.

⓫ 我的下巴尖尖的。
I have a sharp chin.

⓬ 我立志當 小臉美女 。
I am determined to be a beauty with a cute face.

⓭ 大家都說我的圓臉很有親和力。
Everyone says that my round face looks friendly.

⓮ 我總是 笑臉迎人 。
I always have a smiling face.

⓯ 我看起來 很兇 。
I look very mean.

013 你的臉蛋？

❶ 你為什麼不喜歡笑？
Why don't you like to smile?

❷ 你的臉型很漂亮。
You have a beautiful facial structure.

❸ 你的臉好小。
Your face is so small.

❹ 你的臉型 比較方正 。
The shape of your face is somewhat square.

❺ 你的 臉變圓 了。
Your face looks rounder than before.

❻ 你圓圓的臉很可愛。
Your round face looks very cute.

❼ 你有一張 娃娃臉 。
You have a baby face.

❽ 你 長得很甜 。
You look so sweet.

❾ 你的臉比你媽媽的還大。
Your face is bigger than your mother's.

❿ 你跟你家人的 臉型完全不同 。
Your face is shaped totally differently from your
family members'.

⓫ 娃娃臉讓你看起來更年輕。
Having a baby face makes you look younger.

⓬ 你的 笑容很迷人 。
Your smile is very charming.

⓭ 你的 顴骨很高 。
You have high cheekbones.

⓮ 你的表情看起來很嚴肅，發生了什麼事？
You look so serious; what happened?

014 我的五官。

❶ 我的 輪廓很深 。
I have a distinct face.

❷ 我的眼睛像媽媽。
My eyes look like my mother's.

❸ 我的 眼皮浮腫 。
My eyelids are swollen.

❹ 我的 眼睛很小 。
My eyes are small.

❺ 大家都說我的眼睛很大。
Everyone says that my eyes are big.

❻ 我的眼睛細長。
My eyes are long and thin.

❼ 我是 單眼皮 。
My eyelids are single-folded.

❽ 我的 眼睫毛 很長。
My eyelashes are very long.

❾ 我的鼻子很挺。
I have a high-bridged nose.

❿ 我的眼珠是黑色。
My eyes are black.

⓫ 我的 眉毛濃密 。
My eyebrows are thick.

⓬ 我有近視。
I am nearsighted.

⓭ 我經常 修眉毛 。
I trim my eyebrows frequently.

⓮ 我的 嘴唇很厚 。
My lips are thick.

⓯ 我的嘴巴很大。
My mouth is large.

014 你的五官？

❶ 你的雙眼 炯炯有神 。
Your eyes are bright and piercing.

❷ 你的眼睛很漂亮。
Your eyes are very beautiful.

❸ 你有雙 水汪汪 的大眼睛。
What big, bright eyes you have.

❹ 你是典型的 瞇瞇眼 。
Your eyes look typically thin and narrow.

❺ 你是 雙眼皮 嗎？
Do you have double-folded eyelids?

❻ 你的眼皮腫腫的。
Your eyelids look swollen.

❼ 你的 藍色眼珠 很美。
Your blue eyes are very beautiful.

❽ 你的眼神很銳利。
You have sharp eyes.

❾ 你有近視嗎？
Do you have a problem with nearsightedness?

❿ 你的 酒窩 很可愛！
Your dimples are very cute!

⓫ 你的眉色很深。
The color of your eyebrows is very dark.

⓬ 你的眉型很美。
Your eyebrow shape is very beautiful.

⓭ 你的 嘴唇很性感 。
You have sexy lips.

⓮ 你的 鼻子真挺 ！
You have quite a sharp nose!

⓯ 你的鼻子像你爸爸。
Your nose looks like your father's.

015 我的頭髮。

❶ 我是長髮。
   I have long hair.
❷ 我有 瀏海 。
   I have bangs.
❸ 我的髮型 旁分 。
   My hair is parted to one side.
❹ 我的髮長及腰。
   I have waist-length hair.
❺ 我的頭髮有 自然捲 。
   My hair is naturally curly.
❻ 我的髮型中分。
   My hair is parted in the middle.
❼ 我把頭髮 燙直 了。
   I had my hair straightened.
❽ 我染了頭髮。
   I had my hair dyed.
❾ 我的 髮質很好 。
   I have good hair quality.
❿ 我將頭髮 染成紅色 。
   I dyed my hair red.
⓫ 我每天洗頭。
   I wash my hair every day.
⓬ 我每星期上一次美容院。
   I go to the beauty shop once a week.
⓭ 我的頭髮 又硬又粗 。
   My hair is coarse and thick.
⓮ 我常綁 馬尾 。
   I usually wear my hair in a ponytail.
⓯ 我經常改變髮型。
   I change my hairstyle frequently.

015 你的頭髮？

❶ 你喜歡 直髮 還是 捲髮 ？
Do you like straight or curly hair?

❷ 你 染頭髮 嗎？
Do you dye your hair?

❸ 你喜歡長髮還是短髮？
Do you like long or short hair?

❹ 你每天 花多少時間弄 頭髮？
How much time do you spend doing your hair?

❺ 你有在 護髮 嗎？
Do you condition your hair?

❻ 你每天洗頭嗎？
Do you wash your hair every day?

❼ 何不大膽嘗試染個金髮？
Why not be bold and try dyeing your hair blonde?

❽ 你什麼時候 剪頭髮 的？
When did you cut your hair?

❾ 你頭髮習慣分哪一邊？
Which way do you part your hair?

❿ 你的頭髮真美！
What beautiful hair you have!

⓫ 你想 改變髮型 嗎？
Would you like to change your hairdo?

⓬ 你的新髮型很適合你。
Your new hairstyle suits you.

⓭ 我覺得你比較 適合短髮 。
I think short hair suits you better.

⓮ 你打算把頭髮 留長 嗎？
Do you plan to grow your hair long?

⓯ 你的髮型數十年不變。
Your hairstyle hasn't changed in decades.

016 我的妝扮。

❶ 我 不會化 妝。
I don't know how to put on makeup.

❷ 臉色不好時我會 上妝 。
I apply makeup when my complexion looks bad.

❸ 我想學化妝。
I'd like to learn how to put on makeup.

❹ 我大學時開始化妝。
I started to use makeup when I was a college student.

❺ 我經常使用 睫毛膏 。
I apply mascara regularly.

❻ 大家都說我上妝前後 判若兩人 。
Everyone says that I become another person when I put on makeup.

❼ 我從 不戴任何飾品 。
I never wear any jewelry.

❽ 我只戴我的結婚戒指。
I only wear my wedding ring.

❾ 這條項鍊對我深具意義，我總是戴著它。
I always wear this necklace which means a lot to me.

❿ 我喜歡 戴耳環 。
I like to wear earrings.

⓫ 我戴眼鏡。
I wear glasses.

⓬ 我們 公司規定 上班一定要化妝。
Our company requires its employees to wear makeup to work.

⓭ 我不喜歡戴眼鏡。
I don't like to wear glasses.

016 你的妝扮？

❶ 你每天化妝嗎？
Do you wear makeup every day?

❷ 你怎麼學會化妝的？
How did you learn to put on cosmetics?

❸ 你的耳環真漂亮。
Your earrings are very beautiful.

❹ 你 幾歲開始化 妝的？
How old were you when you began to apply cosmetics?

❺ 你的妝很 時髦 。
The makeup you put on looks very fashionable.

❻ 擦口紅 讓你比較有精神。
Wearing lipstick makes you more energetic.

❼ 你的彩 妝很自然 。
Your makeup looks very natural.

❽ 有時候化妝是一種禮貌。
Sometimes, applying makeup is a matter of good manners.

❾ 這個顏色的 眼影很適合 你。
This color of eye shadow really fits you.

❿ 越來越多的年輕女生開始化妝。
More and more young ladies are beginning to put on cosmetics.

⓫ 你可以教我化妝嗎？
Can you teach me how to put on makeup?

⓬ 你戴 隱形眼鏡 嗎？
Do you wear contact lenses?

⓭ 適度化妝可以 為自己加分 。
An appropriate amount of makeup can really add to your looks.

017 我的穿著。

❶ 我 看場合穿 衣服。
I dress for the occasion.

❷ 我穿 套裝 上班。
I wear a suit to work.

❸ 假日時我穿得很 休閒 。
I dress casually on weekends.

❹ 我們公司允許員工隨興打扮。
Our company allows us to dress casually for work.

❺ 上班時我穿 制服 。
I wear a uniform at work.

❻ 出席宴會我會穿上 小禮服 。
I wear semi-formal clothes when I attend a banquet.

❼ 我喜歡簡單大方的穿著。
I like simple and tasteful clothing.

❽ 我最愛 T恤 及 牛仔褲 。
I love T-shirts and jeans the most.

❾ 我偏愛長裙。
Long skirts are my favorite.

❿ 我有各種款式的牛仔褲。
I have every style of jeans.

⓫ 我喜歡 寬鬆 的衣服。
I like loose-fitting clothes.

⓬ 我經常為了 搭配衣服 而苦惱。
I usually struggle to decide what to wear.

⓭ 我每個月的置裝費約 5000 元。
My monthly clothing budget is about NT$5000.

⓮ 我喜歡穿高跟鞋。
I like to wear high heels.

⓯ 我喜歡色彩鮮豔的衣服。
I like colorful clothing.

017 你的穿著？

❶ 你喜歡穿 裙子 還是 褲子 ？
Do you like to wear skirts or pants?

❷ 你偏好什麼樣的穿著？
Which style of clothing do you like?

❸ 你會注意當季的 流行資訊 嗎？
Do you pay attention to the current season's fashion news?

❹ 你上班穿制服嗎？
Do you wear a uniform to work?

❺ 你今天穿的衣服很適合你。
The clothes you are wearing today really suit you.

❻ 這是 新衣服 嗎？
Are these new clothes?

❼ 你想嘗試高跟鞋嗎？
Would you like to try high heels?

❽ 你很會搭配衣服。
You really know how to put together an outfit.

❾ 你的鞋子很好看。
Your shoes are beautiful.

❿ 你真是 天生的衣架子 。
You really are born to wear anything.

⓫ 你穿西裝 真帥 ！
You look terrific in that suit!

⓬ 女人的 衣服永遠少一件 。
Women's wardrobes are always short one item.

⓭ 你的 置裝費 一定很可觀。
Your clothing budget must be considerable.

⓮ 你的鞋子跟衣服 很搭 。
Your shoes really match your clothes.

⓯ 你可以嘗試色彩鮮豔的衣服。
You can try on colorful clothing.

018 我的工作。

❶ 我還在唸書。
I am still in school.

❷ 我是 朝九晚五 的上班族。
I am part of the 9-to-5 workforce.

❸ 我和朋友經營一間店。
My friends and I manage a shop.

❹ 我自己創業 當老闆 。
I've started my own business and am my own boss.

❺ 我的工作完全與所學無關。
My job has nothing to do with what I learned in school.

❻ 我是 在家工作 的 SOHO 族。
I work at home.

❼ 我在電視台上班。
I work at a TV station.

❽ 我從事 服務業 。
I work in the service industry.

❾ 我是 公務員 。
I am a public servant.

❿ 我們公司在台北市中心。
Our firm is located in downtown Taipei.

⓫ 我 嘗試過很多 不同的工作。
I have tried my hand at various professions.

⓬ 我的工作是目前 最熱門 的行業。
My job is currently the most fashionable profession.

⓭ 我同時兼差好幾份工作。
I currently hold more than one job.

018 你的工作？

❶ 你 從事什麼 工作？
   What do you do for a living?

❷ 你自己創業嗎？
   Do you run your own business?

❸ 你和朋友 共同創業 嗎？
   Do you jointly run a company with your friend?

❹ 你在 哪間公司 上班？
   Which company do you work for?

❺ 你們公司是 做什麼 的？
   What's your company's main business?

❻ 你們公司有多少員工？
   How many employees are in your firm?

❼ 你們公司在哪裡？
   Where is your firm located?

❽ 你們公司很有名。
   Your company is very well known.

❾ 你屬於哪一個部門？
   Which department do you belong to?

❿ 你的 職務 是什麼？
   What is your job title?

⓫ 很多人擠破頭想進你們公司。
   A lot of people would do anything to work for
   your company.

⓬ 你有 兼職 的工作嗎？
   Do you still hold any part-time jobs?

⓭ 你們公司打算徵人嗎？
   Does your company plan to recruit new
   employees?

⓮ 你的工作 跟所學相關 嗎？
   Does your current job relate to what you learned in school?

019 我的工作內容。

❶ 我的工作內容 一成不變 。
The nature of my job is unchanging.

❷ 我的工作很繁瑣。
My work is very complicated.

❸ 我需要經常 出差 。
I have to go on business trips regularly.

❹ 我必須 控管產品 的品質。
I manage quality control.

❺ 我的工作是 負責協助 我的上司。
My job is assisting my manager.

❻ 我的工作需要長時間盯著電腦螢幕。
At work, I have to stare at a computer for long periods of time.

❼ 我必須向客戶 介紹新產品 。
I have to introduce our clients to our new products.

❽ 我負責解決客戶的所有問題。
I am in charge of dealing with all the problems that are brought up by our clients.

❾ 我在公司從基層做起。
I started out at the bottom of the company.

❿ 接聽電話 是我的工作之一。
Answering telephones is part of my job.

⓫ 我常常一整天都在 開會 。
I am often in meetings for the whole day.

⓬ 我負責 行銷企畫 。
I am in charge of planning and marketing.

⓭ 我的工作充滿挑戰。
My job is full of challenges.

019 你的工作內容？

❶ 你的 工作內容 是什麼？
What are your job responsibilities?

❷ 你的工作有趣嗎？
Is your job interesting?

❸ 你的工作 有挑戰性 嗎？
Is your job challenging?

❹ 你的工作必須用到英文嗎？
Does your job require the use of English?

❺ 你有一個 工作團隊 嗎？
Do you work with a team?

❻ 你都是 獨立作業 嗎？
Do you work independently?

❼ 你用 Skype 和客戶聯絡嗎？
Do you use Skype to contact your clients?

❽ 你必須公司 大小事一手包 嗎？
Are you responsible for every issue, large and
small, in your company?

❾ 你 有助理 嗎？
Do you have an assistant?

❿ 你有整天接不完的電話嗎？
Do you have phone calls that never stop coming?

⓫ 你在公司 從基層做起 嗎？
Did you start out at the bottom of your company?

⓬ 你必須經常出差嗎？
Do you need to take frequent business trips?

⓭ 你必須經常 拜訪客戶 嗎？
Do you need to visit clients frequently?

⓮ 你有開不完的會嗎？
Do you have meetings that never seem to end?

⓯ 你的工作一成不變嗎？
Does your work never change?

020 我的工作時間。

❶ 我每天九點 上班 ，六點 下班 。
I arrive to work at nine am and leave at six pm.

❷ 我每天 工作八小時 。
I work eight hours a day.

❸ 我們公司 午休 是一個小時。
Our company's lunch break is one hour long.

❹ 公司午休時間是十二點到下午一點。
The company's lunch break is from 12:00 pm to 1:00 pm.

❺ 我的工作時間 不固定 。
My work schedule is not fixed.

❻ 我們公司採 輪班制 。
Our company adopts a shift-work system.

❼ 我已經好幾個月沒休假了。
It's been several months since my last vacation.

❽ 我們公司 週休二日 。
Our company has a two-day weekend.

❾ 我從 不遲到早退 。
I have never arrived late or left early.

❿ 我一年有七天 年假 。
I get a seven-day annual leave.

⓫ 我經常假日也到公司加班。
I often have to work overtime even on holidays.

⓬ 我經 常加班 到深夜。
I often work late into the night.

⓭ 我來公司五年了。
I have been working with this company for five years.

⓮ 我來公司還不到一個月。
I have been working with this company for less than a month.

020 你的工作時間？

❶ 你的 上班時間 是幾點到幾點？
What is your work schedule?

❷ 你們公司什麼時候午休？
When does your office take a lunch break?

❸ 你常工作到很晚嗎？
Do you usually work late into the night?

❹ 你們公司午休時間多長？
How long is your company's lunchtime?

❺ 你幾點到公司？
What time do you arrive at the office?

❻ 你今晚 要加班 嗎？
Do you need to work overtime tonight?

❼ 你一天工作幾小時？
How many hours a day do you work?

❽ 你經常假日加班嗎？
Do you have to work on holidays a lot?

❾ 你 工作幾年 了？
How long have you been working?

❿ 你們要輪班嗎？
Do you have to work different shifts?

⓫ 你在這間公司多久了？
How long have you been working in your current company?

⓬ 你經常 請假 嗎？
Do you often ask for leave?

⓭ 你經 常遲到 嗎？
Are you often late for work?

⓮ 你上 早班 還是 夜班 ？
Do you work the day shift or the night shift?

⓯ 你們公司要 打卡 嗎？
Does your company require you to punch in and out?

021 我的工作心得。

❶ 我熱愛我的工作。
I love my job.

❷ 我是個 工作狂 。
I am a workaholic.

❸ 工作給我很大的壓力。
Work puts me under a lot of pressure.

❹ 我做這份工作 游刃有餘 。
I am more than good enough to do this job.

❺ 我以我的 工作為榮 。
I am proud of my work.

❻ 我覺得我的工作很有挑戰性。
I think my work is full of challenges.

❼ 我的工作可以讓我一展長才。
My job enables me to show my abilities.

❽ 工作中我獲得很多 成就感 。
I derive a great sense of achievement from my job.

❾ 我覺得 自己不適合 這份工作。
I don't think I am suitable for this job.

❿ 我總有 忙不完 的工作。
I always have too much work to finish.

⓫ 工作中我 學到很多 東西。
I have learned a lot from my work.

⓬ 我試著提高我的工作效率。
I have been trying to improve my work efficiency.

⓭ 我 喪失工作熱忱 。
I have lost my enthusiasm for work.

⓮ 工作使我認識很多朋友。
Work has helped me meet many friends.

⓯ 超時工作影響我的健康。
Working overtime affects my health.

021 你的工作心得？

❶ 你喜歡你的工作嗎？
Do you like your job?

❷ 你的工作讓你 學以致用 嗎？
Does your job allow you to use what you have learned?

❸ 你覺得這份工作適合自己嗎？
Do you think this job is suitable for you?

❹ 你的工作能讓你 一展長才 嗎？
Does your job allow you to display your talent?

❺ 你從工作中學到什麼？
What have you learned from your job?

❻ 你以工作為榮嗎？
Are you proud of your job?

❼ 你曾試著改變工作方法嗎？
Have you ever tried to change your work methods?

❽ 工作時你 最大的挫折 是什麼？
What was the most discouraging thing you ever experienced while working?

❾ 你希望成為一個 怎麼樣的職場人 ？
What kind of working person do you want to be?

❿ 你覺得自己不斷在進步嗎？
Do you feel like you are constantly improving?

⓫ 你對工作 充滿幹勁 嗎？
Are you very enthusiastic about your work?

⓬ 你是工作狂嗎？
Are you a workaholic?

⓭ 工作中你能 接觸不同行業 的人嗎？
Do you come in contact with people from other fields when working?

022 我的工作態度。

❶ 我每天 樂在工作 。
I find pleasure in my work every day.

❷ 我 全心投入 工作。
I devote myself to work.

❸ 我會在時間內完成工作。
I will finish my work in time.

❹ 我不遲到早退。
I never arrive late for work, or leave early.

❺ 上班時間我 不做私事 。
I don't engage in my personal affairs while working.

❻ 我會盡力完成公司交付的工作。
I will do my best to finish the tasks that are assigned to me by my company.

❼ 我努力 滿足客戶 需求。
I always strive to satisfy my customers' needs.

❽ 我小心做事 避免出錯 。
I work very carefully in order to avoid making mistakes.

❾ 我不隨便請假。
I don't ask for time off without a good reason.

❿ 我希望 從工作中學習 與成長。
I hope to learn and grow from my work.

⓫ 我希望 今日事今日畢 。
I never put off till tomorrow what should be done today.

⓬ 我不讓個人情緒影響工作。
I don't let my personal emotions influence my work.

⓭ 我希望自己永遠 保持最佳狀態 。
I hope I can always keep myself in the best possible condition.

022 你的工作態度？

❶ 你樂在工作嗎？
Do you find pleasure in your work?

❷ 你 認真工作 嗎？
Do you take your job seriously?

❸ 從工作中，你希望學到什麼？
What do you hope to learn from your job?

❹ 你常請假嗎？
Do you often ask for leave?

❺ 你經常遲到早退嗎？
Do you often arrive late to work and leave early?

❻ 你可以臨危不亂嗎？
Can you remain calm in a crisis?

❼ 工作低潮時 ，你會怎麼辦？
How do you deal with bad times at work?

❽ 你會努力 吸取專業知識 嗎？
Do you work hard to gain professional knowledge?

❾ 你會 主動要求 加薪嗎？
Do you actively request raises?

❿ 被同事抹黑，你怎麼處理？
How do you handle colleagues who try to discredit you?

⓫ 你 積極參與 會議嗎？
Do you actively participate during meetings?

⓬ 你勇於發問嗎？
Are you brave enough to ask questions?

⓭ 你擅長 危機處理 嗎？
Are you good at dealing with crises?

⓮ 你 勇於開發 新產品嗎？
Do you strive to develop new products?

⓯ 你有創新的精神嗎？
Do you have an innovative spirit?

023 我的工作異動。

❶ 我 失業 了。
I lost my job.

❷ 我被 加薪 了。
I got a raise.

❸ 我們公司大幅精簡人事。
Our company cut down on personnel.

❹ 我被減薪了。
My salary has been cut.

❺ 我被 升職 了。
I have been promoted.

❻ 我被 降職 了。
I have been demoted.

❼ 我換工作了。
I switched jobs.

❽ 我將被 派往海外 。
I will be assigned abroad.

❾ 我將被 調到總公司 。
I will be transferred to headquarters.

❿ 我被調到其他部門。
I have been assigned to another department.

⓫ 我才剛 通過試用期 。
I've just made it through the trial period.

⓬ 我將增加兩名助手。
I will have two additional assistants.

⓭ 我的部門來了一位 新同事 。
There is a new employee in my department.

⓮ 我有一個新主管。
I have a new manager.

⓯ 我明年要退休。
I will retire next year.

023 你的工作異動？

❶ 你為什麼離職？
Why did you leave your job?

❷ 你 想換工作 嗎？
Do you want to change jobs?

❸ 你的 新工作 是什麼？
What is your new job?

❹ 聽說你升官了？
I heard that you got promoted.

❺ 你滿意新的職稱嗎？
Are you satisfied with your new title?

❻ 你通過試用期了嗎？
Have you made it through the trial period?

❼ 你是不是 被挖角 ？
Have you been approached by other companies?

❽ 你願意到大陸發展嗎？
Are you willing to develop in China?

❾ 你什麼時候 遞辭呈 的？
When did you hand in your resignation?

❿ 你什麼時候要 退休 ？
When will you retire?

⓫ 你為什麼 被炒魷魚 ？
Why did you get fired?

⓬ 你們公司今年 有調薪 嗎？
Did your company give raises this year?

⓭ 你習慣新主管了嗎？
Have you gotten used to your new manager?

⓮ 你們公司面臨 財務危機 嗎？
Is your company facing any financial difficulties?

⓯ 你的新同事何時就任？
When will your new colleague begin work?

024 我想從事的工作。

❶ 我想做個 規律上下班 的上班族。
I want to work the same hours every day.

❷ 我想在 時尚界 工作。
I want to work in the fashion industry.

❸ 我想做自己 有興趣的 工作。
I want a job that I am interested in.

❹ 我希望自己 創業 。
I hope to start my own business.

❺ 我希望工作與所學相關。
I wish my job was related to what I learned in school.

❻ 我想 開一間店 。
I want to open a shop.

❼ 我想當個自由的 SOHO 族。
I want to be free and work from home.

❽ 我一直希望到 外商公司 上班。
I have always hoped to work in a foreign trading company.

❾ 我想到國外工作。
I want to work abroad.

❿ 我希望在大城市工作。
I wish I worked in a big city.

⓫ 我希望 從政 。
I hope to work in politics.

⓬ 我希望從事媒體相關工作。
I hope to have a job related to the mass media.

⓭ 我想從事 3C 產業。
I want to work in the 3C industry.

⓮ 我想從事服務業。
I want to work in the service industry.

⓯ 我想從事必須 與人接觸 的工作。
I want a job that requires contact with people.

024 你想從事的工作？

❶ 你希望 從事哪一行 ？
   What kind of career do you hope to have?

❷ 你希望工作充滿挑戰嗎？
   Do you wish your work was full of challenges?

❸ 你曾經夢想 當一個大明星 嗎？
   Have you ever dreamt of being a superstar?

❹ 你希望擁有一間小店嗎？
   Do you hope to own a small shop?

❺ 你希望自己創業嗎？
   Do you hope to start your own business?

❻ 你想當 SOHO 族嗎？
   Do you want to work from home?

❼ 你能接受 需要輪班 的工作嗎？
   Can you accept a job with shifts?

❽ 你能接受 24 小時的 工作嗎？
   Can you accept a 24-hour job?

❾ 工作對你有什麼意義？
   What meaning does your job hold for you?

❿ 你希望 到國外 工作嗎？
   Do you hope to work overseas?

⓫ 你想朝 傳播業 發展嗎？
   Do you want to work in mass media?

⓬ 你對 3C 產業有興趣嗎？
   Do you have any interest in the 3C industry?

⓭ 你對服務業有興趣嗎？
   Are you interested in the service industry?

⓮ 你動過 不要工作 的念頭嗎？
   Have you ever thought about not working?

⓯ 你必須 繼承家業 嗎？
   Do you have to inherit your family business?

025 我喜歡的工作環境。

❶ 我希望公司 福利完善 。
   I wish my company had more benefits.

❷ 我希望到員工 100 人以上的大公司。
   I wish I could work in a large company with more than 100 employees.

❸ 我希望 錢多事少 。
   I wish I had less work and more income.

❹ 我希望到員工 20 人以下的小公司。
   I wish I could work in a small company with less than 20 employees.

❺ 我希望公司重視員工培訓。
   I wish my company would focus on employee training.

❻ 我希望公司 交通便利 。
   I wish my firm was conveniently located.

❼ 我希望公司 離家近 。
   I wish my firm was close to my home.

❽ 我希望公司有完善的升遷制度。
   I wish my firm had a complete system for promotion.

❾ 我希望能 準時下班 。
   I wish I could leave work on time.

❿ 我希望每年有 10 天年假。
   I wish I had ten days' leave every year.

⓫ 我希望有 豐厚的年終 獎金。
   I hope to get a substantial year-end bonus.

⓬ 我希望 同事好相處 。
   I wish my colleagues were easier to get along with.

⓭ 我希望公司 供餐 。
   I wish my firm offered meals.

025 你喜歡的工作環境？

1 你希望 薪水多少 ？
How much do you hope your salary will be?

2 你希望多久調薪一次？
How often do you hope to get a raise?

3 你希望年終 獎金幾個月 ？
How much of an annual bonus do you hope to receive?

4 你希望 幾點上班 ？
What time would you like to start work?

5 你希望公司附近有捷運站嗎？
Do you wish there was an MRT station around your office?

6 你希望公司 分紅配股 嗎？
Do you wish your firm offered bonuses and stock options?

7 你希望到 大公司 還是 小公司 ？
Do you hope to work in a big company or a small one?

8 你希望上下班不打卡嗎？
Do you wish you didn't have to punch in and out of work?

9 你希望 月休幾天 ？
How many days off do you wish you had per month?

10 你希望天天準時下班嗎？
Do you wish you could leave work on time every day?

11 你希望公司有更完善的 升遷制度 嗎？
Do you wish your company had a more complete system for promotion?

12 你希望公司在市中心嗎？
Do you wish your firm was located in the downtown area?

13 你希望公司提供 哪些福利 ？
What kinds of benefits do you wish your firm provided?

14 你希望有幾天年假？
How many annual vacation days do you wish you had?

026 我希望外表⋯。

1 我希望 變美 。
I wish I could become more beautiful.

2 我希望自己是眾人 目光的焦點 。
I wish I could be the focus of everyone's attention.

3 我希望 皮膚完美無瑕 。
I wish I had flawless skin.

4 我希望看起來更年輕。
I wish I could look younger.

5 我希望雀斑變少。
I wish I had fewer freckles.

6 我希望 眼睛大一點 。
I wish I had bigger eyes.

7 我羨慕膚色白皙的人。
I envy people with fair skin.

8 我羨慕別人的小臉。
I am jealous of people with small faces.

9 我希望 變成雙眼皮 。
I wish I had double-fold eyelids.

10 我想要又長又翹的眼睫毛。
I want to have long, raised eyelashes.

11 我希望 鼻子變挺 。
I wish I had a pronounced nose.

12 我想要性感渾厚的嘴唇。
I want to have thick, sexy lips.

13 我努力減少臉上細紋。
I am trying to reduce my facial wrinkles.

14 我希望 沒有黑眼圈 。
I wish I didn't have bags under my eyes.

15 我希望看起來 有自信 。
I wish I looked more self-confident.

026 你希望外表…？

❶ 你滿意自己的長相嗎？
Are you satisfied with your appearance?

❷ 你希望 減少細紋 嗎？
Do you want to reduce your wrinkles?

❸ 你最 不滿意的五官 是哪一個？
What is the facial feature that you are most dissatisfied with?

❹ 你羨慕小臉的人嗎？
Are you envious of people who have smaller faces than you?

❺ 你希望 皮膚更白 嗎？
Do you wish you had whiter skin?

❻ 你打算曬成古銅色嗎？
Do you plan to get a bronze tan?

❼ 你希望自己看起來充滿自信嗎？
Do you wish you looked full of confidence?

❽ 你 打算整型 嗎？
Do you plan to have plastic surgery?

❾ 你希望自己看起來 成熟穩重 嗎？
Do you want to look mature and dignified?

❿ 你打算利用雷射 除斑 嗎？
Do you plan to have your blemishes removed by laser?

⓫ 你希望自己看起來更年輕嗎？
Do you wish you looked younger?

⓬ 你希望 永遠迷人 嗎？
Do you hope that you will be charming forever?

⓭ 你希望給別人什麼樣的印象？
What impression do you hope to give others?

⓮ 你想要 改變髮色 嗎？
Do you want to change your hair color?

027 我希望身材…。

❶ 我希望 永遠保持 好身材。
I hope that I can maintain my figure forever.

❷ 我希望身材更完美。
I wish I had a more attractive body.

❸ 我希望 維持目前體重 。
I hope that I can maintain my current weight.

❹ 我想減肥。
I want to lose some weight.

❺ 我 想減重 5公斤。
I want to lose five kilos.

❻ 我 想增胖 3公斤。
I want to gain three kilos.

❼ 我希望長高。
I wish I were taller.

❽ 我希望 別再長高 了。
I hope that I won't get any taller.

❾ 我希望身上毫無贅肉。
I wish that I didn't have any excess weight.

❿ 我希望有雙美腿。
I wish that I had a pair of beautiful legs.

⓫ 我希望 胸部豐滿 。
I wish I had a larger bust.

⓬ 我希望 消除小腹 。
I wish that I could get rid of my gut.

⓭ 我希望雙腿纖細修長。
I wish my legs were slim and slender.

⓮ 我希望手臂結實。
I wish I had sturdy arms.

⓯ 我想要 小蠻腰 。
I want to have a small waist.

027 你希望身材⋯？

❶ 你希望自己的體重多少公斤？
How many kilograms do you wish you were?

❷ 你希望自己 再瘦一點 嗎？
Do you wish you were a bit thinner?

❸ 你覺得自己的體重標準嗎？
Do you think your weight is average?

❹ 你覺得自己的身高標準嗎？
Do you think your height is normal?

❺ 你 希望身高 多少？
How tall do you wish you were?

❻ 你滿意你的身材嗎？
Are you satisfied with your figure?

❼ 你希望自己 永遠吃不胖 嗎？
Do you wish you could eat as much as you wanted
and never gain weight?

❽ 你羨慕模特兒的好身材嗎？
Do you envy the good figure of models?

❾ 你理想的 完美身材 是什麼樣子？
What is your ideal figure?

❿ 你希望能 更強壯 嗎？
Do you wish you were a bit stronger?

⓫ 你 最不滿意 全身哪一個部位？
Which part of your figure are you most dissatisfied
with?

⓬ 你努力 消除贅肉 嗎？
Are you trying to get rid of excess fat?

⓭ 你希望 穿得下 S 號 的衣服嗎？
Do you wish you could wear size small clothes?

⓮ 誰是你心目中的完美身材代表？
Who do you think has the most ideal body?

028 我的生涯規畫。

❶ 我對未來有很多計畫。
I have many plans for my future.

❷ 我對未來 沒有想法 。
I don't have any plans for my future.

❸ 我打算 出國留學 。
I intend to study abroad.

❹ 我只想 走一步算一步 。
I just want to take life one step at a time.

❺ 我希望闖出 一番事業 。
I hope to develop a career for myself.

❻ 我計畫 5 年後創業。
I plan to have my own business in five years.

❼ 我希望 27 歲前結婚。
I hope that I can get married before I turn 27.

❽ 30 歲後我想開一間店。
I want to open a store after I turn 30.

❾ 我想當 頂客族 。
I want to be a DINK (Double Income, No Kids).

❿ 我計畫 60 歲退休。
I plan to retire at age 60.

⓫ 我希望 30 歲前生小孩。
I hope to have a child before I turn 30.

⓬ 我想 生兩個 小孩。
I intend to have two children.

⓭ 一生中我一定要 環遊世界 。
I absolutely must travel around the world at some point in my life.

⓮ 我希望 有經濟基礎 再結婚。
I hope to get married after I have some economic stability.

028 你的生涯規畫？

1 你希望 成為怎麼樣的 人？
What kind of person do you hope to become?

2 十年後，你希望成為什麼樣子？
What kind of person do you hope to be in ten years?

3 你計畫 幾歲結婚 ？
When do you plan to get married?

4 你想過你的未來嗎？
Have you ever considered your future?

5 你有計畫生小孩嗎？
Do you plan to have a child?

6 你打算出國留學嗎？
Do you have plans to study abroad?

7 你打算 一輩子單身 嗎？
Do you plan to be single for the rest of your life?

8 你計畫 幾歲退休 ？
When do you plan to retire?

9 你計畫生幾個小孩？
How many children do you plan to have?

10 你想從事什麼樣的工作？
What kind of career would you like to have?

11 你 退休後 想做什麼？
What do you want to do after you retire?

12 你打算創業嗎？
Do you intend to start your own business?

13 你希望找什麼樣的 人生伴侶 ？
What kind of life partner do you hope to find?

14 你打算 移民 嗎？
Do you plan to immigrate to another country?

15 你準備 考證照 嗎？
Are you prepared for the certification tests?

029 我的理財規畫。

1 我每天 記帳 。
I keep track of my expenses every day.

2 我每個月儲蓄薪水的三分之一。
I save one-third of my salary every month.

3 我投資 股票 。
I invest in stocks.

4 我打算 30 歲買房子。
I plan to buy a house when I am 30.

5 我 每個月儲蓄 5000 元。
I save five thousand every month.

6 我希望 25 歲擁有 第一個 100 萬 。
I hope to have earned my first million by the time I'm 25.

7 我做期貨買賣。
I do futures trading.

8 我希望 10 年內付清車貸。
I hope to pay off my car loan within ten years.

9 我跟會。
I've joined a credit cooperative.

10 我 不隨便花 錢。
I don't spend money carelessly.

11 我把錢在銀行 定存 。
I deposit my money in a savings account.

12 我為自己 買保險 。
I bought insurance for myself.

13 我完全不懂理財。
I don't know how to manage my money at all.

14 我必須準備 小孩的教育費 。
I have to save for my child's education.

15 我花錢完全 不做規畫 。
I spend money without thinking.

029 你的理財規畫？

❶ 你如何理財？
   How do you manage your money?

❷ 你一個月 存多少 錢？
   How much do you save per month?

❸ 你 如何運用 薪水？
   How do you make use of your salary?

❹ 你定期儲蓄嗎？
   Do you save money regularly?

❺ 你有投資 房地產 嗎？
   Do you invest in real estate?

❻ 你每天記帳嗎？
   Do you keep track of your finances every day?

❼ 你 有貸款 嗎？
   Do you have a loan?

❽ 你很清楚 錢花到哪裡去了 嗎？
   Do you know exactly how you spend your money?

❾ 你看理財雜誌嗎？
   Do you read magazines about financial management?

❿ 你做 什麼投資 ？
   What do you invest in?

⓫ 你每個月的薪水都 花個精光 嗎？
   Do you blow your salary every month?

⓬ 你 跟會 嗎？
   Are you part of a credit cooperative?

⓭ 你用錢有計畫嗎？
   Do you have any spending plans for your money?

⓮ 你希望退休時 有多少現金 ？
   How much cash do you hope to have when you retire?

⓯ 沒錢的時候你怎麼辦？
   What would you do if you didn't have any money?

030 我的起床。

❶ 我習慣 早起 。
I am used to getting up early.

❷ 我通常 8點起床 。
I usually wake up at eight o'clock.

❸ 我早上都會自己醒來。
I wake myself up every morning.

❹ 星期六日我 睡到很晚 。
I get up late on weekends.

❺ 我習慣 睡到自然醒 。
I am used to waking up naturally.

❻ 我每天都要別人叫我起床。
I need someone to wake me up every day.

❼ 我常因為爬不起來而 遲到 。
I am usually late because I can't get out of bed.

❽ 我都用手機當鬧鐘。
I use a mobile phone as my alarm clock.

❾ 我需要鬧鐘叫我起床。
I need an alarm clock to wake me up.

❿ 我喜歡 賴床 。
I like to stay in bed.

⓫ 鬧鐘根本叫不醒我。
An alarm clock can't wake me up at all.

⓬ 起床後我仍然覺得 沒睡飽 。
Even after I get up, I still feel like I didn't get enough sleep.

⓭ 我一睡著誰都叫不醒我。
As long as I'm asleep, nobody can wake me up.

⓮ 我剛起床會一直 打呵欠 。
I always yawn just after getting up.

⓯ 起床後 30 分鐘我就出門。
I go out 30 minutes after I wake up.

030 你的起床？

❶ 你通常 幾點起床 ？
What time do you usually wake up?

❷ 你每天早上會 自己醒來 嗎？
Do you get up by yourself every morning?

❸ 假日你都比平常晚起嗎？
Do you always sleep in when you have the day off?

❹ 你會賴床嗎？
Do you lie around in bed?

❺ 你一向晚起嗎？
Do you always get up late?

❻ 你要我 叫你起床 嗎？
Do you need me to wake you up?

❼ 你沒聽到 鬧鐘響 嗎？
Didn't you hear the alarm clock ringing?

❽ 你用鬧鐘嗎？
Do you need to use an alarm clock?

❾ 鬧鐘叫得醒你嗎？
Do alarm clocks wake you up?

❿ 家人會叫你起床嗎？
Does your family wake you up?

⓫ 你常 被吵醒 嗎？
Does noise usually wake you up?

⓬ 你還要睡多久？
How long do you still need to sleep?

⓭ 你 清醒了嗎 ？
Are you awake?

⓮ 你都睡到這麼晚嗎？
Do you always get up so late?

⓯ 你每天 折被子 嗎？
Do you make your bed every day?

031 我的睡眠。

❶ 我習慣 晚睡 。
I am used to going to bed late.

❷ 我每天晚上 10 點就寢。
I go to bed at ten pm every night.

❸ 我都是 一覺到天亮 。
I always sleep right through until dawn.

❹ 我很容易被吵醒。
I am easily awakened by noise.

❺ 我每天睡足 8 小時。
I sleep a full eight hours every day.

❻ 我經常 失眠 。
I frequently get insomnia.

❼ 我很容易入睡。
I fall asleep easily.

❽ 我睡覺 常作夢 。
I usually dream while sleeping.

❾ 沒事的話我可以 睡一整天 。
I can sleep for a full day if there's nothing going on.

❿ 我會 認床 。
I have to sleep in my own bed.

⓫ 我的 睡相不好看 。
I don't look good when I sleep.

⓬ 我睡覺會打鼾。
I snore in my sleep.

⓭ 我嚴重睡眠不足。
I have serious sleep deprivation.

⓮ 我經常熬夜。
I often stay up late.

⓯ 我習慣 裸睡 。
I am used to sleeping naked.

031 你的睡眠？

❶ 通常都 幾點睡覺 ？
What time do you usually go to sleep?

❷ 你一天睡 幾個小時 ？
How many hours of sleep a night do you get?

❸ 你很早睡嗎？
Do you go to bed early?

❹ 你常 熬夜 嗎？
Do you usually stay up late?

❺ 你 容易入睡 嗎？
Do you fall asleep easily?

❻ 你容易被吵醒嗎？
Are you a light sleeper?

❼ 你的睡眠品質好嗎？
Do you get good-quality sleep?

❽ 你常作夢嗎？
Do you often have dreams?

❾ 你會認床嗎？
Can you sleep in other beds?

❿ 睡前你會聽音樂嗎？
Do you listen to music before going to bed?

⓫ 你睡覺會 打鼾 嗎？
Do you snore?

⓬ 你會 踢被子 嗎？
Do you kick the blanket off while sleeping?

⓭ 你 睡眠不足 嗎？
Is your sleep insufficient?

⓮ 你會裸睡嗎？
Do you sleep in the nude?

⓯ 你 開燈睡 覺嗎？
Do you sleep with a light on?

032 我的美容。

1 我很重視皮膚保養。

I pay a lot of attention to skin care.

2 我很重視 保養品 的成分。

I pay a lot of attention to the ingredients of skin care products.

3 我沒有固定使用同一個品牌的保養品。

I don't use a specific brand of skin care products.

4 我每週用 面膜敷臉 一次。

I apply a facial mask once a week.

5 我早晚各洗一次臉。

I wash my face once in the morning and once in the evening.

6 我每天 徹底卸妝 。

I completely remove my makeup every day.

7 避免毛孔粗大，我只用冷水洗臉。

I only wash my face with cold water to avoid enlarging my pores.

8 我定期做皮膚 去角質 。

I exfoliate my skin regularly.

9 夏天出門我一定 擦防曬 乳。

In the summertime, I am sure to put on sunblock when I go out.

10 為了美容，我 不熬夜 不抽煙。

To maintain my appearance, I never stay up late or smoke.

11 我很喜歡 做 spa 。

I like to go to the spa.

12 洗完手我立刻 擦護手霜 。

Right after I wash my hands, I apply hand cream.

13 冬天我會加強皮膚保濕。

In the winter, I work on moisturizing my skin.

032 你的美容？

1 你 怎麼保養 皮膚？
How do you take care of your skin?

2 你現在是用 哪一個品牌 的保養品？
Which brand of skin care products are you using right now?

3 你 定期敷臉 嗎？
Do you apply a facial mask regularly?

4 你用過 瘦身霜 嗎？
Have you ever used weight-loss cream?

5 每個人都希望更年輕更漂亮。
Everyone wants to be younger and more beautiful.

6 你的皮膚需要去角質。
You need to have your skin exfoliated.

7 你怎麼卸妝？
How do you remove the cosmetics you put on?

8 你應該注重 皮膚清潔 。
You should pay attention to the cleanliness of your skin.

9 你應該用溫水或冷水洗臉。
You should use either warm or cold water to wash your face.

10 你做過 spa 嗎？
Have you ever been to a spa?

11 熬夜是 美容大敵 。
Staying up late is the arch-enemy of beauty.

12 眼睛周圍的皮膚要 輕柔對待 。
You should treat the skin around your eyes gently.

13 你應該加強皮膚 保濕 。
You should work on moisturizing your skin.

14 泡溫泉可以美容。
Soaking in hot springs can make you more beautiful.

033 我的健康。

① 我一直都很健康。
I have always been very healthy.

② 我很 容易感冒 。
I catch colds easily.

③ 我從小就 體弱多病 。
I have been weak and sickly since childhood.

④ 我習慣看西醫。
I am used to seeing Western doctors.

⑤ 我常頭痛。
I often get headaches.

⑥ 我 討厭吃藥 。
I dislike taking medicine.

⑦ 我有 經痛 的毛病。
I'm having menstrual pains.

⑧ 我每天吃綜合維他命補充營養。
I take vitamins every day to supplement my diet.

⑨ 我 腸胃不好 。
I have a bad digestive system.

⑩ 我有蛀牙。
I have cavities.

⑪ 我很 重視養生 。
I pay a lot of attention to my health.

⑫ 我每年做 健康檢查 。
I get a physical examination each year.

⑬ 我是 過敏 體質。
I have allergies.

⑭ 我動過一次手術。
I had an operation once.

⑮ 我經常全身痠痛。
I often feel soreness throughout my whole body.

033 你的健康？

❶ 你 常生病 嗎？
Do you get sick often?

❷ 你覺得自己健康嗎？
Do you think you're healthy?

❸ 你看 西醫 還是 中醫 ？
Do you go to see a traditional Chinese doctor or a Western doctor?

❹ 你定期做健康檢查嗎？
Do you regularly go in for a physical?

❺ 你常感冒嗎？
Do you often catch colds?

❻ 你 容易頭疼 嗎？
Do you get headaches easily?

❼ 你有蛀牙嗎？
Do you have any cavities?

❽ 你 害怕打針 嗎？
Are you afraid of having an injection?

❾ 你 動過手術 嗎？
Have you ever had an operation?

❿ 生理期 你會不舒服嗎？
Do you feel uncomfortable during your period?

⓫ 你有 職業病 嗎？
Do you have any occupational sicknesses?

⓬ 你如何保養身體？
How do you keep yourself in good health?

⓭ 你經常全身痠痛嗎？
Do you often feel soreness throughout your whole body?

⓮ 你 擔心癌症 嗎？
Are you worried about cancer?

034 我的運動。

1 我喜歡運動。
I like to exercise.

2 我 | 每天運動 | 。
I exercise every day.

3 我討厭運動。
I dislike exercising.

4 我 | 很少運動 | 。
I seldom exercise.

5 我每週運動三次。
I exercise three times a week.

6 我是個 | 體育白癡 | 。
When it comes to athletics, I'm completely ignorant.

7 我的 | 運動神經 | 很發達。
I am very athletic.

8 運動完我立即補充水分。
I rehydrate immediately after exercise.

9 醫生說我 | 缺乏運動 | 。
The doctor said I don't get enough exercise.

10 游泳是我最愛的運動。
Swimming is my favorite sport.

11 我喜歡各種球類運動。
I like playing every sport with a ball.

12 我偶爾打保齡球。
Every once in a while I go bowling.

13 我定期 | 上健身房 | 。
I work out at the gym regularly.

14 做家事就是我的運動。
My exercise consists of doing the housework.

15 我最近 | 迷上瑜珈 | 。
Recently, I have become very interested in yoga.

034 你的運動？

① 你每週 運動幾次 ？
How many times a week do you exercise?

② 你喜歡運動嗎？
Do you like to exercise?

③ 你 常做什麼 運動？
What do you usually do for exercise?

④ 你的運動神經好嗎？
Are you athletic?

⑤ 你通常 什麼時間 運動？
When do you usually exercise?

⑥ 你到健身房運動嗎？
Do you go to the gym to exercise?

⑦ 你覺得自己的 運動量夠 嗎？
Do you think you get enough exercise?

⑧ 你會游泳嗎？
Can you swim?

⑨ 你經常走路嗎？
Do you walk often?

⑩ 運動絕對有益健康。
Exercise is definitely good for one's health.

⑪ 你喜歡 慢跑 嗎？
Do you like to jog?

⑫ 你可以把 爬樓梯當運動 。
You can climb stairs for exercise.

⑬ 我想你缺乏運動。
I guess you don't exercise enough.

⑭ 你運動是 為了維持身材 嗎？
Do you exercise to stay in shape?

⑮ 你應該養成 運動的好習慣 。
You should develop good exercise habits.

035 我的寵物。

1 我喜歡養寵物。
I like pets.

2 我有 養寵物 。
I have a pet.

3 我們都叫牠小白。
We call it Snowball.

4 我 養狗 。
I have a dog.

5 牠是男生。
It is a male.

6 牠是我 領養 的。
I adopted it.

7 我的狗狗是 朋友送的 。
My dog was given to me by my friend.

8 我每天帶狗狗去散步。
I take my dog for a walk every day.

9 我 養牠 7 年 了。
I have had it for seven years.

10 我的狗一個禮拜洗一次澡。
I bathe my dog once a week.

11 牠現在 3 歲。
It is three years old.

12 牠是我們 全家的寶貝 。
It is our family's baby.

13 我餵牠吃飼料。
I feed it pet food.

14 牠很 貪吃 。
It likes to eat.

15 牠很 受寵 。
It is spoiled.

035 你的寵物？

❶ 你有養寵物嗎？
Do you have a pet?

❷ 你會想要養寵物嗎？
Do you want to own a pet?

❸ 你 養什麼 寵物？
What kind of pets do you have?

❹ 你的寵物叫什麼名字？
What's your pet's name?

❺ 牠年紀多大了？
How old is it?

❻ 你飼 養牠多久 了？
How long have you had it?

❼ 牠是 公的 還是 母的 ？牠是什麼顏色？
Is it male or female? What color is it?

❽ 你每天 遛狗 嗎？
Do you walk your dog every day?

❾ 你喜歡你的寵物嗎？
Do you like your pet?

❿ 牠 幾天洗一次 澡？
How often does it take a bath?

⓫ 你都餵牠吃什麼？
What do you feed it?

⓬ 牠有被寵壞嗎？
Does it ever act spoiled?

⓭ 牠會 亂叫 嗎？
Does it bark a lot?

⓮ 牠會 咬人 嗎？
Does it bite?

⓯ 你的寵物 乖不乖 ？
Is your pet well behaved?

036 我的交通工具。

❶ 我 搭捷運 上班。
I take the MRT to work.

❷ 捷運後我 轉公車 。
I transfer to a bus after taking the MRT.

❸ 我不常搭公車。
I rarely take the bus.

❹ 我偶爾搭計程車上班。
Sometimes I take a taxi to work.

❺ 我 騎機車 上學。
I ride a motorcycle to school.

❻ 我 開車 上班。
I drive to work.

❼ 我害怕 搭飛機 。
I am afraid of flying.

❽ 我有車。
I have a car.

❾ 我容易 暈車 。
I get carsick easily.

❿ 我剛貸款買車。
I just bought a car with a loan.

⓫ 我有汽車駕照。
I have a driver's license.

⓬ 我用 悠遊卡 搭捷運。
I take the MRT using EasyCard.

⓭ 我的油錢很可觀。
My fuel expenses are quite considerable.

⓮ 上個月我收到三張罰單。
I got three traffic violation tickets last month.

⓯ 我定期 保養愛車 。
I have my car serviced regularly.

036 你的交通工具？

❶ 你 怎麼去上班 ？
   How do you get to work?

❷ 你搭捷運上班嗎？
   Do you get to work by MRT?

❸ 你開車上班嗎？
   Do you drive to work?

❹ 你打算換車嗎？
   Do you plan to change cars?

❺ 你 有車 嗎？
   Do you have a car?

❻ 你容易 暈船 嗎？
   Do you get seasick easily?

❼ 你害怕搭飛機嗎？
   Are you afraid of flying?

❽ 你出過車禍嗎？
   Have you ever been in a car accident before?

❾ 你有汽車 駕照 嗎？
   Do you have a driver's license?

❿ 你有悠遊卡嗎？
   Do you have an EasyCard?

⓫ 你通常搭公車嗎？
   Do you usually take the bus?

⓬ 你害怕晚上 搭計程車 嗎？
   Are you afraid of taking a taxi at night?

⓭ 你的 油錢 一個月多少？
   How much is your monthly fuel cost?

⓮ 你常 吃罰單 嗎？
   Do you get traffic tickets often?

⓯ 你多久保養一次愛車？
   How often do you service your car?

037 我的網路活動。

❶ 我覺得網路很方便。
I think that the Internet is very convenient.

❷ 我幾乎 每天上網 。
I go online almost every day.

❸ 我偶爾利用 網路購物 。
Sometimes I shop online.

❹ 我對上網沒興趣。
I don't have any interest in going online.

❺ 我常上網跟朋友聊天。
I usually go on the Internet to talk with my friends.

❻ 我每天 上網 1 個小時 。
I go online for an hour every day.

❼ 我透過網路結交很多朋友。
I've made a lot of friends via the Internet.

❽ 我偶爾跟朋友 玩視訊 。
Sometimes I will use a webcam with my friends.

❾ 我常用網路 搜尋資料 。
I usually use the Internet to search for information.

❿ 我用 email 聯絡客戶。
I use email to contact my clients.

⓫ 我從網路 下載 東西。
I download material from the Internet.

⓬ 我經常因為上網而熬夜。
I always stay up late because of the Internet.

⓭ 我很迷 線上遊戲 。
I am obsessed with online games.

⓮ 我有兩個電子郵件信箱。
I have two email addresses.

⓯ 我常 泡網咖 。
I hang out at Internet cafés a lot.

037 你的網路活動？

❶ 你喜歡上網嗎？
Do you like to go online?

❷ 你經 常上網 嗎？
Do you regularly go online?

❸ 你的電子信箱帳號是什麼？
What is your email account?

❹ 你每天 收 email 嗎？
Do you check your email every day?

❺ 你有 電子信箱 嗎？
Do you have an email address?

❻ 你上網 跟朋友聊天 嗎？
Do you talk with friends online?

❼ 你每天 花多少時間 上網？
How much time do you spend online every day?

❽ 你玩過視訊嗎？
Have you ever used a webcam before?

❾ 你從網路下載東西嗎？
Do you download things from the Internet?

❿ 你會上網找資料嗎？
Do you search for information online?

⓫ 你上網都在做什麼？
What do you do when you go online?

⓬ 你有 網友 嗎？
Do you have any Internet friends?

⓭ 你在網路上買過東西嗎？
Have you ever bought anything online?

⓮ 你用 臉書 嗎？
Do you use Facebook?

⓯ 你去過網咖嗎？
Have you ever been to an Internet café before?

038 我與便利商店。

❶ 我 很少去 便利商店。
I seldom go to the convenience store.

❷ 我常到便利商店買東西。
I often go shopping at the convenience store.

❸ 我利用便利商店 繳費 。
I pay my bills at the convenience store.

❹ 我每天去便利商店買報紙。
I go to the convenience store to buy a newspaper every day.

❺ 便利商店讓我的 生活更方便 。
Convenience stores make my life more convenient.

❻ 我喜歡便利商店的便當。
I like the boxed lunches from the convenience store.

❼ 我偶爾到便利商店傳真。
Sometimes I go to the convenience store to send a fax.

❽ 我住的地方離便利商店很遠。
I live far away from any convenience store.

❾ 我常利用便利商店的 提款機 。
I usually use the ATM in the convenience store.

❿ 我最常到便利商店買口香糖。
I mostly buy gum from the convenience store.

⓫ 我常利用便利商店 寄宅配 。
I usually use the convenience store's home delivery service.

⓬ 我喜歡嘗試便利商店的 新產品 。
I like to try out the convenience store's new products.

⓭ 有時候我到便利商店 買午餐 。
Sometimes I will go to the convenience store to buy lunch.

⓮ 我覺得 逛便利商店 是種樂趣。
I think shopping in the convenience store is fun.

038 你與便利商店？

❶ 你 常去 便利商店嗎？
Do you go to the convenience store frequently?

❷ 你喜歡逛便利商店嗎？
Do you like shopping in the convenience store?

❸ 你喜歡便利商店的食物嗎？
Do you like the food in the convenience store?

❹ 你到便利商店 提款 嗎？
Do you withdraw money from the ATM in the convenience store?

❺ 你到便利商店 影印 嗎？
Do you make copies in the convenience store?

❻ 你有 7-11 的 i-cash 卡嗎？
Do you have a 7-11 i-cash card?

❼ 你利用便利商店繳費嗎？
Do you pay your bills at the convenience store?

❽ 你家附近 有便利商店嗎？
Is there a convenience store around your home?

❾ 你喜歡 7-11 還是全家？
Do you like 7-11 or Family Mart?

❿ 你寄過便利商店的宅配服務嗎？
Have you ever used the convenience store's home delivery service?

⓫ 你每天在便利商店 買報紙 嗎？
Do you buy newspapers in the convenience store every day?

⓬ 很多便利商店 全年無休 。
Many convenience stores are open all year round.

⓭ 在台灣，便利商店 隨處可見 。
Convenience stores are everywhere in Taiwan.

⓮ 你到便利商店買早餐嗎？
Do you go to the convenience store to buy breakfast?

039 我的早餐。

❶ 我每天吃早餐。
I have breakfast every day.

❷ 我 從不吃 早餐。
I never eat breakfast.

❸ 我常因睡過頭而 沒吃早餐 。
I often skip breakfast because I oversleep.

❹ 我不吃早餐會沒體力。
I have no energy without breakfast.

❺ 我常在公車上吃早餐。
I often have my breakfast on the bus.

❻ 我 在家裡吃 早餐。
I have my breakfast at home.

❼ 我媽媽每天幫我做早餐。
My mom makes me breakfast every day.

❽ 我吃三明治當早餐。
I have sandwiches for breakfast.

❾ 我 自己做 早餐。
I make myself breakfast.

❿ 我到便利商店買早餐。
I get my breakfast from the convenience store.

⓫ 我喜歡中式早餐。
I like Chinese-style breakfasts.

⓬ 我今天早餐很豐盛。
I had a sumptuous breakfast.

⓭ 我的早餐 常換花樣 。
I'll have various kinds of breakfasts.

⓮ 我每天早上都吃 吐司夾蛋 。
I have a piece of toast with egg every morning.

⓯ 我覺得早餐是一天中 最重要的一餐 。
I think that breakfast is the most important meal of the day.

039 你的早餐？

❶ 你 每天吃 早餐嗎？
Do you have breakfast every day?

❷ 你通常 幾點吃 早餐？
What time do you usually have breakfast?

❸ 你 為什麼不吃 早餐？
Why don't you want to have breakfast?

❹ 你自己弄早餐嗎？
Do you make breakfast yourself?

❺ 你的早餐 吃什麼 ？
What did you have for breakfast?

❻ 你在辦公室吃早餐嗎？
Do you have breakfast at the office?

❼ 你在 早餐店 吃早餐嗎？
Do you have your breakfast at the breakfast shop?

❽ 你常因睡過頭而沒吃早餐嗎？
Do you skip your breakfast due to oversleeping?

❾ 你常吃 西式 早餐還是 中式 早餐？
Do you usually eat a Western-style or Chinese-style breakfast?

❿ 你覺得早餐很重要嗎？
Do you take breakfast seriously?

⓫ 你早餐吃漢堡嗎？
Do you have hamburgers for breakfast?

⓬ 你在 公車上吃 早餐嗎？
Do you have your breakfast on the bus?

⓭ 你到便利商店買早餐嗎？
Do you get your breakfast from convenience stores?

⓮ 你今天早餐 很豐盛 嗎？
Did you have a sumptuous breakfast?

⓯ 你的早餐常換花樣嗎？
Do you often try different kinds of breakfasts?

040 我的午餐。

❶ 我今天中午 吃很少 。
I had a small lunch.

❷ 我今天午餐很簡單。
I had a simple lunch.

❸ 我今天跟同事一起吃午餐。
I had lunch with my coworkers.

❹ 我今天午餐 吃便當 。
I had a boxed lunch for lunch.

❺ 我常約客戶吃午餐。
I often invite my clients to have lunch with me.

❻ 我通常在下午兩點前吃完午餐。
I usually finish my lunch before two pm.

❼ 我們公司免費供應午餐。
There's a free lunch offered by our company.

❽ 我今天在 員工餐廳 吃午餐。
I had lunch at the employee cafeteria.

❾ 我中午習慣吃飯。
I'm used to having rice for lunch.

❿ 我自己 帶便當 。
I bring my own lunch box.

⓫ 我偶爾吃 商業午餐 。
I have a business lunch from time to time.

⓬ 我們常在學校附近吃午餐。
We often have lunch somewhere near the school.

⓭ 我經常 忙到沒時間吃 午餐。
I'm often too busy to have lunch.

⓮ 我今天午餐 只吃沙拉 。
I had only a salad for lunch.

⓯ 中午 吃太飽 我會想睡覺。
If I eat too much for lunch I get sleepy.

040 你的午餐？

❶ 你吃午餐了嗎？
Did you have lunch yet?

❷ 你要 一起吃 午餐嗎？
Do you want to join us for lunch?

❸ 你通常 一個人吃 午餐嗎？
Do you usually have lunch alone?

❹ 你和同事一起吃午餐嗎？
Do you have lunch with your coworkers?

❺ 你們 公司供應 午餐嗎？
Is lunch provided by your company?

❻ 你的午餐通常吃什麼？
What do you usually have for lunch?

❼ 你自己帶便當嗎？
Do you bring your own lunch box?

❽ 你通常 忙到幾點吃 午餐？
What time can you usually have lunch?

❾ 你今天中午吃飯還是吃麵？或是別的？
Did you have rice or noodles for lunch?
Or something else?

❿ 你中午要和 客戶聚餐 嗎？
Do you need to have lunch with your clients?

⓫ 你中午有 約人吃飯 嗎？
Do you have an appointment with anyone for lunch?

⓬ 你中午只吃水果嗎？
Do you only have fruit for lunch?

⓭ 你的午餐都吃這麼少嗎？
Do you usually have so little for lunch?

⓮ 你在 公司附近吃 午餐嗎？
Do you have lunch near the office?

⓯ 你的午餐 吃得太油膩 了！
You're having too much greasy food for lunch!

041 我的晚餐。

1 我 買晚餐回家 吃。
I bring food home for dinner.

2 我通常 在家吃 晚餐。
I usually have dinner at home.

3 我很少跟家人一起吃晚餐。
I seldom have dinner with my family.

4 我 自己下廚 煮晚餐。
I cook dinner myself.

5 我常跟家人上館子吃晚餐。
I often eat out for dinner with my family.

6 我常跟朋友共進晚餐。
I often have dinner with my friends.

7 我習慣 很晚吃 晚餐。
I'm used to having a late dinner.

8 朋友邀我今晚一起吃飯。
My friend asked me to dinner tonight.

9 我常忙到沒空吃晚餐。
I'm often too busy to have dinner.

10 我偶爾 吃泡麵 當晚餐。
I have instant noodles for dinner sometimes.

11 我很久沒回家吃晚餐了。
I haven't gone home for dinner in a long time.

12 晚餐我總是 吃太多 。
I always eat too much for dinner.

13 我總是 草草解決 我的晚餐。
I always take care of my dinner in a hurry.

14 我偶爾在 高級餐廳 吃晚餐。
I'll go to a fancy restaurant for dinner occasionally.

15 為了減肥我晚餐吃得少。
I eat a light dinner to lose weight.

041 你的晚餐？

❶ 你吃晚餐了嗎？
Did you have your dinner?

❷ 你為什麼不吃晚餐？
Why didn't you have your dinner?

❸ 你 真的不吃 晚餐嗎？
Do you really not want any dinner?

❹ 你通常幾點吃晚餐？
What time do you usually have dinner?

❺ 你都 這麼晚吃 晚餐嗎？
Do you always have your dinner this late?

❻ 你的晚餐通常吃什麼？
What do you usually have for dinner?

❼ 你會自己下廚煮晚餐嗎？
Do you cook dinner yourself?

❽ 你常 在外面吃 晚餐嗎？
Do you often go out for dinner?

❾ 你每天 回家吃 晚餐嗎？
Do you go home for dinner every day?

❿ 你晚上常跟 朋友聚餐 嗎？
Do you often have dinner with your friends?

⓫ 加班時你怎麼解決晚餐？
What do you do for dinner when you have to work overtime?

⓬ 你常 去餐廳吃 晚餐嗎？
Do you often go to restaurants for dinner?

⓭ 你的晚餐會吃泡麵嗎？
Do you have instant noodles for dinner?

⓮ 今晚你 想吃什麼 嗎？
What would you like for dinner?

⓯ 晚上你有 吃飽 嗎？
Did you get enough to eat at dinner?

042 我的飲料。

1 我最 愛喝可樂 。
Coke is my favorite.

2 我 只喝開水 。
I drink only water.

3 我每天至少 喝 2000cc 的水。
I drink at least two liters of water every day.

4 我每天早上喝牛奶。
I have milk every morning.

5 我偏愛冷飲。
I'm partial to cold drinks.

6 我從不喝冰飲。
I never touch iced drinks.

7 我經常嘗試各種不同的飲料。
I'm always trying all kinds of drinks.

8 我冬天常喝熱巧克力。
I often drink lots of hot chocolate during winter.

9 我習慣 飯後喝 一杯茶。
I'm used to having a cup of tea after meals.

10 我很少喝運動飲料。
I seldom drink sports drinks.

11 我每天喝一杯 鮮榨果汁 。
I have a glass of fresh juice every day.

12 我一直都不喝汽水。
I've never drunk any soda.

13 我 喝咖啡提神 。
I drink coffee to wake myself up.

14 我 不喝酒 。
I never drink.

15 我都喝 黑咖啡 。
I drink my coffee black.

042 你的飲料？

❶ 你要喝茶、喝咖啡還是喝水？
Do you want tea, coffee or water?

❷ 你每天喝水嗎？
Do you drink water every day?

❸ 你 常喝哪些 飲料？
What do you usually drink?

❹ 你喜歡 冷飲 還是 熱飲 ？
Do you like cold or hot drinks?

❺ 你喜歡可樂嗎？
Do you like Coke?

❻ 你 喝茶會失眠 嗎？
Can you sleep after drinking tea?

❼ 你一天 喝多少水 ？
How much water do you drink per day?

❽ 你每天喝咖啡嗎？
Do you have coffee every day?

❾ 你 喝酒 嗎？
Do you drink alcohol?

❿ 你喝運動飲料嗎？
Do you drink sports drinks?

⓫ 你喜歡 嘗試不同口味 的飲料嗎？
Do you like to try different-flavored drinks?

⓬ 你喝 優酪乳 嗎？
Do you drink yogurt?

⓭ 每人每天應該攝取 2000cc 的水分。
Everyone should drink two liters of water every day.

⓮ 你喜歡喝汽水嗎？
Do you like soda?

⓯ 小孩子大多愛喝 甜的飲料 。
Most kids prefer sweet drinks.

043 我的飲食習慣。

❶ 心情不好我就 食不下嚥 。
I can't eat when I'm sad.

❷ 我喜歡重口味。
I prefer strong-flavored food.

❸ 我 沒有胃口 。
I have no appetite.

❹ 我 挑食 。
I'm picky on food.

❺ 我的食量很大。
I eat like a horse.

❻ 我喜歡吃辣。
I enjoy spicy food.

❼ 我吃東西的速度很快。
I eat quickly.

❽ 我吃素。
I'm a vegetarian.

❾ 我吃得很清淡。
I have a light diet.

❿ 我喜歡嘗試沒吃過的食物。
I like to try food I've never tried before.

⓫ 我經常 暴飲暴食 。
I often eat and drink excessively.

⓬ 我習慣睡前 吃宵夜 。
I'm used to having night snacks.

⓭ 我的三餐 定時定量 。
I have three square meals a day.

⓮ 我通常只 吃八分飽 。
I normally don't eat until I'm full.

⓯ 我的晚餐經 常外食 。
I often dine out.

043 你的飲食習慣？

1 你的 食量大 嗎？
Are you consuming a lot of food?

2 你都吃的 這麼清淡 嗎？
Do you always have such light meals?

3 你 吃素 嗎？
Are you a vegetarian?

4 你的 食慾好 嗎？
Do you have a good appetite?

5 你挑食嗎？
Are you a picky eater?

6 你經常在外吃晚餐嗎？
Do you usually dine out?

7 你自己下廚嗎？
Do you cook for yourself?

8 你能 吃辣 嗎？
Can you handle spicy food?

9 你三餐定時定量嗎？
Are you having three square meals?

10 你 吃東西速度快 嗎？
Do you eat quickly?

11 你習慣吃宵夜嗎？
Are you used to having nighttime snacks?

12 你喜歡嘗試各種食物嗎？
Do you like to try different kinds of food?

13 你都吃這麼少嗎？
Do you always eat like a bird?

14 你習慣 吃零食 嗎？
Are you used to having snacks?

15 你是 有厭食症 嗎？
Are you anorexic?

044 我喜歡的食物。

❶ 我愛吃的食物很多。
There are many kinds of food that I love.

❷ 我 不能一天不吃 水果。
I can't go one day without fruit.

❸ 我是標準的 肉食主義 者。
I'm a total meat lover.

❹ 我喜歡吃蔬菜。
I like vegetables.

❺ 我超 愛吃辣 。
I'm crazy about spicy food.

❻ 我對甜食和零嘴來者不拒。
I love all kinds of sweets and snacks.

❼ 我喜歡 到夜市吃 小吃。
I love going to the night market for snacks.

❽ 我偏愛中國料理。
I have a weakness for Chinese food.

❾ 我喜歡 焗烤 食物。
I love food cooked au gratin.

❿ 我偏愛油炸食物。
I prefer deep-fried foods.

⓫ 我最近迷上義大利麵。
I've been crazy about spaghetti lately.

⓬ 夏天一定 要吃刨冰 。
Shaved ice is a must in summertime.

⓭ 冬天我喜歡吃 熱騰騰的 食物。
I love steaming hot food in wintertime.

⓮ 我喜歡 台灣特有的 木瓜牛奶。
I like papaya milk, which is peculiar to Taiwan.

⓯ 我喜歡吃義大利麵。
I like pasta.

044 你喜歡的食物？

❶ 你 喜歡什麼樣的 食物？
What kind of food do you like?

❷ 你喜歡吃飯、吃麵還是麵包？
Do you like rice, noodles or bread?

❸ 你喜歡肉類還是海鮮？
Do you like meat or seafood?

❹ 你最喜歡什麼水果？
What kinds of fruit do you like the best?

❺ 你喜歡喝湯嗎？
Do you like soup?

❻ 你偏好 哪一國的料理 ？
Which nation's cuisine do you prefer?

❼ 你喜歡 速食 嗎？
Do you like fast food?

❽ 你常到夜市吃東西嗎？
Do you often eat at the night market?

❾ 你喜歡熱騰騰的食物嗎？
Do you like your food steaming hot?

❿ 你喜歡 重口味 的食物嗎？
Do you like strongly flavored food?

⓫ 你喜歡義式料理嗎？
Do you like Italian food?

⓬ 你喜歡 又酸又辣 的食物嗎？
Do you like spicy and sour food?

⓭ 你喜歡 燒烤 的食物嗎？
Do you like roasted food?

⓮ 你喜歡 吃生的 東西嗎？
Do you like to eat raw food?

⓯ 哇，我以前不知道你 這麼愛甜食 ！
Wow, I didn't know you were such a lover of sweet food!

045 我討厭的食物。

❶ 我 很挑食 ，很多東西不吃。
I'm picky; there is a lot of food that I won't eat.

❷ 我從來不吃青菜。
I never touch green vegetables.

❸ 我討厭 油膩的 食物。
I hate greasy food.

❹ 我討厭食物 沒有嚼勁 。
I don't like food that's not chewy.

❺ 我討厭吃米飯。
I detest rice.

❻ 我最討厭吃 苦瓜 了。
I hate bitter gourd the most.

❼ 我不愛喝湯。
I don't like soup.

❽ 我 不吃零食 。
I don't eat snacks.

❾ 我不喜歡吃酸的食物。
I'm not fond of sour food.

❿ 我討厭 蔥的味道 。
I hate the smell of green onions.

⓫ 我覺得 臭豆腐 很臭。
I think that stinky tofu is really smelly.

⓬ 我不敢吃生食。
Ew, I don't want to eat raw food.

⓭ 我討厭 魚腥味 。
I hate fishy food.

⓮ 我小時候最 怕吃青椒 。
I hated to eat green peppers when I was little.

⓯ 我不吃肥肉。
I don't eat fat.

045 你討厭的食物？

❶ 你討厭什麼樣的食物？
What kinds of food don't you like?

❷ 你很多東西不吃嗎？
Is there much you won't eat?

❸ 你和我一樣 不吃青菜 嗎？
Do you not eat green vegetables, like me?

❹ 你討厭吃肉嗎？
Do you hate meat?

❺ 你完全不碰 過度加工 的食物嗎？
So you completely avoid over-processed food?

❻ 你 為什麼討厭 吃青菜？
Why do you hate green vegetables?

❼ 你討厭吃苦瓜嗎？
Do you hate bitter gourd?

❽ 你受不了魚腥味嗎？
So you can't stand the smell of fish?

❾ 你從來不吃水果嗎？
Haven't you ever eaten fruit?

❿ 你害怕 蒜的味道 嗎？
Are you afraid of the smell of garlic?

⓫ 你對甜食完全沒興趣嗎？
Are you completely immune to the charms of sweets?

⓬ 你害 怕吃肥肉 嗎？
Are you avoiding fat?

⓭ 你 不喜歡吃酸的 東西嗎？
Don't you like things that taste sour?

⓮ 你覺得臭豆腐很臭嗎？
Do you think that stinky tofu smells?

⓯ 你都沒吃，食物 不合胃口 嗎？
You haven't had a bite. Isn't this to your liking?

046 我的父母親。

❶ 我的父母親離婚了。

My parents are divorced.

❷ 我的父親已經 退休 。

My father is retired.

❸ 我必須照顧父母親。

I have to take care of my parents.

❹ 我的父親 身體不好 。

My father's health is not so good.

❺ 我的母親已經 過世了 。

My mother passed away.

❻ 做決定前，我會找父母親商量。

I consult my parents before I make any decisions.

❼ 我和父親 有代溝 。

There is a generation gap between my father and me.

❽ 我的母親 像我的朋友 一樣。

My mother is like my friend.

❾ 父母親贊成我的工作。

My parents approve of my job.

❿ 父母親 對我很嚴格 。

My parents are strict with me.

⓫ 我的父母親希望我趕快結婚。

My parents hope that I will get married soon.

⓬ 父母親從 不干涉我 的生活。

My parents never interfere in my life.

⓭ 我的父母親 結婚三十年 了。

My parents have been married for 30 years.

⓮ 我的母親有自己的工作。

My mother has her own job.

⓯ 我很少和母親見面。

I seldom see my mother.

046 你的父母親？

❶ 你的 父親幾歲 ？
How old is your father?

❷ 你的父親退休了嗎？
Is your father retired?

❸ 你的父親身體 健康嗎 ？
Is your father healthy?

❹ 你必須照顧父母親嗎？
Do you need to take care of your parents?

❺ 你和母親感情好嗎？
Do you get along with your mother?

❻ 你和父親有代溝嗎？
Is there a generation gap between you and your father?

❼ 你常 和父親聊天 嗎？
Do you chat with your father frequently?

❽ 你會和父母親商量事情嗎？
Do you discuss things with your parents?

❾ 你的父母親 給你零用錢 嗎？
Do your parents give you an allowance?

❿ 你和父母親 多久聯絡一次 ？
How often do you contact your parents?

⓫ 你的父母親結婚幾年了？
How many years have your parents been married?

⓬ 你的父母親 對你有什麼期望 ？
What are your parents' expectations for you?

⓭ 你的母親會 催你結婚 嗎？
Does your mother urge you to get married soon?

⓮ 你的父母親會 干涉你的私生活 嗎？
Do your parents interfere in your privacy?

⓯ 你的母親喜歡你交的朋友嗎？
Does your mother like the friends you make?

047 我的兄弟姊妹。

❶ 我只有 一個哥哥 。
I only have an elder brother.

❷ 我有兩個姊姊和一個弟弟。
I have two elder sisters and a younger brother.

❸ 我和兄弟姊妹感情很好。
I have a close relationship with my siblings.

❹ 我是大家庭，有很多兄弟姊妹。
I have a big family with many brothers and sisters.

❺ 我姊姊 很照顧我 。
My elder sister takes care of me.

❻ 我是獨生子。
I am the only son in my family.

❼ 我跟兄弟姊妹 無話不談 。
There are no secrets between me and my siblings.

❽ 我很希望有個妹妹。
I wish I had a younger sister.

❾ 我和兄弟姊妹的 性格截然不同 。
My personality is totally different from my siblings.

❿ 我和妹妹 常吵架 。
I'm always quarrelling with my younger sister.

⓫ 我和兄弟姊妹經常 互相幫忙 。
My siblings and I usually help each other.

⓬ 我和哥哥是 雙胞胎 。
My elder brother and I are twins.

⓭ 我們兄弟姊妹從事不同的行業。
My siblings and I are engaged in different occupations.

⓮ 我的弟弟妹妹 還在唸書 。
My younger brother and sister are still studying right now.

047 你的兄弟姊妹？

❶ 你有兄弟姊妹嗎？

Do you have any siblings?

❷ 你和兄弟姊妹的 感情好嗎 ？

Do you get along with your brothers and sisters?

❸ 你 有幾個 兄弟姊妹？

How many brothers and sisters do you have?

❹ 你是家裡 唯一的小孩 嗎？

Are you the only child in your family?

❺ 你和兄弟姊妹 經常說話 嗎？

Do you often speak to your siblings?

❻ 你的弟弟妹妹還在唸書嗎？

Are your younger brother and sister still studying now?

❼ 你的姊姊 多大 ？

How old is your elder sister?

❽ 你會照顧弟弟妹妹嗎？

Do you take care of your younger brother and sister?

❾ 你的哥哥姊姊很照顧你嗎？

Do your elder brother and sister look after you?

❿ 你的兄弟姊妹 在工作 了嗎？

Are your brothers and sisters working right now?

⓫ 你和兄弟姊妹互相幫忙嗎？

Do you and your siblings help each other?

⓬ 你和兄弟姊妹之間 有秘密 嗎？

Do you keep secrets from your brothers and sisters?

⓭ 你和兄弟姊妹 長得像 嗎？

Do you look like your brothers and sisters?

⓮ 你跟你哥哥是雙胞胎嗎？

Are you and your elder brother twins?

⓯ 你會穿姊姊的衣服嗎？

Do you wear your elder sister's clothes?

048 我的情人。

❶ 我 深愛 我的男朋友。
I love my boyfriend very much.

❷ 我和我的女朋友 一見鍾情 。
I fell in love with my girlfriend at first sight.

❸ 我的男朋友很體貼。
My boyfriend is very considerate.

❹ 我的女朋友是個 醋罈子 。
My girlfriend is a jealous person.

❺ 我男朋友是我同事。
My boyfriend is my colleague.

❻ 我和男朋友 交往五年 。
My boyfriend and I have been dating each other for five years.

❼ 我跟老婆經常起口角。
My wife and I constantly have quarrels.

❽ 我和女朋友是 遠距離戀愛 。
My girlfriend and I have a long-distance relationship.

❾ 我和女朋友 每天黏在一起 。
My girlfriend and I are joined at the hip.

❿ 女朋友和我家人感情融洽。
My girlfriend gets along with my family.

⓫ 我跟女朋友 剛分手 。
My girlfriend and I just broke up.

⓬ 我和男朋友正是 熱戀期 。
My boyfriend and I are passionately in love.

⓭ 老公是我的 初戀情人 。
My husband was my first love.

⓮ 我跟老公個性完全不同。
My husband and I have totally different personalities.

⓯ 老公每天接我上下班。
My husband picks me up from work every day.

048 你的情人？

❶ 你有 心儀的對象 嗎？
Is there someone you are interested in?

❷ 你有女朋友嗎？
Do you have a girlfriend?

❸ 你 喜歡什麼類型 的男生？
What type of guys do you like?

❹ 你們怎麼認識的？
How did you meet each other?

❺ 你們 交往多久 了？
How long is your relationship?

❻ 你們看起來 很甜蜜 。
You two look very close.

❼ 你們每天黏在一起嗎？
Do you two spend every second together?

❽ 你們常吵架嗎？
Do you fight often?

❾ 男朋友什麼特質 吸引你 ？
What is it that attracted you to your boyfriend?

❿ 你們吵架通常是 誰先低頭 ？
Who is the first one to apologize when you quarrel?

⓫ 老公幫你做家事嗎？
Does your husband help you with the household chores?

⓬ 你們 為什麼分手 ？
Why did you break up?

⓭ 你最喜歡你老公哪一點？
What do you like most about your husband?

⓮ 你最受不了你老婆哪一點？
What can't you bear about your wife?

⓯ 你們看起來 很登對 。
You two look like a perfect match.

125

049 我的朋友。

❶ 我很喜歡交朋友。
  I like to make friends.
❷ 我有很多好朋友。
  I have many good friends.
❸ 我不擅長交朋友。
  I am not good at making friends.
❹ 朋友和我有 很多共同點 。
  My friends and I have many things in common.
❺ 我喜歡和朋友講電話。
  I like to chat with my friends on the phone.
❻ 我和朋友爭執後總 能和好如初 。
  My friends and I always make up after we have a quarrel.
❼ 我和朋友 年紀相仿 。
  My friends and I are about the same age.
❽ 我和朋友有 聊不完 的話題。
  My friends and I can chat forever.
❾ 我和朋友經 常見面 。
  My friends and I get together frequently.
❿ 我透過網路結交不少朋友。
  I've made many friends online.
⓫ 我和朋友 彼此關心 。
  My friends and I care about each other.
⓬ 我的朋友都很熱情。
  All my friends are very enthusiastic.
⓭ 我和很多朋友 失去聯絡 。
  I have lost contact with many friends.
⓮ 我有一兩個 知心好友 。
  I have one or two intimate friends.
⓯ 我和朋友偶爾起爭執。
  Sometimes my friends and I get into fights.

049 你的朋友？

① 你有很多 好朋友 嗎？
Do you have many good friends?

② 你常和朋友聯絡嗎？
Do you speak to your friends frequently?

③ 你 喜歡交朋友 嗎？
Do you like to make friends?

④ 你和朋友感情好嗎？
Do you have a good relationship with your friends?

⑤ 你會找朋友 聊心事 嗎？
Will you tell your friend what's on your mind?

⑥ 你有網友嗎？
Do you have any online friends?

⑦ 你有 外國朋友 嗎？
Do you have any foreign friends?

⑧ 你和朋友 興趣相同 嗎？
Do you share the same interests as your friends?

⑨ 你和朋友多久碰面一次？
How often do you meet with your friends?

⑩ 你和朋友會起爭執嗎？
Do you ever have arguments with your friend?

⑪ 你和朋友大多 怎麼認識 的？
How did you meet most of your friends?

⑫ 你的朋友曾經欺騙你嗎？
Have your friends ever cheated you?

⑬ 你的朋友都很 瞭解你 嗎？
Do your friends understand you?

⑭ 你願意向朋友道歉嗎？
Are you willing to apologize to your friends?

⑮ 你有 可以信任的 朋友嗎？
Do you have any friends you can trust?

050 我的老闆。

❶ 我的老闆很 有生意頭腦 。
My boss is very business savvy.

❷ 我的老闆很明理。
My boss is very reasonable.

❸ 我的老闆腦筋動很快。
My boss has a keen mind.

❹ 我的老闆 年輕有為 。
My boss is young and promising.

❺ 我的老闆白手起家。
My boss started his own business.

❻ 我的老闆是個 腳踏實地 的人。
My boss is a practical person.

❼ 我的老闆 知人善任 。
My boss knows how to assign tasks to employees according to their abilities.

❽ 我的老闆是 企業家第二代 。
My boss is a second-generation entrepreneur.

❾ 我的老闆 人脈很廣 。
My boss has a broad social network.

❿ 我的老闆社交手腕高明。
My boss is good at socializing.

⓫ 我的老闆深 受公司員工愛戴 。
My boss is deeply respected by his/her employees.

⓬ 我的老闆非常信任自己的員工。
My boss trusts in his employees very much.

⓭ 我非常敬佩我們老闆。
I admire our boss very much.

⓮ 我的老闆很 愛罵人 。
My boss loves to yell at people.

050 你的老闆？

1 你和老闆的關係好嗎？
Do you have a good relationship with your boss?

2 你的老闆很 好溝通 嗎？
Is your boss easy to communicate with?

3 你喜歡你的老闆嗎？
Do you like your boss?

4 你的老闆會接受員工的意見嗎？
Does your boss accept his/her employees' opinions?

5 你的老闆 信任你 嗎？
Does your boss trust you?

6 你的老闆 欣賞你 的才華嗎？
Does your boss appreciate your talent?

7 你的老闆每天進公司嗎？
Is your boss in the office every day?

8 你的老闆 很囉唆 嗎？
Does your boss nag?

9 你的老闆通常 幾點進公司 ？
What time does your boss usually arrive at the office?

10 你對你的老闆有什麼感覺？
How do you feel about your boss?

11 你的老闆經 常發脾氣 嗎？
Does your boss lose his temper often?

12 你的老闆 白手起家 嗎？
Did your boss start his own business?

13 你的老闆是個 怎麼樣的人 ？
What kind of person is your boss?

14 你瞭解老闆的脾氣嗎？
Do you know your boss's temper?

15 你的老闆幾歲？
How old is your boss?

051 我的同事。

❶ 我跟同事 關係很好 。
I have a good relationship with my colleagues.

❷ 我的同事都很好相處。
All my colleagues are easy to get along with.

❸ 我的同事都已婚。
All my colleagues are married.

❹ 我只認識 同部門 的同事。
I only know colleagues from my own department.

❺ 我的同事以 男性居多 。
My colleagues are mostly male.

❻ 我和同事會互相幫忙。
My colleagues and I always help each other.

❼ 我的同事工作 能力很強 。
My colleague is quite good at his/her work.

❽ 我的同事是我的 最佳拍檔 。
My colleague is my best partner.

❾ 我的同事喜歡 聊八卦 。
My colleagues like to gossip.

❿ 我有些同事喜歡打小報告。
Some of my colleagues like to snitch.

⓫ 我的同事上班 常摸魚 。
My colleagues are always slacking off at work.

⓬ 我的同事對公司抱怨連連。
My colleagues have repeatedly complained about our company.

⓭ 我很多同事最近 要離職 。
Many of my colleagues are going to quit.

⓮ 我有些同事 喜歡挑撥離間 。
Some of my colleagues like to cause mischief among others.

051 你的同事？

❶ 你和同事感情好嗎？
Do you have a good relationship with your colleagues?

❷ 你的同事 好相處 嗎？
Are your colleagues easy to get along with?

❸ 你和同事 互動頻繁 嗎？
Do you interact with your colleagues frequently?

❹ 你和同事 常有摩擦 嗎？
Do you often have disputes with your colleagues?

❺ 你的同事男性居多還是女性？
Do you have more male colleagues or female colleagues?

❻ 同事常 向你吐苦水 嗎？
Do your colleagues spill their complaints to you?

❼ 你的同事會幫你嗎？
Do your colleagues help you?

❽ 你的同事喜歡 打小報告 嗎？
Do your colleagues like to inform on each other?

❾ 你曾受到同事陷害嗎？
Have you ever been framed by your colleagues?

❿ 你的同事彼此 勾心鬥角 嗎？
Do your colleagues ever plot against each other?

⓫ 你的同事愛聊八卦嗎？
Do your colleagues like to gossip?

⓬ 你的同事都 比你資深 嗎？
Are your colleagues senior to you?

⓭ 你的同事已婚？還是未婚？
Is your colleague married or single?

⓮ 你的同事會 在背後說你 的壞話嗎？
Do your colleagues talk about you behind your back?

⓯ 公司的同事你都認識嗎？
Do you know every employee in your company?

052 我的近況。

❶ 我最近很幸運。
I have been very lucky recently.

❷ 我最近過得 馬馬虎虎 ，沒什麼特別的。
I've been all right lately—nothing special.

❸ 我 大病初癒 。
I am just recovering from a serious illness.

❹ 我最近一直很忙。
I have been busy recently.

❺ 我最近 累壞了 。
I have been exhausted lately.

❻ 我最近 壓力很大 。
I have been under a lot of pressure recently.

❼ 我剛搬家。
I just moved.

❽ 我剛買新房子。
I've just bought a new house.

❾ 我 戀愛了 。
I've fallen in love.

❿ 我懷孕了。
I'm pregnant.

⓫ 我最近常 常生病 。
I've been sick a lot lately.

⓬ 我最近 很倒楣 。
I have been very unlucky lately.

⓭ 我剛換了 新工作 。
I just changed jobs.

⓮ 我 剛當爸爸 。
I've just become a father.

⓯ 我剛從國外回來。
I just returned from overseas.

052 你的近況？

① 最近過得如何？
How are you doing?

② 最近 在忙什麼 ？
What have you been so busy with lately?

③ 最近忙嗎？
Have you been busy recently?

④ 你身體好嗎？
How's your health?

⑤ 爛攤子 收拾好了嗎？
Has the mess been cleaned up yet?

⑥ 最近 有什麼好事 發生？
Has anything positive happened lately?

⑦ 你怎麼失蹤了好一陣子？
How come you disappeared for a while?

⑧ 你上次的 感冒好了嗎 ？
Have you gotten over the cold you had last time?

⑨ 你怎麼最近看起來很累的樣子？
Why do you look so tired lately?

⑩ 你的 工作順利 嗎？
Has work been going smoothly?

⑪ 你買車了嗎？
Did you buy a car?

⑫ 你的新工作如何？
How is your new job going?

⑬ 你最近怎麼 氣色不太好 ？
How come you don't look so well lately?

⑭ 你搬家了嗎？
Did you move?

⑮ 你 當媽媽了 嗎？
Did you become a mother?

053 我最近的心情。

1 我最近 心情很好 。
I have been in a terrific mood as of late.

2 我的心情 不好不壞 ，沒啥特別的。
I am just so-so, nothing special.

3 我最近情緒不太穩定。
My moods have been unstable recently.

4 我陷入 低潮 。
I am in low spirits.

5 我最近很怕寂寞。
Lately I've been afraid of being lonely.

6 我這陣子 很沮喪 。
I have been very depressed lately.

7 我覺得人生沒意義。
I feel that life is meaningless.

8 我 充滿鬥志 。
I am full of fight.

9 我好煩。
I am so annoyed.

10 我最近對任何事都 提不起興趣 。
I have been losing interest in everything lately.

11 我最近常流淚。
I have been crying a lot lately.

12 我充滿自信。
I am full of confidence.

13 我好像得了憂鬱症。
I think I am suffering from depression.

14 我今天 心情跌到谷底 。
I am feeling down today.

15 一切 雨過天晴 。
Everything has been cleared up.

053 你最近的心情？

❶ 你最近 心情如何 ？
How have you been feeling recently?

❷ 你 心情不好 ？
Are you in a bad mood?

❸ 你的心情好點沒？
Has your mood improved lately?

❹ 你最近常常這麼低落嗎？
Have you often been low-spirited recently?

❺ 你 走出低潮 了嗎？
Have you made it through your rough period?

❻ 你覺得寂寞嗎？
Do you feel lonesome?

❼ 一切雨過天晴了嗎？
Has everything cleared up?

❽ 你最近常 情緒不穩 嗎？
Have your emotions been unstable recently?

❾ 你過得快樂嗎？
Do you lead a happy life?

❿ 你最近常發脾氣嗎？
Have you been losing your temper very easily of late?

⓫ 你在 煩什麼 ？
What is annoying you?

⓬ 你什麼時候變得這麼多疑？
Since when did you become so suspicious?

⓭ 你得了 憂鬱症 嗎？
Are you suffering from depression?

⓮ 你怎麼 心事重重 的樣子？
Why do you look so upset?

⓯ 你 找回自信心 了嗎？
Has your confidence returned yet?

054 我正在進行的事。

❶ 我正在 找工作 。
I am looking for a job.

❷ 我正在 努力戒煙 。
I am trying to give up smoking.

❸ 我正在學英文。
I am studying English right now.

❹ 我正在減肥。
I am trying to lose some weight.

❺ 我正在 學開車 。
I am learning how to drive.

❻ 我正在整修房子。
I am repairing my house right now.

❼ 我正在 籌備婚禮 。
I am arranging the wedding ceremony right now.

❽ 我正在 準備出國深造 。
I am preparing to study abroad.

❾ 我正在準備搬家。
I am preparing to move.

❿ 我正在 享受我的假期 。
I am enjoying my vacation right now.

⓫ 我正在抉擇要選哪一間學校。
I am in the process of choosing a school.

⓬ 我正在 準備考試 。
I am preparing for an exam right now.

⓭ 我正在考慮換房子。
I am thinking about moving.

⓮ 我正在 考慮到海外發展 。
I am considering working overseas.

⓯ 我正在爭取一個大客戶。
I am trying to win over a big client right now.

054 你正在進行的事？

❶ 你最近 有什麼計畫 ？
What plans have you made recently?

❷ 你戒酒了沒有？
Have quit drinking yet?

❸ 你有考慮畢業之後的出路嗎？
Have you thought about what to do after graduation?

❹ 你正 在減肥 嗎？
Are you on a diet?

❺ 你在找工作嗎？
Are you looking for a job?

❻ 你 找到房子 了嗎？
Have you found a house yet?

❼ 你正在學日文嗎？
Are you studying Japanese?

❽ 你在 考慮換工作 嗎？
Have you thought about changing jobs?

❾ 你打算花多久時間學好英文？
How much time do you plan to spend studying English?

❿ 你 開始運動 了嗎？
Have you begun exercising?

⓫ 你 忙著籌備 婚事嗎？
Are you busy with the wedding?

⓬ 你的家人支持你的計畫嗎？
Does your family support your plans?

⓭ 你的考試 準備得如何 ？
How is your exam preparation going?

⓮ 你在準備留學的事嗎？
Are you preparing to study abroad?

⓯ 你 決定到哪一間 公司上班了嗎？
Which company have you decided to go to work for?

055 我快樂。

❶ 我興奮得不得了。

I'm so excited.

❷ 我的 心情很好 。

I'm in a good mood.

❸ 我的精神很好。

I feel great.

❹ 這氣氛真 令人陶醉 。

This atmosphere intoxicates me.

❺ 我 樂歪了 ！

I'm so happy.

❻ 最近我的運氣一直很好。

I've been lucky recently.

❼ 我中了「樂透」，我真是樂透了！

I won the lottery; I am so happy!

❽ 聽你這樣說，真是讓我 心花怒放 。

What you've said makes me feel incredibly happy.

❾ 今天是我最快樂的一天。

Today is the happiest day of my life.

❿ 人逢喜事 精神爽。

Happy occasions give you energy.

⓫ 我 打從心裏 替你感到高興。

I'm so happy for you, from the bottom of my heart.

⓬ 考試總算過關，真棒！

I passed the exam, that's great!

⓭ 我玩到 樂不思蜀 。

I had so much fun that I forgot to go back home.

⓮ 沒想到事情這麼順利。

I never expected to do so well.

⓯ 我快樂得 像隻小鳥 。

I'm as happy as a jaybird.

138

055 你快樂嗎?

❶ 你最近快樂嗎?
Have you been happy recently?

❷ 你開心嗎?
Are you having fun?

❸ 你怎麼看起來 春風滿面 ?
Why do you look so cheerful?

❹ 什麼事 這麼高興 ?
What makes you so happy like this?

❺ 要結婚了,開心吧?
Are you happy that you're getting married?

❻ 最近有什麼 好事發生 嗎?
Any happy thing happened to you recently?

❼ 最近看起來 氣色很好 喔!
You've been looking good these days!

❽ 一切 如你所願 ,你滿意了吧?
Everything is as you hoped it would be—are you satisfied?

❾ 很久沒看到你這麼開心了。
It's been a long time since I've seen you so happy.

❿ 考試過關了,開心吧?
You passed the exam—are you happy?

⓫ 要當爸爸了, 興奮吧 ?
Are you excited about being a father?

⓬ 要休假了!開心嗎?
Time for vacation! Happy?

⓭ 我一直很快樂,你呢?
I'm always happy—what about you?

⓮ 升官了,應該很高興吧?
You're happy about your promotion, right?

⓯ 談戀愛啦? 笑這麼甜 !
Are you in love? You're smiling so sweetly!

056 我驚訝。

1 是真的嗎？
Is that true?

2 太令人驚訝了！
That's really surprising!

3 有這回事 嗎？
Has such a thing happened?

4 誰說的？
Who said that?

5 這真是 太神奇了 。
This is really a miracle.

6 事情怎麼會變成這樣？
How did it become like this?

7 真是不可思議。
That's really amazing.

8 電影結局真是 出乎意料 。
This movie ended really unexpectedly.

9 真是 怪事年年有 。
Strange things happen all the time.

10 真讓我 目瞪口呆 。
It really amazed me.

11 我一定是在作夢。
I must be dreaming.

12 你一定是 在說笑 吧！
You must be kidding me!

13 真是 嚇出一身冷汗 。
Really scared me into a cold sweat.

14 真是令人歎為觀止。
Absolutely magnificent.

15 這事真是好得令人 難以置信 ！
This is really too good to be true!

056 你驚訝嗎？

❶ 看你 臉色發青 ，還好吧？
You look pale, are you okay?

❷ 嚇到你 了嗎？你還好吧？
Did I scare you? Are you all right?

❸ 出乎意料之外，不是嗎？
Not what you expected, is it?

❹ 嚇一跳 吧？
Made you jump?

❺ 你不覺得太意外了嗎？
Don't you think that it's too unexpected?

❻ 想都 沒想到吧 ？
You've never thought about that, have you?

❼ 你不覺得奇怪嗎？
Don't you feel it is strange?

❽ 有沒有覺得很驚訝？
Are you surprised?

❾ 怎麼樣， 令人驚豔 吧？
What do you think—pretty amazing, eh?

❿ 這點小事就嚇到你啦？
Are you scared of such a tiny thing?

⓫ 你不覺得這事情太不尋常？
Don't you think that this is unusual?

⓬ 是我太 大驚小怪 了嗎？
Am I acting too surprised?

⓭ 有什麼不對嗎？
Is there anything wrong?

⓮ 如何？這個生日禮物 夠特別吧 ？
What do you think? Is this birthday present special enough?

⓯ 有這麼需要 小題大作 嗎？
Is it really worth making such a big deal over?

141

057 我感動。

1 真令人感動。
It's really touching.

2 這部戲真是 賺人熱淚 。
The film's such a tear-jerker.

3 哭得我死去活來。
I cried my eyes out.

4 他 打動了我 的心。
He touched my heart.

5 我蠻感動的。
I'm really touched.

6 他的故事讓我深受感動。
His story really touched me.

7 快拿 面紙給我 ！
Hurry and pass me a tissue!

8 聽到這樣悲慘的故事，真是 令人鼻酸 。
Hearing such a story really puts a lump in your throat.

9 我沒有辦法不感動。
I can't help being touched.

10 我 感同身受 。
I know exactly how you feel.

11 他用熱情感動了我。
His enthusiasm touched me.

12 好感人 的故事。
It's really a touching story.

13 這場景真令人感動。
This scene moves people.

14 我 快哭了 。
I'm almost crying.

15 災民們的處境令人感到難過。
The condition of the victims is saddening.

142

057 你感動嗎？

❶ 你覺得這部電影 感人嗎 ？
Do you think this movie is touching?

❷ 這本書感人嗎？
Is this book touching?

❸ 他這樣說，會影響你的情緒？
Will his words affect your emotions?

❹ 你 被他感動 了嗎？
Were you moved by him?

❺ 你覺得難過嗎？
Are you feeling sad?

❻ 被我感動了嗎？
Did I move you?

❼ 你 在哭 嗎？
Are you crying?

❽ 怎麼這麼 容易感動 你啊！
How easily you are moved!

❾ 你怎麼啦？
What happened to you?

❿ 你的表情看起來怪怪的。
Your expression looks strange.

⓫ 大家都說這個劇本很感人，你覺得呢？
Everyone says this script is really touching, don't you think so?

⓬ 別把感情 悶在心裏 。
Don't seal your feelings in your heart.

⓭ 如果 想哭就哭 吧。
Cry if you want to.

⓮ 你不覺得這實在太悲慘了嗎？
Don't you think that it's really tragic?

⓯ 你是 鐵石心腸 啊？
Do you have a cold heart?

058 我有信心。

❶ 我保證一切 沒問題 。
I promise that everything is okay.

❷ 我可以勝任。
I can handle that.

❸ 有我在，別怕！
I'm here, don't be afraid!

❹ 交給我 準沒錯。
You can count on me.

❺ 我 辦得到 。
I can do it.

❻ 大家都說我很聰明。
Everyone says that I'm very bright.

❼ 我有信心。
I have confidence.

❽ 我 不會辜負你 的期望。
I will not let you down.

❾ 我 有把握 。
I've got it under control.

❿ 我有辦法。
I have a plan.

⓫ 我相信我一定可以 度過難關 。
I'm sure I can overcome the difficulties.

⓬ 我會解決問題的。
I'll solve the problem.

⓭ 相信我。
Trust me.

⓮ 我會 完成老闆交代的 任務。
I will complete the task my boss gave me.

⓯ 我向你保證。
You have my word.

058 你有信心嗎？

❶ 你 可以勝任 這份工作嗎？
Can you handle this job?

❷ 你辦得到嗎？
Can you do it?

❸ 你覺得自己聰明嗎？
Do you think you're smart?

❹ 你 有信心 嗎？
Are you confident?

❺ 你有辦法解決問題嗎？
Do you have a plan to solve the problem?

❻ 要不要 找人幫忙 ？
Do you want to look for help?

❼ 你感到 害怕嗎 ？
Do you feel scared?

❽ 沒問題吧？
No problem?

❾ 是臨時出狀況嗎？
Anything unexpected happen?

❿ 行得通嗎？
Will it work?

⓫ 你 有辦法拿到 這個案子嗎？
Do you have any way to get this case?

⓬ 你自己能處理好嗎？
Can you deal with this by yourself?

⓭ 撐得住 嗎？
Can you hold on?

⓮ 你要失去信念了嗎？
Are you losing your faith?

⓯ 你 能保證 嗎？
Do I have your word?

059 我生氣。

1 我非常 生氣 。
I'm very angry.

2 我 想打人 。
I really want to hit someone.

3 我不想和你說話。
I don't want to talk to you.

4 敢碰我 一根寒毛試試看！
How dare you try and touch me!

5 我不想多說。
I don't want to talk.

6 不要跟我 頂嘴 ！
Don't talk back to me!

7 少 廢話 。
Stop talking nonsense.

8 別理我。
Leave me alone.

9 別來煩 我！
Get off my back!

10 讓我靜一靜。
Give me a little peace and quiet.

11 滾遠點！
Get out of here!

12 小心我 揍你 。
Careful, or I'll smack you.

13 我會報仇的。
I will get revenge.

14 少惹我！
Don't push me!

15 我再也忍 受不了 了！
I can't stand it anymore!

059 你生氣嗎？

❶ 你 在生氣 嗎？
Are you angry right now?

❷ 你在生我的氣嗎？
Are you angry with me?

❸ 為什麼不說話？
Why don't you speak?

❹ 我 做錯了什麼 嗎？
Have I done something wrong?

❺ 為什麼 不理我 ？
Why did you ignore me?

❻ 我又沒有怎麼樣。
I didn't do anything.

❼ 想殺我啊？
Want to kill me?

❽ 你有什麼好生氣的？
What are you mad about?

❾ 想打架嗎？
Do you want to fight me?

❿ 眼睛瞪這麼大 做什麼？
What are you staring at?

⓫ 別生我的氣啦！
Don't be mad at me!

⓬ 拜託！ 生什麼氣 啊？
Come on! What are you angry for?

⓭ 你 冷靜一點 好嗎？
Calm down, will you?

⓮ 這樣就生氣啦？
Do you get angry just like that?

⓯ 有 這麼嚴重 嗎？
Is it really that serious?

060 我難過。

1 我蠻難過的。
I feel miserable.

2 真令人感到 遺憾 。
What a shame.

3 真讓人傷心。
It really makes you miserable.

4 我的心好像 被挖空 了。
My heart seems empty.

5 我 受傷太深 。
I've been hurt very deeply.

6 事情怎麼會演變到這樣？
How could it happen like this?

7 我整天 以淚洗面 。
I cried all day.

8 不曉得什麼時候，事情才會過去。
I don't know when it will be over.

9 我沒辦法快樂起來。
I can't be happy anymore.

10 真令人 心碎 。
It really breaks your heart.

11 我的心好像 被人捅了一刀 。
My heart feels like it has been stabbed.

12 這樣的 日子真是難過 。
Such days are really difficult.

13 我的 心好痛 。
My heart bleeds.

14 真令人心痛。
It really makes my heart bleed.

15 最近心情一直很低潮。
My spirits have been low recently.

060 你難過嗎？

1 感到難過嗎？
Do you feel sad?

2 感到心痛 是嗎？
Feeling heartbroken, are you?

3 你 不快樂 嗎？
Are you unhappy?

4 你看起來不太舒服。
You look uncomfortable.

5 要面對這一切並不容易，對吧？
It's not very easy to face everything, is it?

6 有心事 嗎？
Is there anything on your mind?

7 心情不好嗎？
In a bad mood?

8 發生了什麼事 嗎？
Is there anything that has happened?

9 有什麼我可以幫忙的嗎？
Is there anything that I can help you with?

10 怎麼把自己搞成這樣 不成人形 ？
Why do you torture yourself like this?

11 還思念著他嗎？
Still miss him?

12 想 找人聊聊 嗎？
Want to talk to someone?

13 你也覺得不開心，是嗎？
You feel unhappy too, don't you?

14 想家 了嗎？
Miss home?

15 沒辦法快樂 起來嗎？
Can't seem to cheer yourself up?

061 我失望。

❶ 真令人失望。
It's really disappointing.

❷ 太 可惜 了。
It's too bad.

❸ 我 又失敗 了。
I've failed again.

❹ 差點 就過關了，真是的！
I almost made it, darn it!

❺ 你 讓我失望 了。
I'm really disappointed in you.

❻ 真是找錯人了。
That's really not the right person to count on.

❼ 你浪費了我對你的信任。
You wasted my trust in you.

❽ 我 放棄 了。
I give up.

❾ 哀莫大於心死。
There is no grief greater than the death of the heart.

❿ 我再也 無所謂了 。
It doesn't matter anymore.

⓫ 我 不想再做 任何努力了。
I don't want to try anymore.

⓬ 沒救 了。
It's no use.

⓭ 不可能成功了。
It can't be done.

⓮ 別再努力了。
Don't bother giving it another try.

⓯ 好想死喔！
I want to die!

061 你失望嗎？

❶ 你 灰心 了嗎？
Are you discouraged?

❷ 要放棄了嗎？
Want to give up?

❸ 不再努力 了嗎？
Don't want to try anymore?

❹ 很心痛吧？
Really heartbroken, aren't you?

❺ 失去鬥志 了嗎？
Have you lost your will to fight?

❻ 你覺得無所謂嗎？
Are you apathetic?

❼ 你還 要繼續 支持他嗎？
Are you going to keep supporting him?

❽ 完全 沒有機會 了嗎？
Is there no chance at all?

❾ 要 再試試 嗎？
Want to try again?

❿ 也許還有機會啊。
There might still be a chance.

⓫ 還 不願意放棄 嗎？
Still not giving up?

⓬ 真的有這麼糟嗎？
Is it that bad?

⓭ 有這麼嚴重嗎？
Is it really that serious?

⓮ 還 想奮鬥 嗎？
Still want to fight on?

⓯ 你還是認為事情不是他做的嗎？
Do you still think that he didn't do it?

062 我寂寞。

❶ 我好 想你 。
I miss you very much.

❷ 我 沒有朋友 。
I don't have any friends.

❸ 我想和你說話。
I want to talk to you.

❹ 我 怕黑 。
I'm afraid of the dark.

❺ 屋子裡空蕩蕩的。
The house is empty.

❻ 整個房子都是你的影子。
There are traces of you all over the house.

❼ 你可以 過來陪我 嗎？
Can you come and stay by my side?

❽ 四周 好安靜 ，我可以聽到時鐘的滴答聲。
It's really quiet around here; I can hear the clock ticking.

❾ 我只聽到自己的心跳聲。
I can only hear my own heart beating.

❿ 我 總是一個人 去看電影。
I always go to the movies alone.

⓫ 沒有人在乎我。
Nobody cares about me.

⓬ 我只有一個人。
I'm only one person.

⓭ 我的心 沒人瞭解 。
Nobody understands what's in my heart.

⓮ 沒有人要和我說話。
There's no one who wants to talk to me.

⓯ 我總是一個人吃飯。
I always eat alone.

062 你寂寞嗎？

❶ 想我嗎？
Miss me?

❷ 想哭 嗎？
Want to cry?

❸ 怕黑嗎？
Afraid of the dark?

❹ 自己過日子還好嗎？
Do you not mind being alone?

❺ 要一起 用餐嗎？
Want to eat together?

❻ 寂寞 嗎？
Lonely?

❼ 喜歡 一個人過 生活嗎？
Do you like to live alone?

❽ 要 我陪你 嗎？
Want me to accompany you?

❾ 有心愛的人嗎？
Is there anyone you love?

❿ 有想做的事嗎？
Is there anything you want to do?

⓫ 想交個朋友嗎？
Would you like to make friends with me?

⓬ 你 有朋友 嗎？
Do you have any friends?

⓭ 你覺得 空虛 嗎？
Are you feeling empty?

⓮ 你不喜歡被打擾嗎？
Do you hate being disturbed?

⓯ 你不想被人瞭解嗎？
Don't you want to be understood?

063 我後悔。

❶ 早知道 ，我就不會這樣做。
I wouldn't have done it had I known.

❷ 我後悔死了。
I am really regretful.

❸ 後悔也來不及了。
It's too late for regrets.

❹ 我是豬頭。
I'm really a fool.

❺ 怨不得 人。
It can't be blamed on anyone.

❻ 你打我、罵我吧！
You can beat me and yell at me for all I care!

❼ 都怪我。
It's my fault.

❽ 事到如今只能 怪自己 。
At this point I have only myself to blame.

❾ 我怎麼這麼笨！
How could I be so stupid!

❿ 真是 天不從人願 。
The hopes of man have yet to be fulfilled.

⓫ 我 後悔當初 沒聽朋友的勸告。
I regret ignoring my friend's advice.

⓬ 我這次真的是 學乖了 。
I've really learned my lesson this time.

⓭ 下次，我會多聽聽別人的意見。
Next time, I will listen to others' opinions.

⓮ 我會努力 重新做人 。
I will try to be a new person.

⓯ 我下次一定 不會再犯 錯。
I will not make a mistake next time.

154

063 你後悔嗎？

1 後悔了吧？
Are you regretful?

2 知道錯 了吧？
Have you realized you were wrong?

3 早就跟你說 不要這樣做。
I've told you before not to do that.

4 你還是 不後悔 愛上他？
Do you still not regret loving him?

5 現在說這些是不是太遲了？
Is it too late for saying these things?

6 你是不是覺得自己太傻了？
Don't you think that you've been too stupid?

7 每次說你，你都不聽，現在後悔了吧？
You've never listened to me, now do you regret it?

8 告訴你那是騙人的，你 還不信 ！
I told you that it was a lie, but you still did not
believe me!

9 現在知道 爸媽是為你好 了吧？
Now do you know that your father and I are on
your side?

10 知道老師的用意了吧？
Do you know what your teacher meant?

11 後悔了，就 趕快改正 啊。
If you regret it, then make amends quickly.

12 你是 真心懺悔 嗎？
Are you really repentant?

13 現在 還說這些 幹嘛？
Why are you still saying these things?

14 你後悔嫁給他嗎？
Do you regret marrying him?

15 你還是不後悔？
Do you still not regret it?

064 我覺得無聊。

❶ 無事可做。
I have nothing to do.

❷ 只是 混日子 。
Just fooling around.

❸ 過一天算一天。
Just taking it one day at a time.

❹ 沒什麼大事 發生。
Nothing big has happened.

❺ 每天都一樣。
Every day is the same.

❻ 我閒到快抓狂。
I'm so idle I'm about to go crazy.

❼ 生活就好 像喝白開水 一樣。
Life is like drinking a glass of water.

❽ 好無聊喔！
It's so boring!

❾ 日子 真無趣 。
Life is monotonous.

❿ 好想睡覺。
I really want to sleep.

⓫ 我們可以 換個話題 嗎？
Can we change the subject?

⓬ 再說下去我就 要睡著了 。
I'm going to fall asleep if you keep talking.

⓭ 課本的內容好無趣。
The textbook is so boring.

⓮ 沒什麼事引得起我的興趣。
Nothing interests me.

⓯ 找點新鮮事 做做吧！
Find some new things to do!

064 你覺得無聊嗎？

❶ 你 沒事做 嗎？
Do you have nothing to do?

❷ 你 太閒 了嗎？
Are you too idle?

❸ 你的日子都一成不變嗎？
Are your days all the same?

❹ 想換個工作嗎？
Want to change jobs?

❺ 想去旅行嗎？
Want to go on a trip?

❻ 你不覺得生活很無趣嗎？
Don't you think your life is boring?

❼ 發什麼呆？
What are you staring into space for?

❽ 你每天都做一樣的事嗎？
Do you do the same thing every day?

❾ 怎麼整天 渾渾噩噩 的？
Why have you been muddle-headed all day long?

❿ 想去學些什麼嗎？
Want to learn something?

⓫ 你對這件事 沒興趣 ，是吧？
You are not interested in this, are you?

⓬ 又是這首歌，聽不膩 嗎？
This song again—aren't you sick of it?

⓭ 想來點刺激 的嗎？
Want to have some excitement?

⓮ 你又在 做白日夢 啦！
Daydreaming again!

⓯ 你 沒別的事 可做了嗎？
Don't you have other things to do?

065 我懷疑。

1 一定是你 做的好事。
You must have done something bad.

2 我就是不相信。
I just do not believe that.

3 我 憑什麼 要相信你？
Why should I believe you?

4 我覺得事情 不大對勁 。
Something's fishy.

5 我真的沒辦法相信這個事實。
I really can't believe that this is true.

6 這個 證據太薄弱 。
This evidence is too weak.

7 這是真的嗎？
Is that true?

8 太奇怪了。
It's too strange.

9 怎麼會這樣？
How can it be?

10 很難讓人相信。
It's really hard to convince people.

11 一定 有人說謊 。
Someone must have lied.

12 這事情一定 有問題 。
There must be some problem with this.

13 我沒有辦法不懷疑你。
I can't help doubting you.

14 大家都 各說各話 。
Everybody speaks for himself.

15 這個 理由太牽強 。
This reason is too far-fetched.

065 你懷疑嗎？

❶ 你懷疑他嗎？
Do you doubt him?

❷ 你是 在考驗我 嗎？
Are you testing me?

❸ 你不覺得很 可疑 嗎？
Don't you think it dubious?

❹ 你認為有什麼不對的地方嗎？
Do you think anything is wrong?

❺ 不相信你可以自己去問清楚。
You can go ask yourself if you don't believe it.

❻ 你 不再相信 我了嗎？
You don't believe me anymore?

❼ 那件事 難道是他 做的？
Is it possible that he was the one who did it?

❽ 你相信這是真的嗎？
Do you believe this is true?

❾ 真有這回事嗎？
Has this really happened?

❿ 不會是 騙人的 吧？
It isn't a scam, is it?

⓫ 你總是 疑神疑鬼 。
You always have unfounded suspicions.

⓬ 不要總是懷疑別人。
Don't doubt people so much.

⓭ 別 神經質 了。
Don't be nervous.

⓮ 你不相信，我也沒辦法。
If you don't believe me, there's nothing I can do.

⓯ 會不會是你 想太多 了？
Aren't you thinking too much?

066 我煩惱家人。

❶ 我擔心我父親的健康。

I worry about my father's health.

❷ 我和父母親無話可說。

There's little I can talk to my parents about.

❸ 我很怕我的 小孩會學壞 。

I'm afraid my child will pick up bad habits.

❹ 我跟我的孩子有代溝。

There's a generational gap between me and my children.

❺ 我 不知道如何 跟孩子溝通。

I don't know how to communicate with my kids.

❻ 我常跟太太吵架。

I often quarrel with my wife.

❼ 我先生似乎 有外遇 。

My husband seems to be having an affair.

❽ 我不放心 我父母兩老自己住。

I don't feel comfortable letting my elderly parents live by themselves.

❾ 我擔心我弟弟畢不了業。

I worry that my brother won't be able to graduate.

❿ 我父母成天唸著要抱孫子。

My parents nag me all day long to have a child.

⓫ 我覺得我弟弟 最近怪怪的 。

I feel like my little brother's been acting odd recently.

⓬ 我姊姊的 婚姻出了問題 。

My sister has problems in her marriage.

⓭ 我怕我先生 工作太累 了。

I'm afraid that my husband is working too hard.

⓮ 我們家最近 氣氛不太好 。

The atmosphere in our home isn't very good.

066 你煩惱家人嗎？

❶ 你在 擔心父母親 的健康嗎？
Do you worry about your parents' health?

❷ 你跟父母親還是無法溝通嗎？
Are you still unable to communicate with your parents?

❸ 你知道如何跟孩子相處嗎？
Do you know how to get along with your children?

❹ 你怕你的孩子 交到壞朋友 嗎？
Are you afraid that your child will make bad friends?

❺ 你會擔心你太太有外遇嗎？
Do you worry that your wife is having an affair?

❻ 你擔心你父母會離婚嗎？
Do you worry that your parents will get divorced?

❼ 你太太和你母親之間 有婆媳問題 嗎？
Are there problems between your wife and your mother?

❽ 你母親跟你太太還是 水火不容 嗎？
Do your mother and wife still not get along?

❾ 你在煩惱家裡的什麼事？
What about your family worries you?

❿ 你太太不願意跟你父母同住嗎？
Is your wife not willing to live with your parents?

⓫ 你父母一直催你結婚嗎？
Do your parents keep pressuring you to get married?

⓬ 你父母應該 急著要抱孫子 吧？
Your parents must be eager to have a grandchild, right?

⓭ 你會擔心 孩子的安全 問題嗎？
Do you worry about your child's safety?

⓮ 你不怕孩子會 被你爸媽寵壞 嗎？
Aren't you afraid that your child will be spoiled by your parents?

⓯ 你跟你先生常吵架嗎？
Do you often quarrel with your husband?

067 我煩惱情人。

❶ 我懷疑我男友 劈腿 。
I suspect that my boyfriend is cheating on me.

❷ 我跟我男友經常意見不合。
I often have disagreements with my boyfriend.

❸ 我不知道他對我 是不是真心 的。
I don't know whether he is sincere to me.

❹ 我女友身邊 追求者太多 。
Too many men chase my girlfriend.

❺ 我男友讓我覺得壓力很大。
My boyfriend puts me under a lot of pressure.

❻ 我最怕我女朋友哭了。
I'm afraid when my girlfriend cries.

❼ 我的女友 越來越任性 。
My girlfriend is getting more and more wild.

❽ 我不知道要送她什麼禮物。
I don't know what gift to get her.

❾ 我覺得她不喜歡我了。
I feel that she doesn't like me anymore.

❿ 我的他很 愛吃醋 。
My boyfriend is jealous.

⓫ 我不喜歡他處處管我。
I don't like him trying to control me in every way.

⓬ 我怕她拒絕我的求婚。
I'm afraid she will reject my proposal.

⓭ 我的男朋友遲遲 不跟我求婚 。
My boyfriend still hasn't proposed to me.

⓮ 我不知道 如何維持遠距離 戀愛。
I don't know how to maintain a long-distance relationship.

⓯ 我不懂得 如何討她歡心 。
I don't know how to make her happy.

067 你煩惱情人嗎？

❶ 你跟女友 發生了什麼 問題？
What's the problem between you and your girlfriend?

❷ 你 怕他不愛你 了嗎？
Are you afraid that he doesn't love you anymore?

❸ 你介意她結 交異性朋友 嗎？
Do you mind if she has a friend of the opposite sex?

❹ 你覺得你男友 不在意你 嗎？
Do you feel that your boyfriend doesn't care about you?

❺ 你會為了她吃醋嗎？
Does she make you jealous?

❻ 你們經常意見不合嗎？
Do you two usually disagree?

❼ 你害怕有 三角戀 嗎？
Are you afraid of there being a love triangle?

❽ 你擔心你女友 不答應你 的求婚嗎？
Are you worried that your girlfriend won't accept your proposal?

❾ 你擔心你男友 花心 嗎？
Do you worry that your boyfriend plays around?

❿ 你會為了送她禮物傷腦筋嗎？
Are you stressed out about what to give her?

⓫ 你擔心遠距離戀愛嗎？
Are you worried about having a long-distance relationship?

⓬ 你怕他 腳踏兩條船 嗎？
Do you feel that he isn't loyal to you?

⓭ 你男友讓你覺得有壓力嗎？
Does your boyfriend put you under pressure?

⓮ 你覺得你們已經不行了嗎？
Do you feel there is no way for you two to go on?

⓯ 你信任你女友嗎？
Do you trust your girlfriend?

068 我煩惱人際關係。

❶ 到新環境我會怕生。
Coming to a new environment, I'm shy around strangers.

❷ 我不敢跟陌生人說話。
I don't dare to talk to strangers.

❸ 我說話很 容易得罪人 。
The way I speak easily offends others.

❹ 我最 不會應酬 了。
I just can't socialize.

❺ 我最近常跟朋友吵架。
Lately I've been fighting with my friends a lot.

❻ 我一緊張 舌頭就會打結 。
When I'm nervous, I get tongue-tied.

❼ 我每次都不知道要跟人家聊什麼。
I never know what to chat about with people.

❽ 我常被人惡意中傷。
Other people are often malicious toward me.

❾ 我跟我最好的 朋友絕交 。
I've had a falling-out with my best friend.

❿ 我從小到大都沒什麼朋友。
Ever since I was a child, I've never really had any friends.

⓫ 我在學校 被人排擠 。
I was snubbed in school.

⓬ 我的 生活圈很小 。
My world is too small.

⓭ 我 交不到 男朋友。
I never meet any guys.

⓮ 我分不清損友益友。
I can't distinguish bad friends from good ones.

⓯ 我不容易跟 大家打成一片 。
I don't get along with others easily.

068 你煩惱人際關係嗎？

❶ 你容易交到朋友嗎？
Can you make friends easily?

❷ 你 會怕生 嗎？
Are you afraid of strangers?

❸ 你沒辦法 很快融入大家 嗎？
Do you have a hard time fitting in?

❹ 你都 找不到話題 跟人家聊嗎？
Are you unable to find things to chat about?

❺ 你 沒交過 女朋友嗎？
Have you never had a girlfriend?

❻ 你說話容易得罪人嗎？
Does the way you speak easily offend people?

❼ 你不擅言辭嗎？
Are you not good at speaking?

❽ 你連 說話的對象 都沒有嗎？
Don't you have anyone to talk to?

❾ 你容易和人發生爭執嗎？
Do you get into arguments easily?

❿ 你不擅長 跟人應酬 嗎？
Don't you know how to socialize?

⓫ 你常常誤解別人的好意嗎？
Do you often misunderstand other people's kindness?

⓬ 你在學校 遭人排擠 嗎？
Are you being snubbed in school?

⓭ 你敢跟陌生人交談嗎？
Do you dare to talk to strangers?

⓮ 你能看穿別人的 虛情假意 嗎？
Can you see through false displays of affection?

⓯ 你的生活圈很小嗎？
Is your circle of friends too small?

069 我煩惱工作。

1 我的工作壓力很大。
My job gives me a lot of stress.

2 我一直 沒有加薪 。
I never get raises.

3 我的工作老是趕不上進度。
I'm always behind on my work.

4 我跟同事處得不好。
I don't get along with my colleagues.

5 我有 做不完 的工作。
My work never ends.

6 我沒有一份工作做得長久。
I don't keep jobs for very long.

7 我常 被主管叫去 訓話。
My manager often calls me in to lecture me.

8 我受不了 天天要加班 。
I can't stand working overtime every day.

9 我的工作越來越繁重。
My work is getting heavier and heavier.

10 我最近工作多到 忙不過來 。
I've been swamped with work recently.

11 我很怕 被公司裁員 。
I'm afraid of being laid off.

12 我的工作常要應付 一堆應酬 。
My work often requires me to deal with a slew of
social engagements.

13 我的老闆對我很不滿。
My boss is not satisfied with me.

14 工作讓我 沒時間陪伴 家人。
My work leaves me little time for family.

069 你煩惱工作嗎？

❶ 你工作壓力大不大？
Are you under pressure from work?

❷ 你的工作 忙不過來 嗎？
Are you swamped with work?

❸ 你最近工作還好吧？
Has your work been okay lately?

❹ 你 老闆不滿意 你的工作表現嗎？
Isn't your boss satisfied with your work?

❺ 你最近還是常常加班嗎？
Have you been working overtime a lot lately?

❻ 你已經厭倦這份工作了嗎？
Are you already sick of this work?

❼ 你的工作量又增加了嗎？
Has your workload gotten heavier again?

❽ 你 都沒休息 身體受得了嗎？
You haven't taken any breaks; can your body stand that?

❾ 你又想換工作了嗎？
Are you thinking about changing jobs again?

❿ 你跟同事 相處不好 嗎？
Don't you get along with your colleagues?

⓫ 你擔心自己被裁員嗎？
Do you worry about being laid off?

⓬ 工作讓你沒時間陪家人嗎？
Does work leave you little time for your family?

⓭ 你常常 趕不上工作進度 嗎？
Do you often not make progress at work?

⓮ 你要不要先休息一陣子？
Do you want to take a break for a while?

⓯ 這份工作讓你 很挫折 嗎？
Does work frustrate you?

070 我煩惱金錢。

① 我覺得錢永遠不夠花。
I feel I never have enough money.

② 我是個 窮光蛋 。
I'm as poor as they come.

③ 我沒錢繳電話費。
I don't have enough money to pay the phone bill.

④ 我的薪水根本不夠用。
Frankly, my salary isn't enough.

⑤ 我常 繳不出 房租。
I often can't afford to pay my rent.

⑥ 我有付不完的卡費。
I can never pay off my credit card in full.

⑦ 我被房貸 壓得喘不過氣 來。
My mortgage payments are crushing me.

⑧ 我常常 口袋空空 。
My pockets are usually empty.

⑨ 我朋友常向我 借錢不還 。
My friend often borrows money from me but never pays me back.

⑩ 我常 接到紅色炸彈 。
I often receive wedding invitations.

⑪ 我不想讓家人跟著我吃苦。
I don't want to make my family endure hardships with me.

⑫ 我幾乎每個月都 透支 。
I overdraw my account nearly every month.

⑬ 我這個禮拜只剩 200 元可以用。
I only have NT$200 left to spend this week.

⑭ 我總是 存不了 什麼錢。
I can never save any money.

070 你煩惱金錢嗎？

❶ 你覺得錢 不夠用 嗎？
Do you feel like there's never enough money?

❷ 你有 房貸壓力 嗎？
Do you have pressure from a house loan?

❸ 你的薪水夠你 一個月開銷 嗎？
Is your salary enough for your monthly expenses?

❹ 你這個月繳不出房租嗎？
Can't you pay your rent this month?

❺ 你常會透支嗎？
Do you often overdraw your account?

❻ 你常需要包紅包或白包嗎？
Do you often need to give cash gifts for weddings or funerals?

❼ 你的信用 卡債還清 了嗎？
Have you paid off your credit card debt?

❽ 你擔心自己存不了錢嗎？
Do you worry that you can't save any money?

❾ 你的車貸還完了嗎？
Have you paid off your car loan?

❿ 你煩惱孩子的學費嗎？
Do you worry about your child's tuition?

⓫ 你擔心你連 自己都養不活 嗎？
Do you worry that you won't be able to support yourself?

⓬ 你擔心自己會 窮一輩子 嗎？
Do you worry that you'll be poor for the rest of your life?

⓭ 你擔心沒錢繳水電費嗎？
Do you worry that you won't have enough to pay your utilities?

⓮ 你擔心戶頭的錢 撐不到下個月 嗎？
Do you worry that you didn't make enough deposits to last through the month?

071 我煩惱外表。

❶ 我實在 太胖 了。
I'm really too fat.

❷ 我覺得自己長得不好看。
I don't think I look well.

❸ 我常因為 身材被取笑 。
I'm often made fun of for the way I look.

❹ 我的皮膚不夠白。
My skin isn't white enough.

❺ 我覺得自己是 矮冬瓜 。
I think I'm a munchkin.

❻ 我的眼睛不夠大。
My eyes are not big enough.

❼ 我的腿不夠纖細。
My legs aren't thin enough.

❽ 我討厭我的 大餅臉 。
I hate my moon face.

❾ 我覺得我的 小腹很礙眼 。
I think my belly is an eyesore.

❿ 我全身上下沒有一個地方能看。
Nowhere on my entire body is nice to look at.

⓫ 我恨自己是個 小胸部 。
I hate my small bust size.

⓬ 常有人說我是青蛙。
People often say I'm a frog.

⓭ 腳太大 害我常買不到鞋。
My feet are too big for me to buy shoes that fit.

⓮ 我發福之後很多 衣服都穿不下 。
After I got fat, a lot of my clothes didn't fit me anymore.

⓯ 我的臉色太蒼白了。
My face is too pale.

071 你煩惱外表嗎？

❶ 你不滿意自己的外表嗎？
Aren't you satisfied with your appearance?

❷ 你煩惱你的 腿不夠細 嗎？
Do you worry that your legs are not thin enough?

❸ 你煩惱自己不夠高嗎？
Do you worry that you're not tall enough?

❹ 你煩惱你的臉太大太圓嗎？
Do you worry that your face is too big and round?

❺ 你煩惱你的 眼睛不夠大 嗎？
Do you worry that your eyes are not big enough?

❻ 你嫌自己皮膚不夠白嗎？
Do you complain that your skin isn't white enough?

❼ 你 介意別人評論 你的外表嗎？
Do you mind when others comment on your appearance?

❽ 你不喜歡你的新髮型嗎？
Don't you like your new hairstyle?

❾ 你會因為胸部小而 自卑 嗎？
Do you feel inferior because of your small bust?

❿ 太胖讓你自卑嗎？
Does being too fat make you feel inferior?

⓫ 你會在意自己的氣色好不好嗎？
Do you care if you look well or not?

⓬ 大胸部讓你很困擾嗎？
Does having a large bust bother you?

⓭ 沒化妝你就 不敢出門 嗎？
Are you afraid to go outside without makeup on?

⓮ 長一顆痘痘你就 不想見人 ？
Do you not want to see anyone when you have acne?

⓯ 為什麼你對自己的外表 這麼沒信心 ？
Why are you so insecure about your appearance?

072 我覺得壓力大。

❶ 最近工作多到讓我 喘不過氣來 。
I have so much work I can't breathe.

❷ 真累。
I'm so tired.

❸ 我每天都 加班到很晚 。
I have to work overtime till very late every day.

❹ 我 身心俱疲 。
My body and mind are tired.

❺ 我連假日也要工作。
Even on holidays, I have to work.

❻ 我胃痛， 吃不下 飯。
I can't eat anything, my stomach hurts.

❼ 房貸壓力不小。
Having a mortgage is stressful.

❽ 我忙到 沒時間吃 飯。
I am too busy to have meals.

❾ 我今天還有幾十通電話要打。
I still have dozens of calls to make today.

❿ 我的 行程已經排到 三個月以後了。
My schedule is full for the next three months.

⓫ 我常常腰酸背痛。
I often get a sore waist and an aching back.

⓬ 我很怕 被社會淘汰 。
I'm afraid of being weeded out from society.

⓭ 我像 蠟燭兩頭燒 。
I'm like a candle burning at both ends.

⓮ 我好久沒有好好休息了。
I haven't had a good rest for a long time.

⓯ 家庭和事業 很難兼顧 。
It's really difficult to look after both family and career.

072 你覺得壓力大嗎？

❶ 你常加班嗎？
Do you work overtime often?

❷ 最近 |很勞累| 嗎？
Have you been very tired lately?

❸ 你有黑眼圈了耶。
You have bags under your eyes.

❹ 你假日還要工作啊？
Do you still need to work on weekends?

❺ 要不要 |出去走走|？
Do you want to go for a walk with me?

❻ 你一直都這麼努力嗎？
Do you always work this hard?

❼ 你這樣 |會累出病| 來的。
You will wear yourself out and get sick.

❽ 讓自己 |喘口氣| 吧？
Give yourself a break, will you?

❾ 你每天都工作到晚上九點、十點嗎？
Do you work to nine or ten pm every day?

❿ 你要多照顧自己的身體。
You should take care of your health.

⓫ 你會不會 |壓力太大| 了？
Are you under too much pressure?

⓬ 年紀大了要多注意保養身體。
You should take good care of your health as you
get older.

⓭ |深呼吸| 一下吧！
Take a deep breath!

⓮ 頭還在痛嗎？
Does your head still hurt?

⓯ 你 |透支了| 嗎？
Are you exhausted?

073 我贊成。

1 我舉 雙手贊成 。
I completely agree with that.

2 我 再同意不過 了！
I couldn't agree more!

3 就是這樣！
That's it!

4 有比這個更好的嗎？
Is there anything better than this?

5 當然好！
Of course!

6 你得到我的同意了。
You have my permission.

7 這個計畫 太完美 了！
What a perfect plan this is!

8 算我一份！
Count me in!

9 就 照你說的 做吧！
Just do as you suggest!

10 我想這是最好的了。
I think this is the best.

11 我沒意見。
It doesn't matter to me.

12 都 聽你的 ！
It's all up to you!

13 真是 超乎我想像 的好。
It is beyond my imagination.

14 放手做吧！
Just do it!

15 我 投你一票 。
You've got my vote.

174

073 你贊成嗎？

❶ 你贊成嗎？
Do you agree?

❷ 你有 什麼看法 ？
What is your opinion on this?

❸ 你覺得這樣做好嗎？
Do you think this is a good way?

❹ 你覺得 這主意如何 ？
What do you think about this idea?

❺ 你認為這是最好的方式嗎？
Do you think this is the best method?

❻ 你 同意 我說的嗎？
Do you agree with what I said?

❼ 我希望可以得到你的許可。
I hope that I can have your permission.

❽ 這樣代表你 默許 了嗎？
Does that mean you agree?

❾ 拜託你點個頭嘛！
Please just nod your head and say yes!

❿ 你就 將就點 嘛！
Can't you be a little more flexible?

⓫ 大家都說好，你就答應了吧！
Since everyone has agreed already, would you just
say yes?

⓬ 希望你 能支持我 。
I hope you will support me.

⓭ 我想不出你有什麼理由拒絕。
I don't think there is any reason for you to refuse.

⓮ 我不敢相信你 竟然答應 了！
I can't believe that you just said yes!

⓯ 你在 猶豫什麼 ？
Why do you hesitate?

074 我反對。

❶ 我不會答應的。
I won't approve of it.

❷ 我 無法認同 。
I can't agree with that.

❸ 我反對。
I disagree.

❹ 我 抵死不從 。
I'll die before I agree with that.

❺ 這不是我希望的。
This is not what I wanted.

❻ 我不認為這是個好主意。
I don't think it's a good idea.

❼ 我不想支持你們。
I don't want to support you.

❽ 省省力氣 吧!
Save your strength!

❾ 我想不出比這更糟的提議了!
I can't think of any suggestions worse than this.

❿ 我絕不 和你同流合污 。
I absolutely will not take part in this with you.

⓫ 門兒都沒有!
No deal!

⓬ 不可能說服我的,你放棄吧!
You can't persuade me, give it up!

⓭ 不行就是不行 ,沒什麼好說的。
No means no, there's nothing left to say.

⓮ 這種事我怎麼可能會答應呢?
How can I possibly agree with that?

⓯ 我絕對 不會改變立場 。
I absolutely will not change my position.

074 你反對嗎？

1 你反對嗎？
Are you against that?

2 你 為什麼 反對？
Why don't you agree with that?

3 你不覺得這個點子很棒嗎？
You don't think it's a good idea?

4 你不喜歡這個提議嗎？
You don't like this suggestion?

5 難道你 不再考慮 一下？
Why don't you think about it some more?

6 你不支持我們嗎？
You don't want to support us?

7 我不敢相信你竟然反對。
I can't believe that you are actually against this.

8 請你不要這麼快就說「不」。
Please don't say "no" so quickly.

9 請你不要 為了反對而反對 。
Please don't oppose this just to oppose it.

10 你上回不是贊成嗎？
Didn't you agree last time?

11 你一定要 這麼堅持 嗎？
Must you be so persistent?

12 請你給我一個 合理的理由 。
Please give me a reasonable reason.

13 你反對的理由很奇怪。
Your reason for opposing this is strange.

14 你的 反對是有道理 的。
Your opposition is reasonable.

15 你 有權說「不」 。
You have the right to say "no."

075 我的建議。

❶ 我有個 提議 。
I have a suggestion.

❷ 我沒什麼意見。
I don't have an opinion.

❸ 我想聽聽 大家的意見 。
I would like to listen to everyone's suggestions.

❹ 我可以提個意見嗎？
May I make a suggestion?

❺ 我在想這麼做是不是比較好？
I am considering whether this is a better way to do it.

❻ 這樣也許行得通。
This way might work.

❼ 換個方向 想會比較好。
It will be better if we change the direction of our thinking.

❽ 何不試試 看？
Why don't you give it a try?

❾ 你是否可以考慮一下？
Can you just think about it?

❿ 我建議 找個局外人 來評理。
I suggest that we find an outsider to decide which of us is right.

⓫ 我建議大家 先冷靜 下來。
I suggest that everyone calm down first.

⓬ 我想我們 各做各的 好了。
I think that we should each do our own jobs.

⓭ 我想不出什麼好建議。
I can't think of any good suggestions.

⓮ 大家要不要 參考一下 ？
Does anyone want to consider it?

⓯ 我希望大家都發表意見。
I hope that everyone expresses an opinion.

075 你的建議？

❶ 這件事你有什麼看法？
Do you have any opinion on this matter?

❷ 你有 什麼好建議 嗎？
Do you have any good suggestions?

❸ 這是你的建議嗎？
Is this your suggestion?

❹ 你覺得這個主意如何？
What do you think of this idea?

❺ 你可以 幫忙想想 辦法嗎？
Can you help think of a solution?

❻ 大家一起 腦力激盪 吧！
Let's brainstorm together!

❼ 我很需要你的意見。
I really need your comments.

❽ 我會 尊重你 的意見。
I will respect your opinion.

❾ 謝謝你提供建議。
Thank you for offering your suggestion.

❿ 你 指出了問題 的關鍵。
You've pointed out the key point of this problem.

⓫ 你的意見 很具體 。
Your opinion is very concrete.

⓬ 你的建議解決了大家的難題。
Your recommendation solved everyone's problems.

⓭ 你的建議很 有可行性 。
Your suggestion is quite feasible.

⓮ 我想你一定有很多主意吧？
I bet you probably have a lot of ideas.

⓯ 我等不及要聽你的想法了！
I can't wait to hear your ideas!

076 我需要幫忙。

1 我 有麻煩 了！
I've got a problem!

2 誰來 救我 ！
Who can help me?

3 如果你能幫忙，我會非常感激。
I would appreciate it if you could help me.

4 求求你 嘛！
I am begging you!

5 你介意我耽誤你一些時間嗎？
Would you mind if I kept you here for a moment?

6 我真的 走投無路 了。
There really is no way out for me.

7 你是唯一能幫我的人。
You are the only one who can help me out.

8 也許我該找別人幫忙。
Perhaps I should look for help from someone else.

9 我需要找個 幫手 。
I need to find a helper.

10 我已經絕望了。
I am hopeless.

11 我不知道如何 開口求助 。
I don't know how to ask for help.

12 我不需要別人幫忙。
I don't need help from others.

13 沒有人會憐我的。
Nobody will pity me.

14 你別 假惺惺 了！
Stop pretending!

15 我 說什麼也不接受 你的幫助。
There's no way that I will accept your help.

180

076 你需要幫忙嗎？

1 需要幫忙嗎？
Do you need help?

2 我很 樂意幫忙 。
I am willing to help you.

3 我可以 為你做什麼 嗎？
What can I do for you?

4 我想你可能會需要這個。
I suspect you might need this.

5 真的不用幫你嗎？
You really don't need my help?

6 我想我可以 幫得上忙 。
I think I can help.

7 你願意接受我的幫助嗎？
Are you willing to accept my help?

8 我不知道 該如何幫你 。
I don't know how to help you.

9 讓我試試好嗎？
Let me try, okay?

10 到時候你就會需要我了。
When the time comes, you will need me.

11 我不認為你需要我的幫助。
I don't think you need my help.

12 你說什麼我都會 盡力而為 。
I will do my best to do whatever you ask.

13 請告訴我你的需求。
Please tell me what you need.

14 需要什麼，記得 告訴我一聲 。
Please let me know if you need something.

15 能幫忙是 我的榮幸 。
It is my pleasure to help you.

077 我下定決心。

1 我的 心意已決 。
I've already made up my mind.

2 這就是我的決定！
This is my decision!

3 這個決定 對大家都好 。
This decision will be good for everyone.

4 我需要時間考慮。
I need more time to think about it.

5 我要堅持我的決定。
I have to insist on my decision.

6 沒得商量 了！
There's nothing to negotiate!

7 這是我 仔細考慮後 的決定。
After careful consideration, this is my decision.

8 我常受別人的影響改變決定。
I often change my decisions due to the influence of others.

9 我 做不了主 ！
I can't make the call!

10 我不夠堅持我的想法。
I don't insist enough on my decisions.

11 誰能幫我做決定？
Who can help me make the decision?

12 我 不會後悔 的！
I won't regret it!

13 我一定會盡我 最大的努力 。
I will do my absolute best.

14 這事 我說了算 ！
This is final.

15 誰都不能改變我的決定！
No one can alter my decision!

077 你下定決心嗎？

1 你確定嗎？

Are you sure?

2 你不會後悔嗎？

Won't you regret it?

3 你做出 決定了嗎 ？

Have you made your decision yet?

4 看來你心意堅定。

It seems that you are firm in your decision.

5 你太 優柔寡斷 了。

You are too irresolute.

6 大家都在等你的決定。

Everyone is waiting for your decision.

7 你怎麼會做這種決定？！

How can you make such a decision?!

8 拜託你 快做決定 吧！

Please make up your mind!

9 你的決定 太冒險 了。

Your decision is too risky.

10 你有可能改變決定嗎？

Is it possible that you may change your decision?

11 你不要 匆促下決定 。

Don't make your decision hastily.

12 我信任你的抉擇。

I trust your choice.

13 你要不 要再考慮 一下？

Do you need to think about it again?

14 你這個決定聽起來很不錯。

Your decision sounds good to me.

15 看來是沒有辦法 打消你的念頭 了。

It seems there's no way to make you give up your idea.

183

078 我不瞭解。

1 我不懂乀！
I really can't understand!

2 我 不瞭解 你在說啥。
I don't understand what you are saying.

3 我一點頭緒也沒有。
I don't have a clue.

4 我想我 需要翻譯 。
I guess I need a translation.

5 可以再 解釋清楚 一點嗎？
Can you define that more clearly?

6 怎麼那麼 複雜 ？
How can it be so complicated?

7 有誰能說明一下嗎？
Can anyone take a moment to explain?

8 我怎麼想都 想不透 。
I can't think it through.

9 我真的不明白！
I really don't understand!

10 真是 難懂 ！
It's really difficult to understand!

11 我想這輩子我都不會明白的！
I don't think I will ever understand that!

12 我怎麼 聽不懂 ？
Why can't I understand?

13 我想我們有代溝。
I think there's a generation gap between us.

14 別打啞謎 了！
Don't confuse me like that!

15 你腦袋裡到底裝什麼？
What on earth is in your head?

078 你不瞭解嗎？

1 我該怎麼說明你才懂？
How can I explain this so that you'll understand?

2 你 聽得懂 嗎？
Do you understand?

3 需要我畫圖說明嗎？
Do I need to draw a picture to describe it?

4 我再 加些補充 好嗎？
Is it OK if I make some additional remarks?

5 我講得 夠不夠清楚 ？
Did I explain it clearly enough?

6 可以告訴我 你的問題點 嗎？
Could you tell me the main point of your question?

7 要不要我 再說一次 ？
Do I need to repeat that again?

8 這對你來說太困難嗎？
Is this difficult for you?

9 需要我 把它簡化 嗎？
Do you need me to simplify it?

10 我希望你能瞭解。
I hope you can understand.

11 你需要翻譯嗎？
Do you need it translated?

12 你怎麼那麼 遲鈍 啊？
How can you be so thick-headed?

13 我 換個方式 講好了。
Let me rephrase myself.

14 不懂要問。
If you don't know, then ask.

15 我再說最後一次！
This is the last time I'll tell you!

079 道謝。

❶ 你 人真好 ！
You are a wonderful person!

❷ 讓我 請你吃頓飯 好嗎？
Let me treat you to a meal, okay?

❸ 你是我的英雄！
You are my hero!

❹ 辛苦你了！
Thanks for all your hard work!

❺ 我太感動了。
I'm so touched.

❻ 你真是我的 救命恩人 。
You really are a lifesaver.

❼ 謝謝你 的幫忙！
Thank you for your help!

❽ 請接受我的致謝。
Please accept my thanks.

❾ 我一定會 報答你 。
I will definitely pay you back.

❿ 多謝你的費心！
Thank you for your attention!

⓫ 你不知道你所做的對我意義重大。
You have no idea how much this means to me.

⓬ 我非常喜歡你送的禮物。
I like the gift you gave me very much.

⓭ 真不知該如何報答你。
I really don't know how I can repay you.

⓮ 你的恩情 我不會忘記。
I won't forget your kindness.

⓯ 我真想 給你一個擁抱 。
I really want to give you a hug.

079 回應道謝。

❶ 不客氣。
You're welcome.

❷ 您 過獎 了！
I'm flattered!

❸ 你請我看場電影就算 扯平 ！
We can call it even if you treat me to a movie!

❹ 舉手之勞 而已。
I barely lifted a finger.

❺ 別放在心上。
Don't worry about it.

❻ 我只是盡我所能。
I just did my best.

❼ 區區小事 ，何足掛齒。
Piece of cake, don't mention it.

❽ 您 太客氣 了。
You're too kind.

❾ 這是我 應該做的 。
This is the least I can do.

❿ 我沒你說的那麼好。
I am not as great as you make me out to be.

⓫ 我很高興能幫到你的忙。
I am glad to help you.

⓬ 別這麼說，我會 不好意思 ！
Oh, stop it, you are embarrassing me!

⓭ 你滿意我就開心了。
As long as you are satisfied, I am happy.

⓮ 我才應該謝謝你呢！
It is I who should be thanking you!

⓯ 我 不求什麼回報 。
I don't need any reward.

080 邀請。

❶ 誠摯的邀請你。

You are sincerely invited.

❷ 歡迎攜伴 參加。

Companions are welcome.

❸ 請務必出席。

Please be sure to attend.

❹ 請準時 入座。

Please take your seat on time.

❺ 希望你能前來。

Hope you can participate.

❻ 你不會想錯過的！

You wouldn't want to miss this!

❼ 我們 不能沒有你 。

We would be lost without you.

❽ 你會接受邀約嗎？

Do you accept this invitation?

❾ 我們可以 配合您的時間 。

We can accommodate your schedule.

❿ 我們都 期待見到你 ！

We are looking forward to meeting you in person!

⓫ 你怎麼能不來呢？

How can you not come?

⓬ 你不來我會很失望的。

I will be very disappointed if you do not come.

⓭ 你怎麼可以推辭呢？

How could you decline this invitation?

⓮ 我會 發邀請函 給你。

I will send the invitation to you.

⓯ 有你在場是 我們的榮幸 。

It is our honor to have you here.

080 接受／拒絕邀請。

❶ 謝謝，但我不要。
Thanks, but no thanks.

❷ 我一定到。
I will definitely be there.

❸ 很抱歉，不克前往 。
I am sorry that I will be unable to attend.

❹ 我受寵若驚！
I am flattered!

❺ 太突然了，我無法立刻決定。
It's too sudden; I can't make a decision right away.

❻ 謝謝你的好意。
Thank you for your kindness.

❼ 你的 盛情難卻 。
It would be ungracious not to accept your invitation.

❽ 如果可以我 一定會去 。
I will be there if I can.

❾ 我另外 有約 。
I have another appointment.

❿ 我會把當天的時間空下來。
I will set aside some time on that day.

⓫ 我想我是 沒有藉口推辭 了。
I think I have no reason to refuse.

⓬ 我 恐怕不能 答應。
I am afraid that I can't make it.

⓭ 我可以過幾天回覆嗎？
May I reply in a couple of days?

⓮ 我 要考慮 一下。
I need to think about it.

⓯ 我很 期待那天 的到來。
I'm looking forward to that day.

081 道歉。

1 對不起。
Excuse me.

2 請你原諒。
I beg your pardon.

3 請原諒 我。
Please forgive me.

4 請 恕我冒昧 。
Please excuse my inappropriate behavior.

5 請接受我的道歉。
Please accept my apology.

6 我很抱歉。
I am very sorry.

7 我真不是人!
I am such a jerk!

8 希望你能諒解。
I hope you can understand.

9 請原諒我的 一時糊塗 。
Please forgive me for my stupidity.

10 請原諒我的無知。
Please forgive me for my ignorance.

11 拜託 饒了我 吧!
Please give me another chance!

12 請不要掛在心上。
Don't take it to heart.

13 我誠心的 向你致歉 。
I offer my sincere apologies to you.

14 你不知道 我有多自責 。
You don't know how much I blame myself.

15 可以再 給我一次機會 嗎?
Could you give me one more chance?

081 接受／拒絕道歉。

1 沒關係。
It doesn't matter.

2 忘了吧！
Forget it!

3 別在意了。
Don't mention it.

4 知道錯就好了。
That's fine as long as you realize your mistake.

5 我想你不是故意的。
I am sure you didn't mean it.

6 我原諒你了。
I forgive you.

7 我相信你只是一時糊塗。
I am sure you were just confused at the time.

8 我想你一定有你的難處。
I am sure you must have your own difficulties.

9 以後我們還是好朋友。
We can still continue to be good friends.

10 真是不可原諒！
This is really unforgivable!

11 你怎麼可以那樣做呢？
How could you do that?

12 你這麼做對得起我嗎？
How can you face me after what you have done?

13 我不會輕易放過你的！
I won't let you off easily!

14 你真是太可惡了！
You really are despicable!

15 你要為此付出代價！
You'll pay for this!

082 承認錯誤。

❶ 我錯了。
   I was wrong.

❷ 我真的 很抱歉 。
   I am very sorry.

❸ 我犯了個錯誤。
   I made a mistake.

❹ 我真是不可原諒。
   What I have done is unforgivable.

❺ 我真是個大笨蛋。
   I really am a big fool.

❻ 我真是 錯得離譜 。
   I have made a colossal mistake.

❼ 要我 承認錯誤 真不是一件容易的事！
   It is really not an easy thing for me to admit that I've
   made a mistake.

❽ 看吧，我 又錯了 。
   See? I am wrong again.

❾ 可以 讓我彌補 我的過錯嗎？
   Will you let me make up for the mistake I've made?

❿ 事情變得 一發不可收拾 了。
   Things have gotten out of control.

⓫ 我一定是 昏了頭 ！
   I must have been confused!

⓬ 我真是自私！
   I am so selfish!

⓭ 我犯下了 滔天大錯 。
   I made an extremely serious mistake.

⓮ 我太不用大腦了！
   I am so stupid!

082 原諒錯誤。

1 沒關係啦！
It doesn't matter!

2 別自責 了。
Don't blame yourself.

3 我原諒你了。
I forgive you.

4 人非聖賢，熟能無過 。
Nobody is perfect, everyone makes mistakes.

5 知道錯就好。
It's enough that you realize you were wrong.

6 我 可以諒解 。
I can tolerate that.

7 下次 不要再犯 了。
Don't do it again.

8 沒那麼嚴重啦！
It's not that critical!

9 你要 怎麼補償 我？
How are you going to make it up to me?

10 我可以理解。
I can understand.

11 希望這次你學到教訓了。
I hope that you have learned a lesson from this.

12 下次 眼睛放亮點 ！
Use your head next time!

13 別再這麼迷糊了！
Don't be that foolish again!

14 我 不會記恨 的。
I won't bear a grudge.

15 過去的就 讓它過去 吧。
Just let the past go.

083 請幫我…。

❶ 可以幫我一個忙嗎？

Would you give me a hand?

❷ 我需要你的協助。

I need your help.

❸ 你現在 有空嗎 ？

Are you free right now?

❹ 可憐可憐我吧！

Please have pity on me!

❺ 求求你啦！

Please!

❻ 上回我幫你，這回 換你幫我 了。

I helped you last time, so this time it's your turn.

❼ 你 一定要幫我 這個忙。

You must help me with this.

❽ 我們 是朋友吧 ？

We're friends, aren't we?

❾ 沒有你我做不到。

I can't do it without you.

❿ 今天我請客，但是你要幫我個忙。

Today I'll treat you, but you need to give me a hand.

⓫ 我 只能靠你 了！

I am counting on you!

⓬ 我又 遇上麻煩 了！

I'm in trouble again!

⓭ 怎麼辦 ？沒人幫我！

What should I do? There's no one who'll help me!

⓮ 有事 請教你 。

I need your advice on something.

⓯ 你不可以不幫我。

You can't refuse to help me.

083 答應／拒絕幫忙。

❶ 沒問題，交給我。
No problem, just leave it to me.

❷ 我很樂意幫你。
I am glad to do you a favor.

❸ 我想想怎麼解決。
Let me think about how to solve the problem.

❹ 靜下心來，別急。
Just calm down, don't be in such hurry.

❺ 不好意思，我正在忙…
I'm sorry; I'm in the middle of....

❻ 好！你怎麼報答我？
Good! How will you repay me?

❼ 我忙完馬上去幫你。
I'll help you as soon as I am done with my work

❽ 我真的抽不出時間…
I really can't find the time to....

❾ 我考慮看看。
Let me think about it.

❿ 你找別人幫忙吧！
Find someone else to help you!

⓫ 想得美，我不可能幫你。
Don't even think about it, it's impossible for me to help you.

⓬ 你應該學會自己解決問題。
You should learn how to solve problems by yourself.

⓭ 你總是給我惹麻煩。
You are always making trouble for me.

⓮ 我為什麼要幫你？
Why should I give you a hand?

⓯ 當然！誰叫我們是好朋友。
Of course! We are good friends after all.

084 請借我錢…。

1 我想 和你周轉 一下。
I'd like to borrow some money from you.

2 你有錢可以借我嗎?
Can you lend me some money if you have any?

3 先借我一萬塊好嗎?
Lend me NT$10,000 first, OK?

4 先借我錢繳卡費。
Lend me some money first to pay my credit card bills.

5 你 能借我多少 錢?
How much can you lend me?

6 發薪水就 還你錢 。
I'll pay you back on my payday.

7 我沒有零錢,你有嗎?
I don't have any change, do you?

8 我 忘了帶錢包 ,先借我一百元。
I forgot my purse, can you spot me NT$100?

9 拜託你借我一些錢 應急 。
Please, lend me some money to meet an urgent need.

10 我帶的 錢不夠 ,你身上有錢嗎?
I didn't bring enough money; do you have any on you?

11 借我一些錢吃飯吧?
Will you lend me some money for meals?

12 求你幫幫忙, 借我十萬 元。
I'm begging you for your help; lend me NT$100,000.

13 我的朋友中,就屬你最有錢了。
Of all my friends, you are the richest.

14 我保證 僅此一次 。
I promise that this will be the only time.

15 借不到錢,我就活不下去啦!
I won't be able to live if I can't borrow any money!

084 答應／拒絕借錢。

❶ 沒問題,你 需要多少 ?
No problem, how much do you need?

❷ 需要多少?
How much do you need?

❸ 你遇到了什麼困難嗎?
Are you encountering some difficulties?

❹ 我馬上去 領錢給你 。
I'll go withdraw some money for you right now.

❺ 什麼時候可以還我?
When will you pay me back?

❻ 我從來不借錢給別人,這是我的原則。
I never lend money to anyone; this is my principle.

❼ 我們要 先簽個借據 。
We have to sign an agreement first.

❽ 你不是上個月才向我借錢嗎?
Didn't you just borrow money from me last month?

❾ 我的錢都放在定存不能動ㄟ。
All my money is in the deposit account, and I can't take any out.

❿ 一定要還 我喔!
You must pay me back!

⓫ 我真的沒辦法…
I really can't....

⓬ 免談 ,想都別想!
No way, don't even think about it!

⓭ 我也 沒錢 ㄟ!
I don't have any money either!

⓮ 拜託,你比我還有錢吧!
Come on, you are richer than I am!

⓯ 我 比你還窮 呢!
I'm much poorer than you!

085 請借我東西…。

❶ 這個東西借一下。
Let me borrow this for a while.

❷ 這件衣服明天 借我穿 。
Lend me these clothes for tomorrow.

❸ 可以向你借樣東西嗎？
May I borrow something from you?

❹ 這本書可以借我嗎？
Can you lend me this book?

❺ 外借要錢嗎？
Should I pay you anything to borrow this?

❻ 要不要借啦， 小氣鬼 ？
Are you going to lend it to me or not, you cheapskate?

❼ 外借要辦證件嗎？
Do I need to apply for a certificate to borrow this?

❽ 暫時借用一下， 明天還 。
I just need to borrow it temporarily—I will return it tomorrow.

❾ 借我一下原子筆， 馬上就還 。
Lend me your pen, I'll return it right away.

❿ 我 又不是不還 ，幹麼不借我？
I'm not going to refuse to return it, why not lend it to me?

⓫ 我想到圖書館 借書 。
I want to go to the library to check out some books.

⓬ 我一向 有借有還 。
I always return everything I borrow.

⓭ 你既然用不上，不如借我。
Since you have no use for it, you might as well lend it to me.

⓮ 要借不借 隨便你。
It's up to you whether or not you'll lend it to me.

⓯ 筆記借我抄一下。
Let me copy your notebook for a minute.

085 答應／拒絕借東西。

① 你 儘管拿去 用。
Feel free to use it.

② 沒問題，你用。
No problem, go ahead.

③ 記得還我。
Remember to return it back to me.

④ 可以，這原本就 是公用的 。
Sure, it was for public use originally.

⑤ 你請用，不用客氣。
Go ahead, there's no need to be overly polite.

⑥ 你上次向我借的東西還我了嗎？
Have you returned the thing I lent to you last time?

⑦ 說什麼都 不借 。
No matter what you say, I will not lend anything to you.

⑧ 你自己去買！
Go buy it yourself!

⑨ 你信用不好 ，不借。
You don't have good credit; I will not lend anything to you.

⑩ 我從來不把東西借給別人。
I never lend anything to anybody.

⑪ 這東西 不是我的 ，我不能借你。
I can't lend it to you, it's not mine.

⑫ 我 現在還要用 ，下次再借你。
I'm still using it; I will lend it to you next time.

⑬ 這東西 不能外借 。
It is not for borrowing.

⑭ 借給你我就不能工作了。
I can't work if I lend it to you.

⑮ 我已經 答應借給別人 了。
I've already promised to lend it to someone else.

086 我喜歡。

❶ 我很喜歡。
I like it very much.

❷ 我 會好好珍惜 的。
I will be sure to treasure it.

❸ 我作夢都 夢到 ！
I've dreamt about that!

❹ 我願意用全世界來交換。
I'd give up the whole world for that.

❺ 賠上生命我也 在所不惜 。
Even if it cost me my life, I would not hesitate.

❻ 我 愛死 它了！
I love it to death!

❼ 我想不出還有什麼比這個更棒的了！
I cannot think of anything better than this!

❽ 一看到它我就高興。
As soon as I see it, I feel happy.

❾ 你不覺得這是 全世界最棒 的嗎？
Don't you think this is the best in the whole world?

❿ 真是迷人！
That is quite charming!

⓫ 求求你別將它從我的生命中帶走！
Please do not take it out of my life!

⓬ 多可愛啊！
What a cutie!

⓭ 這真是我的 救命仙丹 ！
This really is my lifesaver!

⓮ 那就是 我想要的 ！
That's the one that I want!

⓯ 你知道它 對我有多重要 嗎？
Do you know how important it is to me?

086 你喜歡嗎？

1 你有 多喜歡 ？
How much do you like it?

2 你喜歡嗎？
Do you like it?

3 你覺得怎麼樣？
What do you think?

4 你會接受這個嗎？
Will you accept this?

5 你比較 喜歡哪一個 ？
Which one do you prefer?

6 這是你想要的嗎？
Is this the one you want?

7 你 為它瘋狂 嗎？
Are you crazy about it?

8 你覺得很棒，對吧？
You think it's pretty great, don't you?

9 你 想擁有 它嗎？
Do you want to have it?

10 你就是 不能沒有它 ，對吧？
You just cannot live without it, can you?

11 你願意用多少錢買它？
How much would you buy it for?

12 你願意 拿什麼跟我交換 ？
What are you willing to exchange with me for it?

13 你願意割捨哪一個？
Which one would you be willing to give up?

14 你想全部擁有，對吧？
You just want to have it all, don't you?

15 你好像 不是很中意 的樣子。
It seems like it doesn't appeal to you.

087 我不喜歡。

❶ 別提了，我不可能接受。
Don't mention it again, there is no way I will accept.

❷ 我已經 忍耐到極限 。
I've already put up with it as long as I can.

❸ 他 以為他是誰 啊？
Who does he think he is?

❹ 我再也不要跟他說話了。
I don't want to talk to him anymore.

❺ 真是 噁心 ！
That's disgusting!

❻ 別在我面前提到他。
Do not mention him around me.

❼ 我 受不了 他的態度。
I can't stand his attitude.

❽ 我 懶得理 她！
I am not in the mood to worry about her!

❾ 想到就想吐！
When I think about that I want to throw up!

❿ 饒了我吧！
Give me a break!

⓫ 窮極無聊！
This is so boring!

⓬ 別來煩我！
Leave me alone!

⓭ 我 恨死 她了！
I absolutely hate her!

⓮ 拜託別找我，我沒興趣。
Please don't count me in, I'm not interested.

⓯ 雞皮疙瘩 掉滿地。
I get goose bumps all over my body.

087 你不喜歡嗎？

❶ 你 不喜歡 嗎？
You don't like that?

❷ 你有多討厭它？
How much do you hate it?

❸ 你連 看都不看 一眼嗎？
You won't even take a look at it?

❹ 你一定要這麼挑剔嗎？
Do you have to be so picky?

❺ 你真的 無法接受 嗎？
Are you really unable to accept it?

❻ 你不能婉轉一點拒絕嗎？
Can't you reject it with a little tact?

❼ 你真的不願意試試嗎？
You really don't want to give it a try?

❽ 你真的覺得 那麼糟 嗎？
Do you really think it is that terrible?

❾ 你真的一點都不考慮嗎？
You really don't even want to give it a little thought?

❿ 這和你 期待的不同 ，對吧？
This is not what you were expecting, is it?

⓫ 你毫無興趣嗎？
Don't you have any interest in it?

⓬ 你為什麼 只看到不好的 一面呢？
Why do you only see the bad side?

⓭ 我很意外你竟然不喜歡。
I am surprised that you didn't like it.

⓮ 這不是 你以前的最愛 嗎？
Wasn't this your favorite before?

⓯ 你不能勉強接受嗎？
Can't you try to accept it?

088 我喜歡/討厭的人。

❶ 我喜歡笑口常開的人。
I like people who smile all the time.

❷ 我喜歡 有禮貌 的人。
I like people who are polite.

❸ 我喜歡熱心公益的人。
I like people who are enthusiastic about the public welfare.

❹ 我喜歡運動型的男生。
I like athletic guys.

❺ 我對溫柔的女生特別有好感。
I especially like tender-hearted girls.

❻ 我敬佩 腳踏實地 的人。
I admire people who are practical.

❼ 斯文的男生深得我心。
Gentlemanly men always capture my heart.

❽ 我討厭 沒禮貌 的人。
I don't like people who are impolite.

❾ 我討厭 不守信用 的人。
I hate people who do not keep their promises.

❿ 我討厭 沒有時間觀念 的人。
I dislike people who have no sense of punctuality.

⓫ 我從不跟 不擇手段 的人打交道。
I refuse to have anything to do with unscrupulous people.

⓬ 自私的人讓我很反感。
Selfish people give me a bad feeling.

⓭ 我瞧不起 馬屁精 。
I look down on people who brown-nose.

⓮ 我討厭別人 自以為是 。
I don't like people who are self-righteous.

⓯ 我討厭陰險的人。
I hate insidious people.

088 你喜歡／討厭的人？

❶ 什麼樣的人 令你心動 ？
What kind of people impress you?

❷ 你有喜歡的人嗎？
Is there anyone you like?

❸ 你喜歡她的 個性還是外表 ？
Do you like her personality or her looks?

❹ 什麼樣的人 令你作嘔 ？
What kind of people make you sick?

❺ 你 喜歡幽默的 男生嗎？
Do you like funny guys?

❻ 你討厭誰？
Who do you dislike?

❼ 你喜歡直率的女生嗎？
Do you like forthright girls?

❽ 你喜歡的人長得好不好看？
Is the person you like good-looking?

❾ 哪種人最 讓你抓狂 ？
What kind of people drive you crazy?

❿ 你瞭解你喜歡的人嗎？
Do you understand the people you like?

⓫ 你 討厭不誠實的 人嗎？
Do you hate dishonest people?

⓬ 他 有那麼好 嗎？
Is he really so nice?

⓭ 你討厭一個人會怎麼做？
What do you do when you dislike someone?

⓮ 他沒有任何優點嗎？
Doesn't he have any virtues?

⓯ 他 哪裡惹你 了？
What has he done to offend you?

089 我喜歡/討厭的顏色。

❶ 我喜歡很多顏色。
I like many colors.

❷ 我 喜歡明亮的 顏色。
I like bright colors.

❸ 我 沒有特別喜歡 的顏色。
I don't have any particular colors that I like.

❹ 我 只喜歡 黑色。
I only like black.

❺ 我喜歡黃色。
I like yellow.

❻ 我喜歡暖色調。
I like warm tones.

❼ 我最近愛上綠色。
Recently I started liking the color green.

❽ 我喜歡 天空 的顏色。
I like the color of the sky.

❾ 紫色是我的最愛。
Purple is my favorite color.

❿ 我喜歡彩虹 繽紛 的顏色。
I like the rich colors of the rainbow.

⓫ 我 偏愛深色 的衣服。
I prefer dark-colored clothing.

⓬ 橘色讓我心情開朗。
Orange makes me feel optimistic.

⓭ 我 討厭暗的 顏色。
I hate gloomy colors.

⓮ 粉紅色很 襯我的膚色 。
Pink is a good shade for my skin.

⓯ 紅色給我溫暖的感覺。
Red gives me a feeling of warmth.

089 你喜歡/討厭的顏色？

❶ 你喜歡明亮的顏色嗎？
Do you like bright colors?

❷ 你 討厭什麼 樣的顏色？
What colors do you dislike?

❸ 你 為什麼喜歡 灰色？
Why do you like the color gray?

❹ 你討厭晦暗的顏色嗎？
Do you hate gloomy colors?

❺ 你偏愛深色還是淺色？
Do you prefer dark colors or light colors?

❻ 你 最喜歡 哪一種顏色？
What colors do you like the most?

❼ 你喜歡 暖色調 還是 寒色調 ？
Do you like warm tones or cool tones?

❽ 每個人對顏色的喜惡很主觀。
Everyone's appreciation of color is subjective.

❾ 你喜歡深藍色還是淺藍色？
Do you like dark blue or light blue?

❿ 你覺得哪個顏色最適合你？
Which color do you think suits you best?

⓫ 你喜歡 買什麼顏色 的衣服？
What color clothes do you like to buy?

⓬ 每一種顏色你 都喜歡 嗎？
Do you like every color?

⓭ 你喜歡什麼顏色的花？
What color flowers do you like?

⓮ 什麼顏色的衣服你 絕對不穿 ？
What color clothing will you never put on?

⓯ 白色給你什麼感覺？
What do you associate with the color white?

090 打招呼。

❶ 嗨！您好。
Hi!

❷ 好久不見。
It's been a long time.

❸ 早安 。
Good morning.

❹ 午安 。
Good afternoon.

❺ 晚安 。
Good evening.

❻ 一切都好嗎？
How's everything?

❼ 你 今天好嗎 ？
How are you today?

❽ 最近 過得如何 ？
How have you been lately?

❾ 工作順利嗎？
Is your work going well?

❿ 之前我們是不是見過面？
Have we met before?

⓫ 最近心情愉快嗎？
Have you been in a good mood lately?

⓬ 吃過飯了嗎？
Have you eaten?

⓭ 有什麼好消息要告訴我嗎？
Do you want to tell me something good?

⓮ 今天天氣 真的很不錯。
The weather is very good today.

⓯ 你的 家人都好嗎 ？
How is your family?

090 回應打招呼。

1 您好。
Hello.

2 是啊，您好嗎？
Yes, how are you?

3 早安！
Good morning!

4 午安，要一起用餐嗎？
Good afternoon, do you want to join us for a meal?

5 晚安，您也好嗎?
Good evening, how are you?

6 我今天心情不錯。
I feel good today.

7 我很好。你呢？
I'm fine, and you?

8 我剛用過餐，你吃過了嗎？
I just had my meal. Have you eaten?

9 是啊，太陽終於露臉了。
Yes, the sun has finally come out.

10 我要結婚了。
I'm getting married.

11 一切都順利。
Everything is going well.

12 是的，我們在艾咪家的聚會上見過一次面。
Yes, we met once at a party at Amy's.

13 謝謝，你也是。
Thanks, you too.

14 託你的福，大家都很好。
Thanks to you, everybody is fine.

15 謝謝。不用替我操心。
Thanks. Don't worry about me.

091 說再見。

1 再見！
See you around!

2 掰掰。
Bye-bye.

3 我會想你 的。
I will miss you.

4 別太想我。
Don't miss me too much.

5 珍重 再見。
Goodbye and take good care of yourself.

6 祝你 一帆風順 。
I hope everything goes smoothly.

7 祝你 有美好的一天 ！
Have a nice day!

8 好好照顧自己。
Take good care of yourself.

9 五點見。
I'll see you at five.

10 晚安。
Good night.

11 路上 小心 。
Take care on the road.

12 好好過週末喔！
Have a nice weekend!

13 要再來喔！
Come again!

14 有個好夢。
Sweet dreams.

15 一夜好眠 喔！
Sleep tight!

091 回應說再見。

1 再見！
Goodbye!

2 掰掰。
Bye-bye!

3 我也會想你的。
I'll miss you, too.

4 別太想我。
Don't miss me too much.

5 我會 照顧自己 的。
I can take care of myself.

6 請 不用為我操心 。
Don't worry about me, please.

7 我會寄明信片給你。
I will send you a postcard.

8 明天見。
See you tomorrow.

9 我 會小心 。
I'll be careful.

10 晚安。
Good night.

11 我一到學校就打電話給你。
Once I arrive at school, I will call you.

12 等我 的消息。
Wait to hear news from me.

13 我又不是不回台北了。
It's not like I am not coming back to Taipei.

14 謝謝大家來送我。
Thank you, everyone, for seeing me off.

15 我只是出去一個星期，馬上就回來 了。
I'm only going away for a week; I'll be right back.

211

092 一般的問候。

1 早安！
Good morning!

2 午安！
Good afternoon!

3 最近好嗎？
How's it been these days?

4 晚安！（打招呼）
Good evening!

5 晚安！（道別）
Good night!

6 最近 身體好嗎 ？
How has your health been these days?

7 你今天 氣色不錯 ㄟ！
Don't you look great today!

8 最近都 在忙什麼 ？
What have you been busy with recently?

9 最近 工作如何 ？
How's your work been going lately?

10 有什麼事困擾著你嗎？
Is there anything that's been bothering you recently?

11 週末 去哪裡玩 啦？
Where did you go over the weekend?

12 有喜事嗎？
Anything positive happen lately?

13 吃飽了 嗎？
Are you full?

14 我有事先走，下次再聊 。
I have something to do; I'll talk to you later.

15 你 好像瘦了 ？
You've lost some weight, haven't you?

092 回應問候。

❶ 早啊。
Morning.

❷ 晚安。（回應打招呼）
Good evening!

❸ 午安。
Good afternoon.

❹ 晚安。（回應道別）
Good night!

❺ 我很好，你呢？
I am fine, and you?

❻ 託您的福，一切都好。
Thanks to you, everything is going fine.

❼ 沒什麼，都是些芝麻蒜皮的小事。
It's nothing, just a few minor things.

❽ 你也是啊。
You too.

❾ 我升官了。
I got a promotion.

❿ 我要結婚了。
I am going to get married.

⓫ 老樣子，還在原來的公司。
Everything is the same; I am still at the same company.

⓬ 我剛吃過。你呢？
I have just eaten. How about you?

⓭ 是啊，雨總算停了。
That's right, the rain has finally stopped.

⓮ 我每個週末爬山。要不要一起去？
I go mountain climbing every weekend. Would you like to join us?

093 早上進公司的寒暄。

① 怎麼一直打哈欠，昨晚熬夜啊？
Why do you keep yawning like that? Did you stay up late last night?

② 大家 早安 。
Good morning, everyone!

③ 哇，難得看你化妝！
Wow, you hardly ever put on makeup!

④ 上班 打卡了嗎 ？
Did you punch in yet?

⑤ 鞋子真漂亮，哪裡買的？
Your shoes are very beautiful. Where did you buy them?

⑥ 一大早在 忙什麼 ？
What are you so busy with this early in the morning?

⑦ 今天要開會嗎？
Do we have a meeting today?

⑧ 穿得真正式，今天要去拜訪客戶嗎？
You are dressed very formally. Are you going to visit clients today?

⑨ 要不要 來杯咖啡 ？
Would you like a cup of coffee?

⑩ 吃過早餐 了嗎？
Have you eaten breakfast yet?

⑪ 昨晚 幾點下班 ？
What time did you leave the office last night?

⑫ 這個月業績如何？
How is your business performance this month?

⑬ 你今天 遇到塞車 啦？
Did you get stuck in traffic today?

093 回應同事的寒喧。

1 早安。
Morning.

2 是啊，我昨晚 又失眠了 。
Yes, you're right; I couldn't sleep again last night.

3 我已經 打卡了 。
Yes, I've already punched my card.

4 我正在準備開會資料。
I am preparing materials for the meeting.

5 想改變一下造型。
I want to change my style.

6 是啊，每天都有開不完的會。
Yeah, we have endless meetings every day.

7 等老闆到就開會。
The meeting will begin whenever the boss arrives.

8 吃了一半，一半還在桌上。
I ate half and left the rest on the table.

9 是的，今天 約了重要客戶 。
Yes, I have an appointment with a major client today.

10 我今天 有一堆事 要處理。
I have a ton of things to deal with today.

11 好啊，謝謝。
OK, thanks.

12 我昨晚 十點才離開 公司。
I didn't leave my office until ten pm last night.

13 馬馬虎虎。
So-so.

14 很不錯。
Very good.

15 是啊，遇到大塞車 。
Yes, you're right, I was stuck in a big traffic jam.

094 認識新朋友。

❶ 可以和你 交換名片 嗎？
May we exchange business cards?

❷ 請問你叫 什麼名字 ？
Excuse me, what is your name?

❸ 我是 瑪莉，想和你認識一下。
I am Mary, and I would like to get to know you.

❹ 我該 怎麼稱呼 你？
What should I call you?

❺ 你是新的同事嗎？
Are you our new colleague?

❻ 你有英文名字嗎？
Do you have an English name?

❼ 我們會變成好朋友的。
We're going to be good friends.

❽ 很高興認識 你。
It's nice to meet you.

❾ 你來自哪裡？
Where are you from?

❿ 你住哪裡？
Where do you live?

⓫ 你結婚了嗎？
Are you married?

⓬ 你在哪裡工作？
Where do you work?

⓭ 你 來台灣多久 了？
How long have you been in Taiwan?

⓮ 我覺得 你很面熟 。
You look familiar to me.

⓯ 我們 見過面嗎 ？
Have we met before?

094 回應新朋友。

① 我是約翰。
I am John.

② 大家都叫我 妮可。
Everyone calls me Nicole.

③ 這是我的名片，請多指教 。
This is my business card; your advice is welcome.

④ 我沒有英文名字。
I don't have an English name.

⑤ 認識你是我的榮幸。
It's really a pleasure to meet you.

⑥ 很高興認識你。
It's nice to meet you.

⑦ 我對你 久仰大名 。
I have been looking forward to meeting you.

⑧ 我們一定會成為好朋友。
We are going to be good friends for sure.

⑨ 業界對 你的風評很好 。
You have a good reputation in this industry.

⑩ 我們 一見如故 。
I feel like we have known each other for a long time.

⑪ 聽說你十分幽默。
I heard that you're very humorous.

⑫ 我結婚了。
I am married.

⑬ 我還是單身。
I am still single.

⑭ 真是 相見恨晚 。
I really wish we had met earlier.

⑮ 我來自台灣。
I am from Taiwan.

095 巧遇老朋友。

❶ 你在忙什麼？
What have you been busy with?

❷ 好久不見！
It's been a long time!

❸ 我們已經 好幾年沒見 啦！
It's been many years since we last saw each other!

❹ 你 一點都沒變 ！
You haven't changed a bit!

❺ 還記得我嗎？
Do you remember me?

❻ 怎麼都不聯絡 一下？
Why didn't you contact me?

❼ 這些年都在忙什麼？
What have you been doing for the past few years?

❽ 都 聯絡不到你 耶。
I haven't been able to get in touch with you at all.

❾ 你 愈來愈年輕 了耶。
You are looking younger and younger.

❿ 還在原來的公司嗎？
Are you still working for the same firm?

⓫ 結婚了嗎？
Are you married?

⓬ 躲哪去 了呀？
Where have you been hiding?

⓭ 你搬家了是嗎？
You've moved, right?

⓮ 不認得我 了呀？
Don't you recognize me?

⓯ 沒良心的。都沒和我聯絡。
That's messed up! You didn't even contact me.

095 回應老朋友。

❶ 好久不見。
It's been a long time.

❷ 是啊，快十年了。
Yeah, it's been almost ten years.

❸ 你 也是都沒變 。
You haven't changed a bit either.

❹ 你也沒和我聯絡！
You didn't contact me either!

❺ 我也聯絡不到你！
I couldn't reach you either!

❻ 哪有， 變老啦 。
Come on, I look a lot older.

❼ 你的電話我打不通啊。
I couldn't get through to your phone.

❽ 都 快不認識你 了。
I can barely recognize you.

❾ 我換工作了。
I changed jobs.

❿ 我已經 結婚了 。
I got married.

⓫ 我現在住美國，很少回台灣。
I live in the U.S. now and seldom come back to Taiwan.

⓬ 你才 沒良心 呢！結婚也不通知一下。
No way! You're the one who's messed up, getting married and not letting me know!

⓭ 我 換電話了 ，所以你聯絡不到我。
You couldn't reach me because I changed my phone number.

⓮ 你現在忙嗎，要不要 找地方聊聊 ？
Are you busy right now? Want to find a place to talk?

096 關心與安慰。

❶ 你 還好嗎 ？
Are you all right?

❷ 需要幫忙嗎？
Do you need any help?

❸ 有心事 嗎？我們可以聊聊。
Is there anything on your mind? We can talk about it.

❹ 你有什麼事要對我說嗎？
Do you have something to say to me?

❺ 別擔心， 事情會好轉 的。
Don't worry, everything is going to be fine.

❻ 別老往壞處想 嘛！
Stop being so pessimistic!

❼ 想想愉快的事情吧！
Think about something happy!

❽ 要休息一下嗎？
Want to take a rest?

❾ 看開一點 吧！
Don't take it so hard!

❿ 別這樣， 你已經盡力 了。
Don't act like that; you did your best.

⓫ 別鑽牛角尖 了！
Stop banging your head against a wall!

⓬ 放輕鬆點！
Take it easy!

⓭ 笑一笑 吧！
Smile!

⓮ 你遇到什麼麻煩嗎？
Have you run into any trouble?

⓯ 如果需要幫忙請讓我知道。
Let me know if you need any help.

096 回應關心與安慰。

❶ 沒事 。我很好。
It's nothing, I'm fine.

❷ 別管我，讓我靜一靜 。
Just leave me alone for a while.

❸ 最近我太太生病了。
My wife has been sick recently.

❹ 我會試試看。
I'll give it a try.

❺ 如果你願意聽 ，我是想找個人聊聊。
If you're willing to listen, I'd love to have someone
to talk to.

❻ 我會想出辦法的。
I'll figure it out.

❼ 你說的 有道理 。
What you've said is reasonable.

❽ 沒辦法，我就是會擔心。
It can't be helped; I'm just a worrier.

❾ 沒關係，我 過一陣子就好 了。
It's OK, I'll be better soon enough.

❿ 我 會振作 。
I'll pull myself together.

⓫ 我的生活會好轉的。
My life will get better.

⓬ 沒辦法，事情就是這樣了。
Nothing to be done—this is it.

⓭ 你就是這麼善體人意。
You are such a thoughtful person.

⓮ 抱歉， 讓你擔心了 。
I'm sorry to make you worry.

⓯ 我知道你的好意。
I know you mean well.

097 提醒。

1 別忘了 帶雨傘。
Don't forget to bring an umbrella.

2 你又忘了 做作業。
You've forgotten to do your homework again.

3 過馬路要小心！
Be careful crossing the street!

4 小心 ！有車。
Watch out! Here comes a car.

5 別忘了你昨天說的話。
Don't forget what you said yesterday.

6 你總是 忘東忘西 。
You always forget something.

7 記得要打電話 回來。
Remember to call back.

8 不怕一萬，只怕萬一 。
Prevention is better than a cure.

9 別太晚回來。
Don't come home too late.

10 明天的約會在十點。
Tomorrow's appointment will be at ten o'clock.

11 請你多保重。
Please take good care of yourself.

12 需要我打電話提醒你嗎？
Do you need me to remind you with a phone call?

13 想想看，有沒有什麼事忘了？
Think about it, is there anything you've forgotten?

14 記得要幫我買東西。
Remember to buy the things for me.

15 昨天答應我的事，你忘了嗎 ？
You promised me yesterday—have you forgotten?

097 回應提醒。

1 謝謝你的提醒。
Thanks for the reminder.

2 我會記住的。
I'll keep that in mind.

3 放心，| 我沒忘 |。
Don't worry, I haven't forgotten.

4 別擔心，我知道。
Don't worry, I remember.

5 | 謝謝你的提醒 |，我差點忘了。
Thanks for the reminder; I almost forgot.

6 我會把事情記在筆記簿上。
I'll make a note of the matter in my notebook.

7 我已經完成了。
I'm already done.

8 | 別再嘮叨 | 啦！
Stop babbling!

9 沒關係，我會處理。
It's OK, I'll handle it.

10 我自己會想辦法。
I'll figure it out by myself.

11 我 | 早就準備好 | 了。
I've been ready for a long time.

12 我真是 | 愈來愈健忘 | 了。
I'm becoming more and more forgetful.

13 我一直記得。
I've always remembered that.

14 | 好在有你 | 提醒我。
Fortunately, you reminded me.

15 天啊！我 | 怎麼忘記了 |？
Gosh! How could I forget about that?

098 勸告。

❶ 別做壞事。

Don't do bad things.

❷ 這樣做不太好。

It's not good to do that.

❸ 你 會遭到報應 。

You will get what you deserve.

❹ 這樣做是錯的。

It's wrong to do that.

❺ 上帝不會原諒你。

God will not forgive you.

❻ 你得 做大家的好榜樣 。

You have to be a good example for everyone.

❼ 請多 多努力 。

Please work harder.

❽ 加油！

Go, go!

❾ 算了，別和他一般見識。

Forget it; don't lower yourself to the same level as him.

❿ 事情 過了就算了 。

It is past, so let it go.

⓫ 別再吵了。

Knock it off.

⓬ 再怎樣做也是於事無補。

It's no use doing anything else.

⓭ 放棄 吧！

Forget it!

⓮ 你一定要 堅持到底 。

You have to stick it out.

⓯ 你應該換個工作。

You should change jobs.

098 回應勸告。

1 謝謝你的勸告。
Thanks for your advice.

2 我會 三思而後行 。
I'll think twice before I act.

3 你說的也有道理。
What you've said is reasonable.

4 我會 照著你的話 去做。
I'll do what you said.

5 我也打算這麼做。
That's just what I intend to do.

6 我 會小心 的。
I'll be careful.

7 我不會這麼做的。
I won't do that.

8 你 把你自己管好 吧。
Mind your own business.

9 只要我喜歡 有什麼不可以 。
If I like it, then why not?

10 我自己會負責。
I'll take responsibility for myself.

11 別管我！
Leave me alone!

12 我不怕，我 就是要這樣 。
I'm not afraid; this is what I want.

13 別用大人的口氣 對我說話。
Don't speak to me as if I were a child.

14 不關你的事。
It's none of your business.

15 我不可能受你影響。
You can't possibly influence me.

099 讚美。

❶ 你穿這件衣服 比我好看 。
This clothing looks better on you than on me.

❷ 你 真帥 。
You are so handsome.

❸ 你真的很聰明。
You are really smart.

❹ 你可以 去當電影明星 了。
You could be a movie star with your looks.

❺ 妳看起來只有 25 歲。
You look like you're only 25 years old.

❻ 我真希望能和妳一樣美。
I really hope that I can be as beautiful as you are.

❼ 美女喔！
What a pretty girl!

❽ 看不出來 妳已經是三個孩子的媽！
You really don't look like a mother with three children!

❾ 帥哥喔！
What a handsome boy!

❿ 我 真羨慕你 的才華。
I really envy your talent.

⓫ 你是班上最聰明的學生。
You're the smartest student in this class.

⓬ 你太棒了！
You are wonderful!

⓭ 做得好！
Good job!

⓮ 妳看起來像她姊姊，不像媽媽。
You look like her sister, not her mother.

⓯ 你讓我們 相形失色 。
We pale in comparison to you.

099 回應讚美。

❶ 謝謝你的讚美。
Thanks for your praise.

❷ 你真 有眼光 。
You really have good judgment.

❸ 大家都這樣說。
Everybody says that.

❹ 沒有啦，你 過獎 了。
It's nothing; you're making too much of it.

❺ 你這樣說，我會不好意思的。
I am embarrassed by what you said.

❻ 再 多說幾句好聽的 吧。
Say some more things that I like to hear.

❼ 別再灌我迷湯了。
Don't flatter me again.

❽ 你是 真心話嗎 ？
Do you mean what you said?

❾ 你說真的嗎？還是逗我開心？
Do you mean it, or are you just joking around?

❿ 聽你這麼說 我心花怒放 。
What you said makes me extremely happy.

⓫ 你才是我學習的對象。
You're really a role model I can learn from.

⓬ 我才羨慕你 呢！
No, I envy you!

⓭ 你比我還棒呢！
You're better than I am!

⓮ 別逗我開心 了。
Don't make fun of me.

⓯ 謝謝你的肯定。
Thanks for your recognition.

100 鼓勵。

❶ 加油！
Go, go!

❷ 一定要 堅持下去 。
You've got to stick it out.

❸ 你 會成功 的。
You'll succeed.

❹ 下一次會更好。
Next time will be better.

❺ 別洩氣。
Don't feel disappointed.

❻ 再試一次。
Try it one more time.

❼ 我們 對你有信心 。
We have confidence in you.

❽ 我們 一起努力 。
We can work hard together.

❾ 失敗為成功之母。
Failure is the mother of success.

❿ 比上不足 比下有餘 啦！
Worse off than some, better off than many!

⓫ 沒關係， 還有機會 。
It's OK, there's still another chance.

⓬ 盡力就好。
Your best is good enough.

⓭ 你已經做得很好了。
You've already done your best.

⓮ 你很 有潛力 。
You have a lot of potential.

⓯ 只差一點就成功了。
You almost succeeded.

100 回應鼓勵。

❶ 我會 全力以赴 的。
I'll do my best.

❷ 我 不會放棄 的。
I will not give up

❸ 我不會讓你失望的。
I will not disappoint you.

❹ 我會堅持下去。
I'll stick it out to the end.

❺ 謝謝你始終這麼支持我。
Thanks for your support from beginning to end.

❻ 謝謝你的鼓勵。
Thanks for your encouragement.

❼ 我會 再試試 的。
I'll give it another try.

❽ 為了你，我要好好表現。
For you, I'll do my best.

❾ 我會 繼續努力 。
I'll keep on striving.

❿ 你說的很對。
What you said is right.

⓫ 我會 試著振作 起來的！
I'll try to pull myself together again!

⓬ 我會試著 往好的一面 想。
I'll try to look on the bright side.

⓭ 聽到你這麼說，我又 有信心了 。
Hearing what you said has given me confidence again.

⓮ 我一定會成功的。
I will succeed.

⓯ 我確實已經盡了全力。
I've really done my best.

101 祝賀。

❶ 新年 快樂！
Happy New Year!

❷ 情人節快樂！
Happy Valentine's Day!

❸ 生日 快樂！
Happy birthday!

❹ 一路順風。
Bon voyage.

❺ 母親節快樂！
Happy Mother's Day!

❻ 聖誕節快樂！
Merry Christmas!

❼ 天作之合。
A match made in heaven.

❽ 祝福你 事業成功 。
Best wishes for your business.

❾ 父親節快樂！
Happy Father's Day!

❿ 恭喜你 高昇。
Congratulations on your promotion.

⓫ 為你的健康 舉杯！
To your health!

⓬ 祝你 青春永駐 。
I wish you eternal youth.

⓭ 恭喜啊， 喜獲麟兒 。
Congratulations on your new son.

⓮ 祝你幸福。
I wish you happiness.

⓯ 喬遷 之喜。
Best wishes for your new home.

101 回應祝賀。

❶ 謝謝。
Thank you.

❷ 你 真貼心 。
You're really kind.

❸ 希望大家都跟你一樣。
I wish everyone were like you.

❹ 你 真是有心 。
You're so thoughtful.

❺ 也 同樣祝福你 。
Same to you.

❻ 謝謝你的禮物。
Thanks for your gift.

❼ 人來就好 了，別太客氣。
Don't be so polite, just come.

❽ 有空常來 坐坐。
Come visit whenever you have time.

❾ 我今天真的 很開心 。
I'm really happy today.

❿ 下回就輪到你啦。
Next time it will be your turn.

⓫ 什麼時候換我祝福你呀？
When will it be my turn to offer you my blessings?

⓬ 你的禮物對我來說實在是太珍貴了。
Your present is really too valuable to me.

⓭ 感謝你 特別前來祝賀我。
Thank you for your congratulating me in person.

⓮ 真不知道怎麼感謝你。
I really don't know how I can thank you.

⓯ 我感銘在心！
I really appreciate it!

102 歡迎客人。

❶ 嗨，請進 。
   Hi, please come in.

❷ 歡迎 歡迎。
   Welcome.

❸ 希望你會喜歡這個派對。
   I hope that you will enjoy my party.

❹ 歡迎來我家玩。
   Welcome to my home.

❺ 地址 好找嗎 ？
   Any problems finding the address?

❻ 路上有塞車嗎？
   Any traffic on the way here?

❼ 你 來得真早 。
   You came early.

❽ 很高興你能來。
   I'm glad that you could come.

❾ 其他的人應該也快到了。
   The others should be here in a moment.

❿ 這下子 全員到齊 囉！
   Now we have a full house!

⓫ 大家 都在等你 呢！
   Everyone is waiting for you!

⓬ 謝謝你的禮物，你太客氣了！
   Thank you for the present, you're too kind!

⓭ 你先生 沒跟你一起 來嗎？
   Didn't your husband come with you?

⓮ 你們能來真是我的榮幸。
   It's my honor to have you here.

⓯ 旁邊這位 是你太太嗎 ？
   Is the person next to you your wife?

102 回應主人的歡迎。

❶ 打擾了！
Sorry to bother you!

❷ 抱歉，我遲到了！
Sorry I'm late.

❸ 謝謝您的邀請。
Thank you for your invitation.

❹ 我 很高興能參加 今天的盛會。
I'm so happy to participate in today's party.

❺ 這是一點 小禮物 。
This is a small present.

❻ 你們這邊 不太好找 呢！
It's very hard to find your place!

❼ 我該不會是最後一個到的吧？
Am I the last one to arrive?

❽ 這是我太太 琳達。
This is my wife Linda.

❾ 約翰來了嗎？
Has John arrived yet?

❿ 我帶太太一起來。
I brought my wife with me.

⓫ 我等一下 有事得先走 。
I have to go early; there's something I need to do.

⓬ 出門前我把小孩托給我的父母。
I dropped the kids off with my parents before I came here.

⓭ 我為了這個派對 特別打扮 一番。
I spent a lot of time dressing up for this party.

⓮ 我今晚是 排除萬難 才趕過來的。
I rearranged my whole schedule so I could make it here.

⓯ 我先生 有事不能來 。
My husband can't come due to a prior commitment.

103 招待客人。

1 怎麼不 找個地方坐 下來？
Why don't you find a place to sit down?

2 請坐。
Please sit down.

3 來這裡坐， 別光站著 。
Come sit here; don't just stand there like that.

4 請 不要拘束 。
Don't stand on ceremony.

5 有任何需要儘管跟我說。
Let me know if you need anything.

6 當自己家 一樣，輕鬆點。
Relax, make yourself at home.

7 你怎麼不過去跟大家聊天？
Why don't you go and socialize with everybody?

8 你喜歡這種氣氛嗎？
Do you like this kind of atmosphere?

9 只是個簡單的聚會， 別緊張 。
It's just a simple get-together, don't be nervous.

10 我 介紹你給大家 認識。
Let me introduce you to everyone.

11 這裡有你認識的人嗎？
Is there anyone you know here?

12 要不要先喝點什麼？
Would you like to have something to drink?

13 要不要聽點音樂？
Would you like to listen to some music?

14 我們 都是自己人； 別跟我客氣。
We're friends; no need to be polite with me.

15 會不會冷？
Are you cold?

103 回應主人的招待。

1 我很好,別擔心我!
I'm fine, don't worry about me!

2 我覺得 很自在 。
I feel comfortable.

3 這個派對真是好!
What a great party this is!

4 我才 不會跟你客氣 呢!
I won't stand on ceremony with you!

5 我需要什麼一定跟你說。
I'll let you know if I need anything.

6 我 第一次參加 這種派對。
It's my first time attending a party like this.

7 我站著就可以了。
Standing is OK for me.

8 你忙你的 ,我四處看看。
Go ahead; I'll look around by myself.

9 這裡 人真的好多 喔!
It's really crowded here!

10 我認識的人好像都還沒來。
It seems like none of the people I know has arrived yet.

11 我覺得有點熱。
I feel a bit hot.

12 人多的地方會令我緊張。
Crowded places make me nervous.

13 我要借 用一下洗手間 。
I need to use the restroom.

14 我等一下自己找地方坐。
I'll find myself a seat later.

15 我想去陽台 透透氣 。
I'm going out to the balcony to get some fresh air.

104 招呼用餐。

❶ 盡量吃，我準備很多菜。
Help yourself; I've prepared lots of dishes.

❷ 多吃一點，不要客氣。
Eat more; don't be so polite.

❸ 有沒有吃飽？
Are you full?

❹ 你 想吃什麼 我幫你拿。
I will get you anything you want.

❺ 你 怎麼都沒吃 ？
Why aren't you eating anything?

❻ 食物 合你的胃口嗎 ？
Does the food suit you all right?

❼ 你有沒有還沒嘗試的東西？
Is there any food you haven't tried yet?

❽ 嚐嚐 我的拿手菜 吧。
Have a taste of my special dish.

❾ 過來 吃點水果 吧！
Come over and have some fruit!

❿ 我可以抄食譜給你。
I can make a copy of the recipe for you.

⓫ 要不要吃些點心？
Would you like some dessert?

⓬ 你們有人 要喝酒嗎 ？
Would anyone like a drink?

⓭ 甜點會不會太甜？
Is the dessert too sweet for you?

⓮ 你們夫妻倆 要不要坐在一起 ？
Do you two want to sit together?

⓯ 大家都有座位了嗎？
Has everyone found a seat?

236

104 回應招呼用餐。

❶ 你也過來一起吃啊。
Come here and eat with us.

❷ 你 別忙了 。
Don't rush.

❸ 你自己也都沒吃東西。
You didn't eat anything either.

❹ 你花 多少時間準備 這些吃的東西啊？
How much time did you spend preparing this food?

❺ 這個 要怎麼吃 呢？
How should I eat this?

❻ 每一道菜看起來都 好好吃 。
Every dish looks delicious.

❼ 我應該跟你拜師學藝。
I should have you teach me how to cook.

❽ 嗯， 我不敢吃 這個。
Ew, I don't want to eat that.

❾ 你可以給我這道菜的食譜嗎？
Can you give me the recipe for this dish?

❿ 甜點是 你自己做的 嗎？
Did you make this dessert?

⓫ 我 吃得好撐 。
I'm stuffed.

⓬ 我想再來杯果汁。
I would like one more glass of juice.

⓭ 我自己來，你 別忙著招呼 我。
I'll help myself; you don't need to wait on me.

⓮ 我好像喝太多了。
I seem to have drunk too much.

⓯ 請把胡椒粉遞給我。
Please pass the pepper.

105 主人送客。

❶ 歡迎隨時來玩。
You're always welcome to come over.

❷ 以後 常來玩 喔！
Come here often!

❸ 下次一定還要賞臉。
Please come again next time.

❹ 謝謝你們肯賞光。
Thank you for coming.

❺ 今天能看到你真的太開心了。
I'm really happy to have seen you today.

❻ 真 捨不得 讓你們走。
It's really hard for me to let you go.

❼ 感謝您 遠道而來 。
Thank you for coming from such a long ways away.

❽ 需要幫你們叫車嗎？
Do you need me to call a taxi for you?

❾ 你們等一下 怎麼回去 ？
How will you get back home?

❿ 你今天有開車嗎？
Did you drive today?

⓫ 我 陪你們走 出去。
Let me walk you out.

⓬ 回去 路上小心 喔！
Be safe on your way home!

⓭ 你要不要 搭他的便車 ？
Would you like to get a ride with him?

⓮ 有沒有東西忘了拿？
Have you forgotten anything?

⓯ 你有 喝酒不要開車 。
You've had a few drinks; don't drive.

105 回應主人送客。

1 我們差不多 該告辭了 。
It's about time for us to leave.

2 你一定累了，早點休息 吧！
You must be tired right now; don't stay up too late!

3 有時候像這樣聚聚也不錯。
It's really nice to get together like this sometimes.

4 下次 還要約我 唷！
Be sure to invite me again next time!

5 你 不用出來送 我們了。
You don't need to come out with us.

6 我真希望可以待久一點。
I really wish that I could stay longer.

7 我們 先走了 。
We're going to take off.

8 外面風大，你趕快進去吧！
It's windy outside; hurry back in the house!

9 打擾你 到這麼晚，真不好意思！
I'm really sorry for bothering you so late!

10 對不起，還要讓你自己善後。
I'm sorry that you'll have to deal with the mess we made.

11 我自己到外面叫車。
I will go outside to call a cab by myself.

12 我搭他的便車回去。
I'll get a ride home with him.

13 我 有開車 來。
I drove my car here.

14 我可以搭公車回去。
I can go back by bus.

15 啊！我的外套沒拿！
Ah! I forgot my coat!

106 主人接受致謝。

❶ 哪裡，招待不周。
I haven't been a good host.

❷ 我今天都沒有好好招呼你。
I didn't take such good care of you today.

❸ 不會啦！一點都不累。
Not at all! I don't feel the least bit tired.

❹ 玩得開心就好。
I'm glad that you had fun.

❺ 很高興你有賓至如歸的感覺。
I'm so glad that you felt at home.

❻ 一直道謝就太客氣了。
You are very welcome for your many thanks.

❼ 過獎了，我也沒做什麼。
I'm flattered; it was nothing.

❽ 哪裡，只是些家常菜。
You're welcome; they were just homemade dishes.

❾ 是你不嫌棄啦！
Well, you must not be too picky!

❿ 好好招待你是應該的。
Taking good care of you is the least I can do.

⓫ 我很高興你喜歡今天的派對。
I'm glad that you liked the party.

⓬ 這是我的榮幸。
It's my pleasure.

⓭ 謝謝你的稱讚。
Thank you for your praise.

⓮ 我手藝不好，讓你們見笑了。
I've embarrassed myself with my bad cooking.

⓯ 下次人來就好，別再帶東西了。
Just come here without anything next time.

106 客人致謝。

❶ 今晚謝啦！
Thanks for tonight!

❷ 謝謝你 熱情的款待 。
Thank you for your enthusiastic hospitality.

❸ 謝謝你邀請我來。
Thank you for your invitation.

❹ 謝謝你讓我有個 愉快的夜晚 。
Thank you for giving me such a pleasant night.

❺ 你真是個 稱職的主人 。
You're a wonderful host.

❻ 謝謝你費心準備的一切。
Thank you for everything that you've prepared.

❼ 謝謝你介紹朋友給我認識。
Thank you for introducing me to new friends.

❽ 你親切的招待讓我 賓至如歸 。
Your kind hospitality really made me feel at home.

❾ 託你的福，我今天很開心。
Thanks to you, I feel very happy today.

❿ 我玩得 非常盡興 。
I had a lot of fun today.

⓫ 派對很成功唷！
What a successful party it was!

⓬ 今天真是 辛苦你 了。
You have really done too much for today.

⓭ 今晚真的是太棒了！
What an amazing night it's been!

⓮ 謝謝你的晚餐。
Thank you for your dinner.

⓯ 下次讓我招待 你吧！
Allow me to reciprocate next time!

107 劃位。

❶ 我要 劃位 。
I would like to book my seat.

❷ 這是我的 護照 和 機票 。
Here are my passport and plane ticket.

❸ 我要靠走道的座位。
I would like to have an aisle seat.

❹ 我有一件 託運行李 。
I have one piece of baggage to check in.

❺ 我 不要中間的 座位。
I don't want a middle seat.

❻ 我要靠窗的座位。
I would like to have a window seat.

❼ 我要靠近逃生門的座位。
I would like to have a seat near an emergency exit.

❽ 請給我前面的座位。
Please give me a seat near the front.

❾ 我需要一份 素食餐 。
I need a vegetarian meal.

❿ 可以給我第一排的座位嗎？
May I have a seat in the first row?

⓫ 我的行李 超重了嗎 ？
Does my luggage exceed the weight limit?

⓬ 這是我的會員卡，請幫我 累積旅程點數 。
This is my membership card; please add my travel mileage to it.

⓭ 這件行李我可以 隨身攜帶 嗎？
Can this bag be a carry-on?

⓮ 何時登機？
When is the boarding time?

107 機場櫃臺人員怎麼說？

❶ 有需要服務的地方嗎？

May I help you?

❷ 請告訴我您預訂的 班機時間 。

Please tell me the time of your flight.

❸ 要 靠窗 還是 靠走道 的位置？

Would you like a window or an aisle seat?

❹ 我需要您的護照和機票。

I need your passport and plane ticket.

❺ 有特別的需要嗎？

Do you have any special needs?

❻ 我需要您的身分證明。

I need your identification.

❼ 對不起，您的 行李超重 了。

I'm sorry, your baggage is overweight.

❽ 要為您訂素食嗎？

Do we need to order vegetarian meals for you?

❾ 要託運行李嗎？

Any baggage to check in?

❿ 這班飛機已經 客滿了 。

This flight is full.

⓫ 請打開行李接受檢查。

Please open your luggage for inspection.

⓬ 十點的飛機， 七號登機門 。

Boarding gate number seven, departing at ten o'clock.

⓭ 您要 候補機位 嗎？

Would you like to be put on standby?

⓮ 祝您旅途愉快。

Have a nice flight.

⓯ 機票已經內 含機場稅 。

The price of the ticket includes airport tax.

108 飛機上。

1 請幫我 放一下行李 。
Please help me stow this suitcase.

2 我需要 一條毛毯。
I need a blanket.

3 請問耳機如何使用？
Excuse me, can you tell me how to use the headphones?

4 可以給我一瓶礦泉水嗎？
May I please have a bottle of mineral water?

5 可以 給我一杯 熱咖啡嗎？
May I have a hot coffee?

6 可以給我一杯熱水嗎？
May I please have a cup of hot water?

7 我身體 不太舒服 。
I'm not feeling well.

8 可以給我白酒嗎？
May I please have a glass of white wine?

9 可以給我入境卡嗎？
May I have an incoming passenger form?

10 可以教我填 寫入境卡 嗎？
Can you please show me how to fill out the incoming passenger form?

11 飛機 什麼時候降落 ？
What time does the plane land?

12 可以給我中文雜誌嗎？
May I please have a Chinese magazine?

13 什麼時候開始賣 免稅商品 ？
When will you start selling the duty-free goods?

14 我訂了一份兒童餐。
I ordered a children's meal.

108 空服人員怎麼說？

❶ 歡迎各位搭乘。
Welcome aboard.

❷ 您的座位 請直走 。
Please walk straight ahead to find your seat.

❸ 有什麼需要 幫忙的嗎？
Do you need any help?

❹ 需要報紙嗎？
Do you need a newspaper?

❺ 需要熱 茶或咖啡 嗎？
Would you like some hot tea or coffee?

❻ 您需要什麼飲料？
What would you like to drink?

❼ 請 把手機關掉 。
Please turn off your cell phone.

❽ 請問您要 牛肉 還是 豬肉 ？
Would you like beef or pork?

❾ 這是您的素食餐盒。
This is your vegetarian meal.

❿ 請 繫好安全帶 。
Please fasten your seatbelt.

⓫ 請把茶杯放在托盤上，我為您倒茶。
Please put your cup on the tray; I will pour some tea for you.

⓬ 請把用過的耳機丟進塑膠袋。
Please put your used headphones into the plastic bag.

⓭ 需要毛毯嗎？
Do you need a blanket?

⓮ 飛機 要降落了 ，請把椅背豎起來。
The plane is going to land; please put your seat back in the upright position.

109 入境海關。

❶ 請問外國人 該排在哪裡 ？
Excuse me, where is the line for foreigners?

❷ 這是本國人士排隊區。
This is the line for citizens only.

❸ 請問需要檢查 哪些證件 ？
Excuse me, what papers need to be checked?

❹ 對不起，我不懂你的意思。
Excuse me, I don't understand what you mean.

❺ 我 排錯隊伍 了嗎？
Am I in the wrong line?

❻ 這些東西需 要報稅嗎 ？
Do these things need to be declared?

❼ 我不知道這些東西要報稅。
I didn't know these things needed to be declared.

❽ 這都是我的 隨身物品 。
These are my personal belongings.

❾ 請問在 哪裡取行李 ？
Excuse me, where can I pick up my baggage?

❿ 有什麼問題嗎？
Is there a problem?

⓫ 有會 說中文的人 嗎？
Is there anyone who speaks Chinese?

⓬ 在幾號行李轉台？
Which luggage carousel is it at?

⓭ 我要 到免稅商店 買香煙和化妝品。
I'm going to buy cigarettes and cosmetics in the
duty-free shops.

⓮ 行李出來了嗎？
Has the baggage come out yet?

109 海關人員怎麼說？

❶ 請 出示護照 。
Please show your passport.

❷ 請出示 台胞證 。
Please show your Mainland Travel Permit for
Taiwan residents.

❸ 要報稅的東西請拿到這邊。
Please bring the items you would like to declare
over here.

❹ 入境單 填了嗎？
Have you filled out the entry form yet?

❺ 你不能攜帶國外的水果入境。
You are not allowed to bring foreign fruit into the
country.

❻ 你會 停留多久 ？
How long will you stay?

❼ 請經 過檢疫區 ，測量體溫。
Please walk through the quarantine area to have
your body temperature measured.

❽ 請在黃線之後等候。
Please wait behind the yellow line.

❾ 請問你來我們國家的 目的 ？
What's the purpose of your visit to our country?

❿ 古柯鹼是 違禁品 。
Cocaine is a prohibited item.

⓫ 護照上的照片是你嗎？
Is the picture in your passport of you?

⓬ 這是你帶的東西嗎？
Did you bring these things with you?

⓭ 請到一旁 接受檢查 。
Please step to the side for inspection.

⓮ 歡迎來到我們國家。
Welcome to our country.

110 行李掛失。

❶ 都半小時了，怎麼還沒有看到我的行李？
It's been half an hour already—how come I haven't seen my baggage yet?

❷ 我的 行李不見 了。
I can't find my luggage.

❸ 我 少了一件 行李。
I'm missing a piece of luggage.

❹ 我的行李箱裡面有我 全部的家當 。
All my personal belongings are in my suitcase.

❺ 遺失行李該 找誰幫忙 ？
Whom should I speak to about lost baggage?

❻ 怎麼樣？發現我的行李了嗎？
Well? Have you found my luggage?

❼ 我還沒拿到行李。
I haven't picked up my baggage yet.

❽ 請你盡快 幫我找 到行李。
Please help me find my luggage as soon as possible.

❾ 我的錢都放在行李箱。
All my money is in the suitcase.

❿ 這個行李箱和我的一樣，但 不是我的 。
This suitcase looks the same, but it's not mine.

⓫ 我留下飯店及房號給你。
I will leave the hotel name and room number with you.

⓬ 我的行李是藍色的。
My bags are blue.

⓭ 這是 你的行李嗎 ？
Is this your luggage?

⓮ 行李外有寫我的 姓名及電話 。
My name and phone number are on my luggage.

110 服務人員怎麼說？

❶ 行李還沒有全部送出來，請您再等等看。
Please wait a moment; not all the luggage has come out yet.

❷ 您的行李箱上 有做記號嗎 ？
Was your baggage marked?

❸ 如果您的行李真的遺失，我們會負起賠償的責任。
If your baggage really is lost, we'll take responsibility for compensation.

❹ 請問您的行李是什麼顏色的？
Excuse me, what color is your baggage?

❺ 請問您 少了幾件 行李？
How many pieces of baggage have you lost?

❻ 可以給我看一下您的 行李條 嗎？
May I see your baggage claim ticket?

❼ 也許是 別人拿錯 了您的行李。
It's possible that someone took your bags by mistake.

❽ 請 留下您的資料 ，找到行李後我們馬上與您聯絡。
Please leave your contact information; we will contact you as soon as we find your luggage.

❾ 您有在行李外寫下姓名及聯絡電話嗎？
Were your name and phone number written on the luggage?

❿ 我幫您查 一下電腦紀錄。
Let me check the computer records for you.

⓫ 不好意思，我們 可能弄丟了 您的行李。
I'm terribly sorry; we may have lost your luggage.

⓬ 對不起，我們把您的行李送到別的地方去了。
I'm sorry, we delivered your baggage to the wrong place.

⓭ 我們 找到 您的行李了。
We've found your luggage.

111 飯店訂房。

1 我要預訂一間 單人房 。
I would like to make a reservation for a single room.

2 這是一個人的價格還是一個房間的價格？
Is the price per person or per room?

3 有打折嗎？
Is there any discount?

4 請問 房價多少 ？
Excuse me, how much is it for a room?

5 請問要如何支付訂金？
Excuse me, how should I pay the deposit?

6 你們有車來機場接我們嗎？
Will you pick us up from the airport?

7 房間有 衛浴設備 嗎？
Does your room have a bathroom?

8 要 先付訂金 嗎？
Do I need to pay a deposit first?

9 這裡是 商務旅館 還是 民宿 ？
Is it a commercial hotel or a bed and breakfast?

10 房間有空調嗎？
Do your rooms have air conditioning?

11 房間有 盥洗用品 嗎？
Are your rooms provided with toiletries?

12 可以使用 信用卡付款 嗎？
Do you take credit cards?

13 可以接受美金付款嗎？
Do you accept American currency?

14 有供應早餐嗎？
Do you offer breakfast?

15 你們的旅館 離車站近嗎 ？
Is your hotel near the train station?

111 飯店櫃臺人員怎麼說？

❶ 歡迎光臨。
Welcome!

❷ 您 有預約嗎 ？
Do you have a reservation?

❸ 只有套房有衛浴設備。
Only the suites have bathroom facilities.

❹ 我們 沒有空房 了。
We have no vacancy right now.

❺ 我們只剩下四人房。
We only have four-person rooms available.

❻ 下午可能有客人退房，您 要等等看嗎 ？
Some our guests might check out this afternoon—
would you like to wait?

❼ 我們 只接受現金 付款。
We only accept payment in cash.

❽ 我們有 供應早餐 。
We offer breakfast.

❾ 樓下健身房可以免費使用。
The gym downstairs is available for free.

❿ 您是已經訂房的黃小姐嗎？
Are you the Miss Huang who made a reservation?

⓫ 請先付 今天的住宿費。
Please pay your bill for today first.

⓬ 我們這裡有腳踏車租借的服務。
We have a bicycle rental service.

⓭ 歡迎您下次再來。
Hope you'll come again.

⓮ 我們的旅館 靠近捷運站 。
Our hotel is near the MRT Station.

112 辦理入住。

1 我想要風景好的房間。
I want a room with a nice view.

2 我要 辦理住宿 。
I want to check in.

3 這是我的證件。
This is my ID.

4 請給我 兩張單人床 。
Please give me a room with two single beds.

5 請給我 一張大床 。
Please give me a room with a king-sized bed.

6 請給我高樓層的房間。
Please give a room on the upper floors.

7 住幾天以上住宿有折扣？
How long do I need to stay to get a discount?

8 只剩下 這間房間了嗎？
Is this room the only one left?

9 住一晚 多少錢 ？
How much per night?

10 早餐幾點開始？
When is breakfast available?

11 如果不滿意我 可以換房間嗎 ？
Can I change rooms if I'm not satisfied?

12 在幾樓吃早餐？
On what floor is breakfast served?

13 我想 多住一晚 。
I want to stay one more night.

14 請幫我把行李送到房間。
Please send my luggage to my room.

15 我想要先 看一下房間 。
I would like to take a look at the room first.

112 飯店櫃臺人員怎麼說？

❶ 歡迎光臨。
Welcome.

❷ 您 有行李嗎 ？
Do you have any luggage with you?

❸ 我查一下電腦紀錄。
Let me check our computer records.

❹ 一間雙人套房，是嗎？
One double suite, right?

❺ 請給我 您的證件 。
May I please see a form of ID?

❻ 我沒有看到您的資料。
I don't see any of your information here.

❼ 您的 訂房日期 是七號到十號，共三個晚上。
Your reservation is from the seventh to the tenth, three nights in total.

❽ 這是您的 房卡 。
This is the keycard for your room.

❾ 請填上您的個人資料。
Please fill in your personal information.

❿ 這是您的 早餐券 。
This is your breakfast coupon.

⓫ 在地下一樓用早餐。
Breakfast is served on B1.

⓬ 三樓的房間可以嗎？
Is a room on the third floor OK for you?

⓭ 退房的時間 在中午十二點前。
Check-out time is at noon.

⓮ 對房間有什麼 特別的要求 嗎？
Do you have any special requests for your room?

113 住宿問題。

❶ 我想 換個房間 。
  I would like to change rooms.

❷ 我的房卡有問題，門打不開 。
  There is a problem with my keycard—it won't
  open the door.

❸ 少一組肥皂和毛巾。
  The room is short one set of soap and towels.

❹ 打開水龍頭都 沒有熱水 。
  There is no hot water when I turn on the faucet.

❺ 有免費洗衣的服務嗎？
  Is there free laundry service?

❻ 冰箱裡的礦泉水是免費的嗎？
  Is the mineral water in the fridge free?

❼ 房間的空調 好像壞了 。
  The air-conditioner in my room seems to be broken.

❽ 冰箱裡的飲料 需要付費嗎 ？
  Do I need to pay for the beverages in the fridge?

❾ 可以幫我送兩雙拖鞋來嗎？
  Could you please bring up two pairs of slippers?

❿ 怎麼打內線電話？
  How do I make a room-to-room call?

⓫ 請幫我送 一些冰塊，謝謝。
  Could you please send me some ice cubes?

⓬ 怎麼打國際電話？
  How do I make an international call?

⓭ 明天早上七點半請打電話 叫我起床 。
  Please give me a wake-up call at seven-thirty
  tomorrow morning.

⓮ 飯店 可以上網嗎 ？
  Is there Internet access at this hotel?

113 飯店服務人員怎麼說？

1 不好意思，全部 房間都客滿 了。
I'm very sorry, but all our rooms are full.

2 我們馬上為您安排其他房間。
We will set up another room for you right away.

3 我們 立即派人 幫您處理。
We will send someone on our staff to take care of that for you immediately.

4 我們立刻送過去給您。
We will send it to you right away.

5 我 幫您檢查 看看是不是出了問題。
Let me check to see if there's a problem.

6 冰箱的飲料需要付費。
Beverages in the fridge need to be paid for.

7 洗衣需要 另外計費 。
There's a separate charge for laundry.

8 房客可以免費使用健身中心。
Our guests can use the gym for free.

9 市內電話不用收費。
Local calls are free.

10 礦泉水是 免費的 。
The mineral water is free.

11 我們飯店 提供無線上網 。
We offer wireless Internet access.

12 房間對房間可以直撥房間號碼。
For room-to-room calls, just dial the room number.

13 好的，我們會準時打電話叫您起床。
All right, we'll give you a prompt wake-up call.

14 游泳池 開放到晚上 十點。
The pool is open until ten pm.

114 我要買…。

❶ 我要 不易破 的材質。
I want the tougher material.

❷ 我要 34 吋，C 罩杯。
I need a size 34C bra.

❸ 我要找棉麻材質的衣服。
I'm looking for cotton-linen clothes.

❹ 我要 吸汗 的材質。
I want the moisture-wicking material.

❺ 我領圍 14 吋 。
My neck size is 14 inches.

❻ 我需要滋潤型的乳液。
I need a moisturizing cream.

❼ 我要 成分天然 的產品。
I need a product with natural ingredients.

❽ 我要 不含油脂 的化妝品。
I need oil-free cosmetics.

❾ 防曬係數 必須在 15 以上。
The SPF has to be above 15.

❿ 我要透明感好一點的粉底。
I need a facial powder with better transparency.

⓫ 我喜歡 尖頭的 鞋子。
I like sharp-tipped shoes.

⓬ 我需要液態的保養品，不要膏狀的。
I need liquid-based care products, not lotion-based.

⓭ 我喜歡 味道清爽 一點的香水。
I like the fresher-smelling perfume.

⓮ 我喜歡三吋以上的高跟鞋。
I like high heels to be more than three inches.

⓯ 我要接近膚色的絲襪。
I need a pair of nude-colored silk stockings.

114 服務人員怎麼說？

1 要我幫您量一下尺寸嗎？

Would you like me to take your measurements?

2 可以告訴我 您的尺寸 嗎？

Can you tell me your measurements?

3 您喜歡一般的款式還是流行的？

Would you like the general style or the new fashion style?

4 要我 幫您介紹 嗎？

Would you like me to tell you more about it?

5 您要 什麼顏色 的口紅？

What kind of lipstick color would you like?

6 您要試試 最新的款式 嗎？

Would you like to try the newest fashion?

7 您是乾性肌膚還是油性肌膚？

Do you have dry skin or oily skin?

8 您喜歡 什麼材質 的衣服？

What kind of clothing material would you like?

9 您需要什麼樣的乳液？

What kind of cream would you like?

10 您喜歡清淡的香水還是味道濃郁的？

Would you like perfume with a light, fresh scent or a heavier scent?

11 您喜歡 皮製的 嗎？

Do you like leather?

12 這個顏色如何？

How do you like this color?

13 您要找 什麼款式 的鞋子？

What kind of shoe style are you looking for?

14 您需要 平底鞋 還是 高跟鞋 ？

Would you like flat-heeled or high-heeled shoes?

115 試穿。

① 可以 試穿 嗎？
Can I try on the clothes?

② 我覺得 還不錯 。
I think it's not bad.

③ 剪裁不夠大方。
The cut doesn't look graceful enough.

④ 這個顏色 不適合我 的膚色。
The color doesn't fit my skin tone.

⑤ 拉鍊不好拉。
The zipper doesn't zip well.

⑥ 這款設計十分優雅。
The design is very graceful.

⑦ 我覺得穿起來 怪怪的 。
I feel weird wearing it.

⑧ 質料蠻好 的。
The material is pretty nice.

⑨ 是這樣穿沒錯嗎？
Is this the right way to wear it?

⑩ 質料不透氣。
The material is airproof.

⑪ 腰圍太鬆了。
It's too loose in the waist

⑫ 太暴露 了。
It's too revealing.

⑬ 穿起來 很舒服 。
It feels comfortable.

⑭ 太緊了。
It's too tight.

⑮ 好土 喔！
It doesn't look cool at all!

115 服務人員怎麼說？

① 要不要試穿 看看？
Would you like to try it on?

② 不好意思，特價品 不能試穿 。
Sorry, the products on sale cannot be tried on.

③ 您比較適合這個顏色。
This color fits you better.

④ 這個顏色 很好搭 配。
This color goes with everything.

⑤ 這個款式 不會退流行 。
This style will never go out of fashion.

⑥ 質料很棒，您可以摸摸看。
The material is really good—feel it.

⑦ 這種材質很容易保養。
The material is easy to care for.

⑧ 我覺得您穿這件衣服很好看。
I think you look great in this.

⑨ 這是我們的 暢銷品 ，前一陣子還缺貨。
This is our best-selling item. In fact, we ran out not too long ago.

⑩ 這是今年最流行的樣式。
This is the most fashionable style this year.

⑪ 這是 義大利進口 的鞋子。
These shoes are imported from Italy.

⑫ 您可以試試最新的款式。
You can try the newest style.

⑬ 您可以 再搭配一件 外套。
You can also wear a coat to match it.

⑭ 這是小牛皮製的。
This is made of calf leather.

⑮ 還 有別的顏色 可以選擇。
We also have other colors for you to choose from.

116 尺寸。

❶ 褲子 太長了 。
The pants are too long.

❷ 大小 剛剛好 。
It fits me well.

❸ 袖子太短了。
The sleeves are too short.

❹ 領口有點緊。
The collar is too tight.

❺ 腰圍太鬆了。
It's too baggy in the waist.

❻ 腰圍太緊了。
It's too tight in the waist.

❼ 拉鍊 拉不上來 。
I can't zip up the zipper.

❽ 扣子 扣不起來 。
I can't button it up.

❾ 我通常 穿 M 號 的。
I usually wear a medium.

❿ 尺寸太小了。
The size is too small.

⓫ 我喜歡穿 合身的 衣服。
I like to wear clothes that fit me well.

⓬ S 號太小，M 號又太大。
The small is too small, but the medium is too big.

⓭ 下擺太寬了。
The lower hem is too wide.

⓮ 有 大一號 的嗎？
Do you have one in a bigger size?

⓯ 有 小一號 的嗎？
Do you have one in a smaller size?

116 服務人員怎麼說？

❶ 要不要試 試別件 ？
Would you like to try on another one?

❷ 不好意思，大一號的 缺貨 。
Sorry, the larger ones are all sold out.

❸ 請告訴我您的尺寸。
Please tell me your size.

❹ 請試試小一號的。
Try the smaller size.

❺ 我們可以 幫您修改 。
We can alter it for you.

❻ 請試試大一號的。
Try the bigger size.

❼ 修改不用另外計費。
Alterations are free of charge.

❽ 可以把褲長放長些。
We can lengthen the pants a bit.

❾ 把腰圍改一下就很漂亮了。
A little alteration to the waistline and it'll look great.

❿ 可以把褲長 改短一點 。
We can make the pants shorter.

⓫ 我們還有 其他的尺寸 。
We still have some other sizes.

⓬ 長度修改到這裡可以嗎？
Is this the length you need?

⓭ 我們可以 量身訂做 。
We can tailor it to your size.

⓮ 我們可以 幫您加個鞋墊 。
We can put a pad in your shoes.

⓯ 今年都流行比較 貼身的設計 。
The more skin-tight design is popular this year.

117 殺價。

❶ 太貴了。
It's too expensive.

❷ 算整數 吧?
How about making it an even price?

❸ 我就只有這些錢了。
This is all the money I've got.

❹ 再便宜一些吧?
Can you go a little lower?

❺ 去掉零頭 可以嗎?
How about cutting it to an even amount?

❻ 兩件算五百,可以嗎?
Two for five hundred, all right?

❼ 別人都賣二百元而已。
Other stores sell it for two hundred.

❽ 算便宜點 我就多買幾件。
I'll buy more if you give me a lower price.

❾ 這件衣服 有些瑕疵 ,算便宜點我就買。
This piece of clothing has some flaws; I'll buy it for a discount.

❿ 我是 老客戶 了,還跟我計較這些。
I am your old customer, and you want to haggle with me?

⓫ 不然你要送我一個小禮物。
Or you can give me a small gift instead.

⓬ 算便宜點,我會 介紹朋友來 給你買啦!
Give me a better price and I'll bring my friends here.

⓭ 算便宜一點我就全部買。
I'll buy them all for a lower price.

⓮ 這好像 快退流行 了。
This one may go out of fashion soon.

117 服務人員怎麼說？

① 我一件只賺十塊錢。
I can only make ten NT on each one.

② 我是 賠本在賣 。
I am selling it at below cost.

③ 趕快賣一賣要回家啦！
I'm in a hurry to sell them out.

④ 少算十塊如何。
How about I give you a ten-dollar discount?

⑤ 三百元， 買不買隨便你 。
Three hundred, take it or leave it.

⑥ 不然你再 多買一件 。
How about you buy one more?

⑦ 不可能再便宜 了。
I can't go any cheaper than that.

⑧ 品質絕對好，不然你可以拿來退。
If the quality isn't what I say it is, I'll give you your money back.

⑨ 不然你說 要算多少 ？
Exactly how much would you be willing to pay for it?

⑩ 就是有小瑕疵，才賣你這麼便宜。
The flaw is why I'm offering you such a low price.

⑪ 老客戶才賣你這個價錢。
Only an old customer like you can get this price.

⑫ 已經非常便宜了。
It's already very cheap.

⑬ 賠錢生意 沒人做啦！
Come on, nobody would do business without profit!

⑭ 你真是 殺價高手 。
You are truly a good bargainer.

⑮ 要介紹朋友來買喔！
Be sure to bring your friends here!

118 包裝。

1 請幫我 用禮盒包 裝。
Please wrap it in a gift box.

2 請給我有提把的袋子，我比較方便拿。
Please give me a bag with a handle so I can carry it easily.

3 我要這一款的紙盒。
I want this type of paper box.

4 我需 要塑膠袋 。
I need a plastic bag.

5 包裝要另外付費嗎？
Is there an extra charge for gift wrapping?

6 請幫我把價錢 貼標撕掉 。
Please tear off the price tag.

7 我要寫一張卡片放進去。
I want to write a card and put it inside.

8 這是要送給女生的禮物，我想要粉紅色的包裝。
This is a gift for a lady. Please wrap it in pink paper.

9 我要送禮 ，請包裝得漂亮一點。
This is a present. Please wrap it nicely.

10 如果需要包裝費，就不用了。
I don't want to wrap it if it costs extra.

11 請 幫我包裝 一下。
Please wrap it up for me.

12 是自己要用的，就 不用包裝 了。
This is for my own use—I don't need to wrap it.

13 有比較特別的包裝方式嗎？
Do you have a more special way to wrap it?

14 我不喜歡這樣的包裝，請你重新包一次。
I don't like this wrapping. Please wrap it again.

15 請幫我 加上緞帶 。
Please tie some ribbons to it.

118 服務人員怎麼說？

❶ 請選一個 包裝紙 的顏色。
Please pick a color of wrapping paper.

❷ 需 要包裝嗎 ？
Would you like it wrapped?

❸ 我幫您把衣服燙一燙再包起來。
I'll iron your clothes before wrapping them.

❹ 這些都放在一起可以嗎？
Can we have them wrapped together?

❺ 您要 挑張卡片 嗎？
Do you need to pick a card?

❻ 你要搭配 其他的裝飾 做包裝嗎？
Are there any decorations you would like to use?

❼ 您要用禮盒裝嗎？
Do you need a gift box for it?

❽ 要紙袋還是塑膠袋？
Paper or plastic?

❾ 要 分開包 嗎？
Do you want to pack them separately?

❿ 您要用 有提把的 袋子嗎？
Do you need a bag with a handle?

⓫ 您需要乾燥劑嗎？
Do you need some desiccant?

⓬ 價錢要撕掉嗎？
Do you want to tear off the price tag?

⓭ 您要紙盤和蠟燭嗎？
Would you like some paper plates and candles?

⓮ 包裝要 另外付費 。
There is a surcharge for gift wrapping.

⓯ 包裝不用另外付費。
There is no surcharge for gift wrapping.

119 結帳。

❶ 只能用現金嗎？
Do you only take cash?

❷ 這些 總共多少 錢？
How much are these in total?

❸ 這兩件總共多少錢？
How much are these two pieces together?

❹ 這件不是賣三百五十元嗎？
Isn't this one priced at NT$350?

❺ 可以 刷卡 嗎？
Can I use a credit card?

❻ 這件衣服不是打八折嗎？
Isn't this twenty percent off?

❼ 不是 有特價嗎 ？
Don't you have a special discount?

❽ 不是有贈品嗎？
Doesn't this come with a gift?

❾ 請幫我分成兩袋， 分開結帳 。
Please put them into two bags and bill me separately.

❿ 對不起，我沒有現金。
Sorry, I don't have cash.

⓫ 我先結帳， 一會兒再過來 拿衣服。
I'll pay the bill first and come back to get the clothes later.

⓬ 我有貴賓卡可以 打幾折 ？
How much of a discount can I get with my VIP card?

⓭ 請等一下，我去隔壁提款機提錢。
Hang on a minute, let me withdraw some cash from the ATM next door.

⓮ 可以 用禮卷 嗎？
Do you take coupons?

119 服務人員怎麼說？

❶ 我來幫您結帳。
I'll be your cashier.

❷ 對不起，我們 只接受現金 付費。
Sorry, we only take cash.

❸ 黑色的貴五十元。
The black one costs fifty dollars more.

❹ 對不起，我們 不接受刷卡 。
Sorry, we don't take credit cards.

❺ 有特價的不是這件衣服。
This is not the one that's on sale.

❻ 有問題可以拿來換。
You can bring your item back to exchange if there's a problem with it.

❼ 七天之內 可以退貨 。
We have a seven-day return policy.

❽ 兩件以上才有特價。
There's only a discount if you buy two or more.

❾ 特價期間 已經過了。
Our sale is over.

❿ 總共是 二千元。
The total amount is two thousand dollars.

⓫ 這也是要結帳的嗎？
Do you want to buy this one too?

⓬ 不好意思，您的 信用卡被拒絕 了。
Sorry, but your credit card was rejected.

⓭ 這是 發票 及 收據 。
Here is the invoice and receipt.

⓮ 提醒您一下，用 禮券不能找錢 喔。
May I remind you that coupons are not exchangeable for cash?

120 退換貨。

❶ 我要 換大一號 的。
I want to exchange it for a larger size.

❷ 我要換長一點的。
I want to exchange it for a longer one.

❸ 我要告你們 廣告不實 。
I want to sue you for running misleading ads.

❹ 我要換顏色深一點的。
I want to exchange it for a darker one.

❺ 這件衣服我穿起來不好看，我要 換別的款式 。
This piece of clothing does not fit me. I want to exchange it for another style.

❻ 我要 退錢 。
I want a refund.

❼ 我要換另一件。
I want to exchange it for another one.

❽ 這件衣服 還沒穿就破 了，我要退貨。
This piece of clothing was torn before I wore it. I want a refund.

❾ 我的 發票不見 了，可以退貨嗎？
My receipt is gone. Can I still return it?

❿ 我想換白色的那件。
I want to exchange it for that white one.

⓫ 這東西和你們型錄上感覺 差太多 ，我要退貨。
This doesn't look anything like the picture in your catalogue. I want to return it.

⓬ 為什麼我不能退貨？
Why can't I return this item?

⓭ 其他產品我都不喜歡，我要退錢。
I don't like any of your other products. I want a refund.

120 服務人員怎麼說？

❶ 好，我幫您辦理退貨。
Yes, I'll accept your return.

❷ 有帶發票嗎？
Did you bring the receipt with you?

❸ 這是特價品，不能退錢。
This is an on-sale item. It can't be returned for cash.

❹ 要有發票 才能退貨。
We require a receipt for all returns.

❺ 這是您自己弄壞的，我們沒有辦法接受退貨。
You have damaged it. We can't accept this return.

❻ 已經 超過七天，不能退貨了。
It has already been over seven days. We can't accept this return.

❼ 包裝已經打開了不能退貨。
The packaging was open. We can't take it.

❽ 只能更換 等價商品。
We can only replace it with something of equal value.

❾ 買的時候就已經說了「貨出概不退換」。
When you were buying it, we told you that it couldn't be returned.

❿ 或是 補差價 購買其他商品。
Or you buy another item and pay for the difference.

⓫ 已經使 用過了 就不能退貨。
Once you have used the item you can't return it.

⓬ 我們已經 沒有同樣的 商品了。
We are out of those items.

⓭ 沒有您需要的尺碼了。
We don't have the size you need.

121 點餐。

❶ 這裡的菜都是 單點 嗎？
Is everything here à la carte?

❷ 有供應 套餐 嗎？
Do you have set meals?

❸ 請給我菜單。
May I have a menu?

❹ 你們有推出母親節特餐嗎？
Do you have a special menu for Mother's Day?

❺ A 餐和 B 餐 有什麼不同 ？
What's the difference between Set A and Set B?

❻ 這道菜會 很辣嗎 ？
Is this dish spicy?

❼ 有什麼推薦菜嗎？
Is there anything you can recommend?

❽ 這道菜是怎麼烹調的？
How is this dish prepared?

❾ 你們的招牌菜是什麼？
What's your house special?

❿ 你可以 幫我們配菜 嗎？
Can you choose some side dishes for us?

⓫ 這是義大利餐廳嗎？
Is this an Italian restaurant?

⓬ 先點這些 ，不夠我們再點。
That's it for now; we'll order more if it is not enough.

⓭ 主菜 是從這三種中任選一樣嗎？
Does the entrée have to be one of these three?

⓮ 這些菜 夠我們五個人吃 嗎？
Are these dishes enough for the five of us?

⓯ 我們想要點甜點。
We would like to order dessert.

121 服務生怎麼說？

1 需要 中文菜單 嗎？
Do you need a Chinese menu?

2 需要我介紹菜單嗎？
Would you like me to introduce our menu?

3 這是我們的 招牌菜 。
This is our house special.

4 要不要點個湯？
Would you like to order soup?

5 這道菜很受歡迎，要不要試試？
This dish is very popular; would you like to try it?

6 我們的料理是法式的。
Our cooking is French.

7 我們都用 天然的食材 。
We always use natural ingredients.

8 我可以 請廚師少放一些 辣椒。
I can ask our chef to add less hot peppers for you.

9 需要 加點甜點 嗎？
Would you like some dessert?

10 我們的廚師是五星級飯店的主廚。
Our chef is from a five-star hotel.

11 主菜加一百元就變成套餐。
You can add NT$100 to the price of an entrée to make it a set meal.

12 請問需要什麼 餐後飲料 ？
What would you like to drink after your meal?

13 需要 白飯 嗎？
Would you like white rice?

14 我重複一遍您點的菜。
I will repeat what you ordered.

122 用餐。

❶ 我們 沒點這道 菜。
We didn't order this.

❷ 這家餐廳的口味不錯。
This restaurant has good food.

❸ 請問這道菜 怎麼吃 ？
May I ask how this dish should be eaten?

❹ 這家餐廳的氣氛很好。
This restaurant's atmosphere is very good.

❺ 這家餐廳的 服務很好 。
This restaurant has very good service.

❻ 請給我辣椒醬。
Please pass me the hot sauce.

❼ 這盤海鮮很新鮮。
This seafood dish is very fresh.

❽ 請問這是 什麼醬汁 ？
Excuse me, what kind of sauce is this?

❾ 這道菜很有異國風味。
This dish has an exotic flavor.

❿ 這道菜很適合 配生啤酒 。
This dish goes well with draft beer.

⓫ 吃不完 可以打包嗎 ？
Can we wrap up what we haven't finished?

⓬ 可以給我們刀叉嗎？
Could you please give us a fork and knife?

⓭ 可以再給我們一副碗筷嗎？
Could we please have a bowl and chopsticks?

⓮ 可以幫我們 加個水 嗎？
Could you please fill our water glasses?

⓯ 我們 還有一道菜 沒上。
We still have one more course that has not been
served yet.

122 服務生怎麼說？

1 沙拉吧可以 自己取用 。
Help yourself to the salad bar.

2 上菜了 ，請小心。
Here you go; be careful.

3 刀叉在餐台的下方。
Knives and forks are underneath the table.

4 這是您需要的 調味醬 。
Here is the sauce you asked for.

5 這盤菜是 免費招待 的。
There is no charge for this dish.

6 這是我們廚師的拿手菜。
This is our chef's specialty.

7 菜都到齊了 嗎？
Have all your dishes been served yet?

8 請等一下，您的菜 馬上送過來 。
Please wait a second; I'll bring your meal right away.

9 需要辣椒醬或是醬油嗎？
Do you need either hot sauce or soy sauce?

10 湯涼了，要再加熱一下嗎？
The soup is cold; would you like it warmed up a bit?

11 餐盤放在桌上 我會來收 。
Just leave your dishes on the table; I'll pick them up.

12 請問您需要甜點或是飲料嗎？
Excuse me, would you like any dessert or beverages?

13 需要我幫您服務嗎？
Can I help you with anything?

14 剩下的菜需 要打包嗎 ？
Would you like to wrap up your leftovers?

15 還滿意我們的菜色嗎？
How was your meal?

123 用餐問題與抱怨。

1 這盤菜的 份量好少 。
The portions of this meal are too small.

2 湯裡面有蚊子。
There is a mosquito in my soup.

3 好鹹 喔。
It's too salty.

4 這道菜和照片上的差太多了。
This dish does not look like the picture.

5 好辣喔。
It's too spicy.

6 食材 不太新鮮 。
The food is not very fresh.

7 這道菜不好吃。
This dish tastes bad.

8 肉 煮得太老 了，咬不動。
The meat is overcooked, I can't chew it.

9 桌巾怎麼這麼髒？
How come the tablecloth is so dirty?

10 我們已經 等了快半個小時 了。
We've waited for almost half an hour.

11 餐具好像 不太乾淨 。
The tableware doesn't look very clean.

12 餐廳好吵喔。
It's too noisy in this restaurant.

13 水的 味道怪 怪的。
The water tastes weird.

14 為什麼最後一道菜遲遲不來？
Why has our last dish not been served yet?

15 這裡的服務生 態度很差 。
The waiters here have bad attitudes.

123 服務生怎麼說？

❶ 對不起，我 幫您問一下 廚房。
I'm sorry, I'll check with our kitchen for you.

❷ 對不起，我們幫您 重新出菜 。
I'm sorry, we'll bring you a new order.

❸ 對不起，這道菜烹調時間要久一點。
I'm sorry, this dish needs some more time to cook.

❹ 不合口味嗎？
It doesn't appeal to your tastes?

❺ 您覺得太辣了嗎？
Do you think it is too spicy?

❻ 我幫您換 一副餐具。
I'll bring you a new set of utensils.

❼ 對不起，我馬上幫您更換。
I'm sorry, I will change that for you immediately.

❽ 菜馬上就來了。
Your food is on its way.

❾ 對不起 讓您久等 。
I'm sorry for keeping you waiting.

❿ 不好意思，我們會 盡力改進 。
I'm terribly sorry; we'll do our best to improve.

⓫ 對不起，我們遺 漏了這道菜 。
I'm sorry, we forgot about your dish.

⓬ 如果份量不夠，我再幫您補充一些。
If the portion is not big enough, I'll bring you
some more.

⓭ 對不起，今天 客人實在太多 了。
I'm sorry, we are very busy today.

⓮ 對不起，這個服務生今天第一天上班。
I'm sorry; this is the waiter's first day.

⓯ 這些小菜由我們免費招待。
These side dishes are on the house.

124 餐後結帳。

1 我要 買單 。
Check, please.

2 可以刷卡嗎？
Can I pay by credit card?

3 只接受現金嗎？
Do you only accept cash?

4 總共 多少錢 ？
How much is the total?

5 錢好像不太對…
The amount does not seem right....

6 零錢 不用找了 ，謝謝。
Keep the change, thanks.

7 請給我看一下 帳單明細 。
Please give me a detailed check.

8 這不是我們的帳單。
This is not our check.

9 有含一成 服務費 嗎？
Does it already include the ten percent service charge?

10 小菜是多少錢？
How much are the side dishes?

11 可以找零錢給我嗎？
May I have the change?

12 你 算錯帳 了。
You made a mistake on this bill.

13 可以 分開找錢 給我們嗎？
Can you give us the change separately?

14 白飯一碗多少？
How much for a bowl of white rice?

15 我這裡有折價餐券。
I have a discount meal coupon.

124 服務生怎麼說？

❶ 這是 |您的帳單| 。
This is your check.

❷ 需要 |開收據| 嗎？
Do you need a receipt?

❸ 還要加上三碗白飯的費用。
I still need to add three bowls of white rice to the bill.

❹ 可以給我您公司的 |統一編號| 嗎？
Can I please have your company's unified invoice number?

❺ 我們有收一成的服務費。
We put in a ten percent service charge.

❻ 這張 |折價券| 可以使用。
You can use this discount coupon.

❼ 一次消費只能使用一張折價券。
You can only use one coupon at a time.

❽ 這張折價券已經過期了。
This discount coupon has expired.

❾ 您需要 |分開結帳| 嗎？
Do you need separate checks?

❿ 剛才離開的客人已經幫您結帳了。
Your check has already been paid by the guest who just left.

⓫ 對不起，我算錯帳了。
I'm so sorry, I miscalculated the bill.

⓬ 請問您 |有零錢嗎| ？
Excuse me, do you have any change?

⓭ 請簽名。
Please sign your name.

⓮ 這是您的 |發票| 。
Here is your receipt.

⓯ 歡迎 |下次再來| 。
Please come again.

125 換錢。

❶ 我要換錢打電話。

I need some change to make a phone call.

❷ 我想換美金。

I'd like to exchange this into U.S. dollars.

❸ 哪裡可以換 零錢？

Where can I get change?

❹ 可以和你換零錢嗎？

Can I get change from you?

❺ 請問需要什麼證件？

What kind of ID do you need?

❻ 請幫我 把錢換開 。

Please change the money into small bills for me.

❼ 請全部換給我零錢。

Please change all my money into coins.

❽ 今天的 匯率是多少 ？

What's the exchange rate for today?

❾ 可以換新台幣嗎？

Can I exchange this into New Taiwan dollars?

❿ 哪裡有 換鈔機 ？

Where can I find a coin machine?

⓫ 紙鈔可以打電話嗎？

Can I use a bill to make a phone call?

⓬ 需要 手續費 嗎？

Is there a service charge?

⓭ 可以給我一些百元鈔票嗎？

Can you give me some hundred-dollar bills?

⓮ 請換零錢給我。

Please give me some coins.

⓯ 這台機器 會找零嗎 ？

Does this machine give change?

125 服務人員怎麼說？

❶ 你 要怎麼換 錢？
How would you like your money?

❷ 你要 換多少 錢？
How much money do you want to exchange?

❸ 你要換 十元 還是 一元 ？
Do you want your money changed into tens or ones?

❹ 請給我你的護照。
Please let me see your passport.

❺ 你要換 美金 還是 日圓 ？
Would you like your money exchanged into U.S.
dollars or Japanese yen?

❻ 這裡也可以換新台幣。
We can exchange money into New Taiwan dollars
here, too.

❼ 不能用零錢打卡式電話。
You cannot use coins for prepaid card phones.

❽ 搭公車要 自備零錢 。
You need change to take a bus.

❾ 手續費是 5 %。
The service charge is five percent.

❿ 這是你的收據。
Here is your receipt.

⓫ 我 看看有沒有 零錢。
Let me see if I have any change.

⓬ 你還需要多少零錢？
How much more change do you need?

⓭ 我 沒有零錢 。
I don't have any change.

⓮ 五張一元和一張五元可以嗎？
Can I give you five ones and one five?

126 問路。

① 請告訴我 怎麼回 麗晶飯店。
Can you please tell me how to get back to the Regent Hotel from here?

② 我 迷路 了。
I am lost.

③ 請問 這裡是哪裡 ？
Excuse me, where is this place?

④ 請問哪裡可以搭計程車？
Can you please tell me where I can find a taxi?

⑤ 請問最近的公車站要 往哪裡走 ？
Excuse me, which way is the nearest bus station?

⑥ 請問捷運站在哪一個方向？
Excuse me, which way is the MRT station?

⑦ 請問火車站在哪裡？
Excuse me, where is the train station?

⑧ 什麼時候要左轉呢？
When should I turn left?

⑨ 請問我在 地圖上的哪裡 ？
Excuse me, where am I on this map?

⑩ 直走就會到我的 目的地 嗎？
If I keep going straight, will I reach my destination?

⑪ 直走之後呢？
And after going straight ahead?

⑫ 請問 還有幾站 ？
Excuse me, how many stations are left?

⑬ 右轉 還是 左轉 ？
Turn right, or turn left?

⑭ 第幾個十字路口該左轉？
At which crossroads should I turn left?

126 對方怎麼說？

❶ 你 走錯方向 了。
You took a wrong turn.

❷ 有 公車可以到 那裡。
There is a bus that goes there.

❸ 往前直走 就到了。
Go straight ahead and you'll be there.

❹ 你可以搭捷運過去。
You can take the MRT to get there.

❺ 搭計程車只要十分鐘。
It only takes ten minutes to get there by cab.

❻ 過馬路 後往前走就看到了。
Cross the street, then walk straight ahead and you'll see it.

❼ 向右轉、再左轉就到了。
Make a right turn and then a left turn and you'll be there.

❽ 直走後看到 紅綠燈右轉 。
Go straight ahead and make a right at the traffic light.

❾ 你現在在地圖的這裡。
On the map, you are right here.

❿ 前面最大的建築物就是火車站。
The train station is the largest building in front of you.

⓫ 你可以在 這一站下車 。
You can get off at this station.

⓬ 直走五分鐘 就到了。
Go straight along this road for five minutes and you'll be there.

⓭ 下一站你就要下車了。
You should get off at the next station.

⓮ 坐計程車過去比較方便。
It would be easier to take a taxi there.

⓯ 不會很遠 ，走路只要五分鐘。
It is not that far from here, only a five-minute walk.

127 詢問打電話。

1 請問哪裡可以買到電話卡？
Can you please tell me where I can buy a phone card?

2 請問附近哪裡有 公共電話 ？
Excuse me, is there a public phone around here?

3 請問打 市內電話 要多少錢？
Excuse me, how much does it cost to make a local call?

4 市內電話要 怎麼打 ？
How can I make a local call?

5 電話卡要多少錢？
How much does a prepaid phone card cost?

6 請問打長途電話要多少錢？
Excuse me, how much does it cost to make a
long-distance call?

7 國際電話 要怎麼打？
How can I make an international call?

8 公共電話可以打國際電話嗎？
Can a public phone be used to make an international
call?

9 長途電話要怎麼打？
How can I make a long-distance call?

10 這個 電話壞掉了 嗎？
Is this phone broken?

11 叫消防隊要 打幾號 ？
What number should I dial to reach the fire
department?

12 公共電話能打 對方付費 電話嗎？
Can I use a public phone to make a collect call?

13 有免費的公共電話嗎？
Are there any toll-free payphones?

14 我的 手機沒電了 ，可以借用你的嗎？
My mobile phone's battery is dead; can I borrow yours?

127 對方怎麼說？

❶ 大馬路旁都有公共電話。
There are always payphones beside major roads.

❷ 先撥區域號碼，再撥對方的電話號碼。
Dial the area code first, and then dial the phone number of the person you want to call.

❸ 你可以到便利商店買電話卡。
You can buy phone cards at convenience stores.

❹ 電話卡有各種面額。
The value of prepaid phone cards varies.

❺ 市內電話每分鐘一元。
One dollar per local call.

❻ 電話卡大部分都是一百元的面額。
The value of most prepaid phone cards is 100 dollars.

❼ 插入卡片，再直撥電話號碼。
Insert the card and then dial the phone number directly.

❽ 你可以用我的手機。
You can use my cell phone.

❾ 你可以不投錢，直撥 110 或 119。
You can dial 110 or 119 directly without inserting any coins.

❿ 長途電話比較貴。
Long-distance calls are more expensive.

⓫ 話機上有特別註明的，才能打國際電話。
Only specially marked phones can be used to make international calls.

⓬ 這台電話不適用這種卡片。
This type of card cannot be used with this phone.

⓭ 你的電話卡金額不夠了。
You do not have enough value on your calling card.

128 搭乘計程車。

1 我已經 打電話叫 計程車了。
I've already called a taxi.

2 我要到 桃園機場。
I want to go to Taoyuan Airport.

3 我要到這上面的地址。
I want to get to this address.

4 這是我住的飯店地址，請帶我到飯店。
This is the address of the hotel I'm staying in; please take me there.

5 請快一點，我 在趕時間 。
Please hurry up; I'm really in a rush.

6 請走不會塞車的路。
Please take a road that will avoid traffic.

7 司機先生，請問你知道怎麼走嗎？
Excuse me sir, do you know how to get there?

8 是不是 走錯路了 ？
Did we go the wrong way?

9 請在下一個紅綠燈 讓我下車 。
Please let me off at the next traffic light.

10 這樣子好像 繞了遠路 。
It seems like this is the long way.

11 請把車轉進第一個巷子。
Please turn down the first alley.

12 計程車資是 多少錢起跳 ？
How much is the initial taxi fare?

13 我在前面的巷口下車，謝謝。
I want to get off at the alley up ahead, thanks.

14 計程車有 夜間加成 嗎？
Do the cabs have a late night surcharge?

128 司機怎麼說？

❶ 請問您 要去哪裡 ？
Where would you like to go?

❷ 你有飯店的名片借我看一下嗎？
Could I have a look at the hotel's business card?

❸ 是在火車站附近嗎？
Is it near the train station?

❹ 要不要 繞到對面 ？
Should I turn around to the other side?

❺ 想 走哪一條路 過去？
What road would you like to take to get there?

❻ 這條巷子太窄， 車子進不去 。
This alley is too narrow; the car can't fit through it.

❼ 你知道怎麼走嗎？
Do you know how to get there?

❽ 要在 這裡下車 嗎？
Do you want to get off here?

❾ 我知道在哪裡。
I know where it is.

❿ 這條路是 捷徑 。
This way is a shortcut.

⓫ 走這條路比較不塞車。
There will be less traffic this way.

⓬ 我 找錢 給你。
Let me give you your change.

⓭ 前面就到了。
It is just ahead.

⓮ 快不了，塞車了。
There's a traffic jam; we can't go any faster.

⓯ 尖峰時間， 到處都塞車 。
It is rush hour; there is traffic everywhere.

129 接電話。

❶ 喂。
Hello.

❷ 我就是。
Speaking.

❸ 請問您是 哪一位?
May I ask who is calling?

❹ 喂, 我是 約翰。
Hello, this is John.

❺ 你好,請問你要 找哪一位 ?
Hello, who are you looking for?

❻ 你要找哪一位林小姐?
Which Miss Lin are you calling for?

❼ 我幫你把電話 轉給她 。
I will transfer your call to her.

❽ 你要找陳小姐是嗎?
You are looking for Miss Chen, right?

❾ 抱歉,我 現在不方便 講電話。
Sorry; I can't take your call right now.

❿ 你介意 再說一次 剛剛的話嗎?
Would you mind repeating what you just said?

⓫ 請稍等。
Please wait a moment.

⓬ 我幫你轉客服部。
I will transfer your call to the customer service department.

⓭ 抱歉, 我聽不清楚 你說的話。
Excuse me, I can't hear you clearly.

⓮ 等一下回你 電話。
I'll call you back later.

⓯ 我在講另外一支電話。
I am on another call right now.

129 打電話。

❶ 可以麻煩史密斯先生聽電話嗎？
May I speak to Mr. Smith?

❷ 喂，我是湯姆。
Hello, this is Tom.

❸ 你好，請問琳達 在嗎 ？
Hello, is Linda there?

❹ 大衛在嗎？
Is David there?

❺ 請幫我 轉客服部 。
Please transfer me to the customer service department.

❻ 我想跟王先生講話。
I would like to speak to Mr. Wang.

❼ 喂，比利嗎？
Hello, Billy, is that you?

❽ 我是他同事。
I am his colleague.

❾ 請 接分機 15。
Extension 15, please.

❿ 電話可以借我用一下嗎？
May I use your phone?

⓫ 你 在忙嗎 ？
Are you busy right now?

⓬ 我是 XYZ 公司的吳大衛。
This is David Wu of XYZ Company.

⓭ 我 有急事 要找林先生。
I would like to speak to Mr. Lin regarding an
urgent matter.

⓮ 我要 找你們老闆 。
I would like to speak to your boss.

⓯ 你剛剛打電話 找我嗎 ？
Did you just call me?

130 告知對方打錯電話。

❶ 你可能撥錯電話號碼了。
You might have the wrong number.

❷ 沒有這個人。
There is nobody by that name here.

❸ 這支電話是我新申請的。
I've only recently started using this number.

❹ 你說你 要找誰 ？
Who did you say you are calling?

❺ 你 打錯了 。
You have the wrong number.

❻ 我們公司 沒有林小姐 。
There is no Miss Lin in our company.

❼ 我們這邊是住家。
This is a residential number.

❽ 號碼沒錯，但沒有你要找的人。
The number you dialed is correct, but there's nobody by that name here.

❾ 她已經 離職了 。
She is no longer working here.

❿ 他已經不使用這個電話號碼了。
He doesn't use this number anymore.

⓫ 他已經 不住在這裡 了。
He doesn't live here anymore.

⓬ 他的分機 號碼改了 。
His extension number has changed.

⓭ 我不是 你要找的人。
I am not the person you are looking for.

⓮ 林小姐的分機是 17。
Miss Lin's extension number is 17.

130 確認是否打錯電話。

① 請問你的電話號碼是幾號？

Sorry, may I ask what your phone number is?

② 你 撥打幾號 ？

What number did you dial?

③ 請問你用這支號碼多久了？

Excuse me, how long have you been using this phone number?

④ 你這支電話是最近申請的嗎？

Have you just recently started using this number?

⑤ 你那邊是 ABC 公司嗎 ？

Is this the ABC company?

⑥ 你確定你沒撥錯號碼？

Are you sure that you didn't dial the wrong number?

⑦ 你的電話號碼是 1234-1234 嗎？

Is your phone number 1234-1234?

⑧ 可以跟你確認一下電話號碼嗎？

May I double-check the phone number with you?

⑨ 請問是 黃先生府上 嗎？

Excuse me, is this the Huangs' residence?

⑩ 請問是 林小姐嗎 ？

Excuse me, is this Miss Lin?

⑪ 喂，剛剛有人打我手機嗎？

Hello, did someone just call my mobile phone?

⑫ 喂， 客服專線 是這支號碼嗎？

Hello, is this the customer service number?

⑬ 這個分機不是陳小姐的嗎？

Isn't this Miss Chen's extension number?

⑭ 我 打錯了嗎 ？怎麼是你接電話？

Did I dial the wrong number? How come it is you who are answering the phone?

131 無法接聽電話。

❶ 他現在不方便接電話。
He can't come to the phone right now.

❷ 你要 在線上等候 嗎？
Would you like to stay on the line?

❸ 他今天休假。
He is taking a day off today.

❹ 他現在 在開會 。
He is in a meeting right now.

❺ 琳達不在。
Linda is not here right now.

❻ 我 請他回你 電話。
I will ask him to call you back.

❼ 她現在在 電話中 。
She is on the phone right now.

❽ 林先生還沒有進公司。
Mr. Lin hasn't come into the office yet.

❾ 愛咪還沒回來。
Amy hasn't come back yet.

❿ 你要找的人 不在座位 上。
The person you're looking for is not at his desk right now.

⓫ 請問他幾點會進公司？
When will he come in?

⓬ 他 外出了 ，他出去拜訪客戶了。
He is out; he went to see some clients.

⓭ 他 什麼時候回來 ？
When will he be back?

⓮ 李先生這個禮拜出差。
Mr. Lee is going on a business trip this week.

⓯ 有什麼辦法可以聯絡到他嗎？
Is there any way to contact him?

131 處理對方留言。

❶ 你要請他回電嗎？
Would you like to have him call you back?

❷ 請問你找他 有什麼事情 嗎？
May I ask what you are calling him about?

❸ 有什麼我可以為你轉達的嗎？
Is there any message I can pass on for you?

❹ 要我告訴湯姆你找他嗎？
Would you like me to tell Tom that you called?

❺ 你 要留言嗎 ？
Would you like to leave a message?

❻ 請問 你哪裡找 ？
May I ask who is calling?

❼ 我會 幫你轉告 他。
I will pass your message on to him.

❽ 你方便留一下 聯絡方式 嗎？
Would you like to leave a contact number?

❾ 請告訴我你的電話號碼。
Please tell me your phone number.

❿ 我等一下要外出，請她 打我手機 。
I'm going out in a minute; please tell her to call my mobile number.

⓫ 你可以請他回電嗎？
Could you have him call me back?

⓬ 我是約翰的母親，請告訴他我找他。
This is John's mother; please tell him that I called.

⓭ 請琳達 盡快回電 給我。
Please have Linda give me a call as soon as possible.

⓮ 他多晚回我電話都沒關係。
It does not matter how late he returns my call.

132 轉達有人來電。

❶ 林先生剛剛 有回你電話 。
Mr. Lin just called you back.

❷ 你不在座位時， 手機有響 。
Your mobile phone rang while you were away from your desk.

❸ 剛剛 有人打來 找你。
Someone just called you.

❹ 你母親要你回電話給她。
Your mother wants you to call her back.

❺ 陳先生現在 在 1 線 電話上。
Mr. Chen is on line one now.

❻ 這是林小姐的電話號碼。
This is Miss Lin's phone number.

❼ 林先生請你撥他手機。
Mr. Lin asked you to call his cell number.

❽ 你不在時，有個女生打電話找你。
A woman called for you while you were out.

❾ 一堆人留言 要你回電話。
A bunch of people left messages for you to call them back.

❿ 林小姐在公司，她請你回電話。
Miss Lin is in her office now, and she asks that you call her back.

⓫ 強尼下午有打電話找你。
Johnny called for you this afternoon.

⓬ 你太太 請你儘速回電 。
Your wife asked you to phone her as soon as possible.

⓭ 林小姐說晚一點會再來電。
Miss Lin said that she would call you again later.

⓮ 珍妮 打了好幾通 電話找你。
Jenny has already called you several times.

132 詢問是否有人來電。

❶ 我不在時 有人找我嗎 ？
Did anyone call for me while I was out?

❷ 對方沒說他 是誰 嗎？
Did he say who he was?

❸ 他有留姓名跟電話嗎？
Did he leave his name and phone number?

❹ 你記得他大概什麼時候打的嗎？
Do you remember when he called?

❺ 他 幾點打來 的？
When did he call?

❻ 他有說是 哪一間公司 的人嗎？
Did he say which company he was from?

❼ 他有說 會再打來嗎 ？
Did he say that he would call again?

❽ 她的聲音聽起來怎麼樣？
What did her voice sound like?

❾ 我母親是下午打給我的嗎？
Did my mother call me this afternoon?

❿ 早上你有幫我代接電話嗎？
Did you take any calls for me this morning?

⓫ 是不是吉米打來的？
Was it Jimmy that just called?

⓬ 吉米有說 找我什麼事 嗎？
Did Jimmy say why he was calling me?

⓭ 李先生有打電話找我嗎？
Has Mr. Lee called for me?

⓮ 剛剛是林小姐找我嗎？
Did Miss Lin just call for me?

⓯ 他有說他 在公司 還是 在家裡 嗎？
Did he say whether he was in the office or at home?

293

133 介紹同事。

1 這位是我們公司的 新進人員 。
This is our new employee.

2 你們 認識嗎 ？
Do you know each other?

3 瑪麗從今天起擔任祕書的職務。
As of today, Mary will be our new secretary.

4 你見過史密斯先生嗎？
Have you met Mr. Smith yet?

5 你要不要 自我介紹 一下？
Would you like to introduce yourself a bit?

6 林先生，讓我介紹我同事給您認識。
Mr. Lin, allow me to introduce to you my colleague.

7 他是職場 新鮮人 。
He is a rookie in the job market.

8 他是我們公司最負責任的員工。
He is the most responsible employee in our company.

9 帶你認識 一下公司同事。
Let me take you to meet our colleagues.

10 這位是我們公司的業務。
This is our company's salesperson.

11 這位史密斯先生是管理部的主管。
Mr. Smith here is the chief of the management department.

12 旁邊這位是 負責業務的大衛。
This man beside me is David, who is in charge of sales.

13 我先介紹你給大家認識。
First, I want to introduce you to everyone.

14 這位是以後 負責帶你的 林小姐。
This is Miss Lin, who is going to be in charge of training you.

15 先帶你去各部門 拜碼頭 。
Let me take you around to each department first.

133 主動認識同事。

❶ 初次見面，你好嗎？
This is the first time we've met; how are you?

❷ 你好，我是 負責業務的約翰。
Hello, I am John, and I'm in charge of sales.

❸ 你好嗎？我是珍‧史密斯。
How are you? I am Jane Smith.

❹ 這是我的名片，請多指教。
This is my business card; your suggestions are welcome.

❺ 很高興認識你。
It's really nice to meet you.

❻ 歡迎加入 我們。
We're so happy you joined us!

❼ 你好，請多指教。
Hello, your advice is welcome.

❽ 很高興能跟你成為同事。
I'm really happy to be your colleague.

❾ 工作上有任何問題都 可以問我 。
You can ask me any question about work.

❿ 久仰大名。
I've heard a lot about you.

⓫ 你好，我是今天 第一天上班 的珍妮。
Hello, I am the new girl, Jennie.

⓬ 我是個 菜鳥 ，請多擔待。
Please excuse me, I am a newcomer.

⓭ 我會盡快進入工作狀況。
I'll do my best to settle into a work routine.

⓮ 我會努力工作，不給大家添麻煩 。
I'll work hard to avoid causing extra work for anyone.

⓯ 叫我珍就可以了。
You can call me Jane.

134 必須請假／有同事請假。

❶ 你可以 幫我請病假 嗎？
Can you help me ask for a sick leave?

❷ 我後天請 喪假 。
I'm taking a bereavement leave the day after tomorrow.

❸ 我明天請半天假。
I'm taking a half-day leave tomorrow.

❹ 我明天請 事假 。
I'm taking a personal day tomorrow.

❺ 我可以請一個禮拜的假嗎？
Can I request a one-week leave?

❻ 我想請假 到月底 。
I would like to request a leave of absence till the end of the month.

❼ 我要請 年假 。
I want to take my annual leave.

❽ 我在等頭兒准假。
I'm waiting for my boss to approve my leave of absence.

❾ 休假期間他是我的 職務代理人 。
He'll fill in for me while I'm away on vacation.

❿ 我請假這段期間，萬事拜託了。
Please take good care of everything for me while I am on leave.

⓫ 他早上有打電話來請假。
He called this morning to ask for a leave of absence.

⓬ 我想 申請留職停薪 。
I would like to apply for unpaid leave.

⓭ 我可以提早一個小時離開公司嗎？
May I leave the office an hour early?

⓮ 我們公司 請假規定 很多。
Our company has a lot of rules about taking time off.

134 尋求協助／提供協助。

❶ 誰來幫我 一下？
Is there anyone who can help me?

❷ 我自己 忙不過來 。
I can't handle it by myself.

❸ 我需要一個人幫忙影印。
I need someone to make copies for me.

❹ 你願意協助我處理這個案子嗎？
Can you help me deal with this case?

❺ 可以 幫我看一下 我的電腦嗎？
Could you have a look at my computer for me?

❻ 可以幫我看一下這份企畫案嗎？
Would you take a look at this proposal for me?

❼ 可以幫我把這些資料輸入電腦嗎？
Can you help me input this data into the computer?

❽ 麻煩你在主管面前 幫我美言幾句 。
Please put in a good word to your manager for me.

❾ 可以 拜託你一件事 嗎？
Can I request a favor from you?

❿ 你願意陪我一起去拜訪客戶嗎？
Would you accompany me to visit this client?

⓫ 我需要借助你的專業技能。
I need to borrow your professional skills.

⓬ 你可以幫我打幾個電話嗎？
Can you help me make some phone calls?

⓭ 可以幫我傳真這份文件嗎？
Can you fax this document for me?

⓮ 有任何需要 儘管說 。
Don't hesitate to tell me if you need anything.

⓯ 我可以幫你什麼嗎？
What can I do for you?

135 接待訪客。

❶ 您好，請問您要 找哪一位 ？
Hello, may I ask who you are looking for?

❷ 您 有預約嗎 ？
Do you have an appointment?

❸ 歡迎您大駕光臨。
Thank you for your visit.

❹ 他的辦公室在這個方向。
His office is this way.

❺ 讓您久等了。
Sorry to keep you waiting for so long.

❻ 請問 有什麼事 嗎？
May I help you?

❼ 我們老闆已經等您很久了。
Our boss has been waiting for you.

❽ 請您 稍待片刻 。
Please wait here for a moment.

❾ 這邊請。
This way, please.

❿ 我帶您 到會客室 。
Let me show you to the reception room.

⓫ 抱歉，他現在有客人。
I'm sorry, he is meeting with a client right now.

⓬ 請坐 這裡。
Have a seat here, please.

⓭ 不好意思，林先生有事外出。
I'm very sorry; Mr. Lin is out.

⓮ 下次 請您先預約 時間。
Next time please make an appointment first.

⓯ 請喝 咖啡。
Have some coffee, please.

135 主動拜訪。

❶ 我是 ABC 公司的業務，想要拜訪你們老闆。
I am a salesperson with ABC Company, and I would like to visit your boss.

❷ 不好意思，可以 幫我通報 一下嗎？
I'm sorry, could you let him know I've arrived?

❸ 你跟他說大衛他就知道了。
Just tell him that David is here; he will know what you mean.

❹ 我是 順道過來 拜訪的。
I happened to be in the neighborhood, so I stopped by to visit you.

❺ 我沒有事先預約。
I haven't made an appointment.

❻ 我有打過 電話預約 。
I made an appointment over the phone.

❼ 他今天都不會再進公司嗎？
Will he not be in the office for the rest of the day?

❽ 那我 改天 再登門拜訪。
OK, I'll come some other day.

❾ 他現在方便會客嗎？
Is he available to meet with visitors right now?

❿ 請問他 大概還要多久 才會有空？
Around what time will he be available?

⓫ 我跟他約三點，不過我早到了。
My appointment with him is for three pm, but I've arrived early.

⓬ 麻煩你 為我帶路 。
Please show me the way.

⓭ 沒關係， 我等他 。
That's fine, I will wait for him.

136 接機。

❶ 請問您是 X 公司的史密斯先生嗎？
Excuse me; are you Mr. Smith of X company?

❷ 公司派我來 機場接您。
My company sent me here to pick you up.

❸ 您好，我是 ABC 公司的陳大衛。
Hello, I am David Chen of ABC company.

❹ 我一直等候您大駕光臨。
I've been waiting for your arrival.

❺ 麻煩您在這裡等我。
Please wait here.

❻ 一路上 還好吧？
Did you have a good flight?

❼ 您在台灣期間由 我負責接待 您。
I am responsible for taking care of you during your stay in Taiwan.

❽ 我幫您拿一些行李吧。
Let me help you carry some of your baggage.

❾ 歡迎您 來到台灣。
Welcome to Taiwan.

❿ 希望您在台灣期間過得愉快。
Hope you have a pleasant time in Taiwan.

⓫ 我先為您說明今明兩天的行程。
First let me explain the itinerary of today and tomorrow.

⓬ 我去把 車子開過來 。
I will pull the car over here.

⓭ 我先帶您 到飯店 休息。
I'll go ahead and drive you to the hotel so you can rest.

⓮ 旅途一切順利嗎？
Is everything on your trip going smoothly?

136 感謝對方接機。

1 你好，我是 X 公司的麥可・史密斯。
Hello, I'm Michael Smith of X company.

2 謝謝 你來接我。
Thank you for picking me up.

3 這樣麻煩你真不好意思。
I'm very sorry to bother you with this.

4 你的 車停哪 ？
Where did you park your car?

5 行李 我自己拿 就可以了。
I can carry my luggage.

6 我在這裡等你開車過來嗎？
Should I just wait for you to drive over here?

7 這真是趟漫長的旅程。
This seems like an endless journey.

8 我想 先回飯店 休息。
I would like to go to the hotel to rest.

9 你可以先帶我去吃點東西嗎？
Can you take me to get a bite to eat?

10 你可以先告訴我 今天的行程 嗎？
Can you tell me about today's schedule first?

11 接下來幾天是你負責接待我嗎？
Are you going to be my guide for the next few days?

12 我這幾天要如何 跟你聯絡 ？
How can I contact you for the next few days?

13 我想直接 去你們公司 。
I want to go directly to your company.

14 你明天早上 會來接我嗎 ？
Are you going to pick me up tomorrow morning?

15 你們老闆現在在公司嗎？
Is your boss in the office right now?

137 拜訪客戶。

❶ 我想找時間 到貴公司拜訪 。
I want to take some time to pay a visit to your company.

❷ 您好，我是 接替傑克職務 的人。
Hello, I am the person who replaced Jack.

❸ 請問什麼時候方便過去拜訪您？
May I ask when would be a suitable time to visit you?

❹ 這是我的名片， 請多指教 。
This is my business card; I look forward to working with you in the future.

❺ 您好，我是 LKK 公司的吳大衛。
Hello, I'm David Wu from LKK company.

❻ 我主要負責 業務方面 的工作。
I'm mainly responsible for business matters.

❼ 以後將由我繼續為貴公司服務。
I will continue to serve your company in the future.

❽ 有任何需要請跟我說。
Please let me know if you need anything.

❾ 很抱歉 臨時來打擾 您。
I'm very sorry to trouble you at the last minute.

❿ 我是 剛剛打電話來 的懷特。
I'm White, the one who just called.

⓫ 請問怎麼稱呼？
May I ask your name?

⓬ 我們的報價是 同業中最便宜 的。
Our price quotes are the cheapest in the business.

⓭ 方便給我一張您的名片嗎？
May I have your business card?

⓮ 希望有幸能為貴公司服務。
I really hope that we have the opportunity to serve your company.

137 瞭解客戶需求。

1 要不要我先 幫您估個價 ？
Would you mind if I made an assessment for you first?

2 請問您有什麼需要？
May I ask what it is that you need?

3 您是希望 降折扣 嗎？
You're looking for a discount, right?

4 您希望我們給您多少的折扣？
How much of a discount would you like us to offer?

5 您的要求我們會 優先考量 。
Your requests will be our top priority.

6 您有任何要求都可以提出來討論。
Go ahead and bring up any requests that you would like to discuss.

7 您需要詳細的 價目表 嗎？
Do you need a detailed price list?

8 請問您希望 何時簽約 ？
When would you like to sign the agreement?

9 您有其他的考量嗎？
Do you have any other considerations?

10 付款方式您可以自由選擇。
You are free to choose the type of payment.

11 您是 考慮成本 的問題嗎？
Are you considering the problem of cost?

12 付款期限 我們可以再商量。
We can discuss the payment terms later.

13 售後服務 的問題您不用擔心。
You don't need to worry about after-sale service.

14 我們隨時有 專人為您服務 。
Our expert staff is always at your service.

138 爭取合作機會。

① 您會 考慮長期 跟我們合作嗎？
Would you consider working with us for the long term?

② 百忙之中勞您抽空見我，非常感謝。
I appreciate that you've found some time in your full schedule to see me.

③ 希望貴公司 再給我們一次機會 。
We hope that your firm will give us another chance.

④ 請問您何時會做出決定？
When will you make the decision, may I ask?

⑤ 希望您好好考慮，我 等您的答覆 。
Hope you will think about it; I'm looking forward to your answer.

⑥ 如果還有任何問題，請與我聯絡。
Please contact me if you have any further questions about that.

⑦ 我要來 跟您簽約 。
I've come to sign a contract with you.

⑧ 明天給您答覆可以嗎？
Can I give you the answer tomorrow?

⑨ 我會盡可能完成您的所有要求。
I'll try my best to fulfill all of your requests.

⑩ 我會 跟公司反應 您的意見。
I'll relay your feedback to our company.

⑪ 我們 非常有誠意 要跟您做生意。
We would sincerely like to do business with you.

⑫ 您要不要先看一下合約？
Would you like to see the contract first?

⑬ 這是 新的報價單 。
This is the new price list.

138 客戶的回應。

1 不要緊，歡迎你來。
That's OK, you're welcome.

2 平時很謝謝你們公司的幫忙。
Thank you for your firm's steady assistance.

3 你好，找我 有什麼事情 嗎？
Hello, what can I do for you?

4 我記得我今天沒跟你約吧？
I don't remember having an appointment with you for today.

5 我等一下要開會，請 長話短說 。
I have a meeting coming up, so please make it short.

6 希望你盡快幫我解決這個問題。
I hope that you can help me solve this problem as soon as possible.

7 上次談的 價錢你評估了嗎？
Have you evaluated the price we discussed last time?

8 我 打算終止 我們的合作關係。
I plan to terminate the cooperative relations between us.

9 我不想跟你們公司合作。
I don't want to work with your company.

10 你什麼時候可以 給我答案 ？
When can you give me your reply?

11 我目前沒有 換廠商 的打算。
I currently don't have any plans to change suppliers.

12 我考慮看看。
Let me think about it.

13 我上次已經清楚表達 我的立場 。
I already made my position very clear last time.

14 你們公司可不可以拿出點誠意？
Could your firm show a little sincerity?

139 我的聯絡方式。

❶ 這是 我的名片 ，上面有我的聯絡方式。
This is my business card; on the front is my contact info.

❷ 我 公司的電話 是 2927-0000。
My company's phone number is 2927-0000.

❸ 我留我的聯絡方式給您。
Let me leave my contact info for you.

❹ 我沒有分機。
I don't have an extension.

❺ 我手機會隨時開著。
My cell phone is always on.

❻ 我的 分機 是 17。
My extension is 17.

❼ 您也可以打手機找我。
You also can reach me through my cell number.

❽ 這是我的電子郵件信箱。
This is my email address.

❾ 有事情可以透過 電子郵件聯絡 。
You can contact me via email if anything occurs.

❿ 不好意思，我剛好 沒帶名片 。
I'm sorry, I ran out of name cards.

⓫ 我 常不在公司 ，請用手機與我聯絡。
I am seldom in my office, so please contact me through my cell phone.

⓬ 您有紙筆嗎？我 抄電話給您 。
Do you have a pen and paper? Let me write down my phone number for you.

⓭ 上班時間您可以打電話到公司。
You can call me at my office during working hours.

139 客戶的聯絡方式？

❶ 請問我 怎麼和您聯絡 ？
How can I contact you?

❷ 方便留一下您的聯絡方式嗎？
Would you mind leaving your contact info?

❸ 可以再跟我說一次 您的電話 嗎？
Could you please tell me your phone number one more time?

❹ 我可以用電子郵件跟您聯繫嗎？
Can I contact you via email?

❺ 您有電子信箱嗎？
Do you have an email account?

❻ 您有備用的電子信箱嗎？
Do you have a backup email account?

❼ 打到公司 找曾小姐就可以了嗎？
Can I just dial your company's number to call Miss Tseng?

❽ 您有分機嗎？
Do you have an extension?

❾ 請等一下，我拿筆寫下您的電子信箱。
Please wait a second, let me grab a pen to write your email address down.

❿ 名片上有 您的手機 嗎？
Is your cell number on your business card?

⓫ 我可以用 Skype 與您保持聯絡嗎？
Can I keep in touch with you via Skype?

⓬ 您會使用 視訊會議 的功能嗎？
Can you use the video conference function?

⓭ 什麼時間 跟你聯絡比較方便？
When is the best time to contact you?

⓮ 晚上找您也是撥這支電話嗎？
Is this also the number to call you at night?

140 介紹產品。

❶ 我想向您介紹本公司的產品。
I would like to introduce our company's product to you.

❷ 這款是我們本月的 主打商品 。
This design is what we're promoting this month.

❸ 這是我們公司最暢銷的產品。
This is our company's most popular product.

❹ 這是我們的 最新產品 。
This is our newest product.

❺ 這項產品頗受好評。
This product has received several positive reviews.

❻ 這個商品下個月 即將上市 。
This product will go on the market next month.

❼ 這是我們 獨家研發 的產品。
This is our exclusively developed product.

❽ 它經過改良後更臻完善。
It is nearing perfection after so much improvement.

❾ 這個產品我們主打 年輕人市場 。
We are promoting this product mainly to the youth market.

❿ 操作人性化 是本產品的特色。
User-friendliness is this product's feature.

⓫ 價格便宜是它最大的優勢。
A low price is its biggest advantage.

⓬ 這是目前 最受歡迎 的款式。
This is currently our most popular design.

⓭ 它已經在網路上引起熱烈討論。
It has provoked fervent discussion on the Internet.

⓮ 這項商品堪稱本公司的 代表作 。
This product can be considered our company's signature work.

140 客戶需要的產品？

1 您需要怎樣的產品呢？
What kind of product do you want?

2 您的預算 大概是多少？
Approximately how much is your budget?

3 這項產品不符合您的需求嗎？
Doesn't this product meet your needs?

4 您比較注重 實用性 是嗎？
You are concerned with practicality, right?

5 您要不要看我們的 產品型錄 ？
Would you like to take a look at our product catalogue?

6 請問您需要 哪些功能 ？
What functions do you need, may I ask?

7 您希望功能及外觀兩者兼顧嗎？
Are you hoping to consider both function and appearance?

8 您有 指定品牌 嗎？
Do you have a designated brand?

9 外型是你選購產品的重點嗎？
Is the external appearance the key point for you when buying products?

10 需要我 為您推薦 嗎？
Do you need me to make a recommendation for you?

11 這項產品非常符合您的需要。
This product definitely meets your requirements.

12 我比較 建議您 選購這個商品。
I would suggest that you buy this product.

13 您的產品想要強調什麼呢？
What does your product try to emphasize?

14 您有設計圖嗎？
Do you have the design drawings?

141 說明交貨時間。

1 我們即將完成。

We are about finished with it.

2 我們保證 如期交貨 。

We guarantee on-time delivery.

3 明天交貨沒問題。

Delivery tomorrow is no problem.

4 交貨時間 可以商量嗎 ？

Can we talk about the delivery time?

5 我們目前 進度落後 。

We are currently behind schedule.

6 恐怕得向您 延後交貨 時間。

I'm afraid of that we probably will have to delay
the time of your delivery.

7 我們的交貨期限通常是一個禮拜。

Our delivery time is usually one week.

8 我們盡量 幫您趕趕看 。

We'll try our best to do that for you.

9 您給我們的期限真的很短。

The deadline you gave is really short.

10 我們需要一個月的生產時間。

We need one month's time for production.

11 機器故障，恐怕 無法如期 出貨。

I'm afraid that we can't make the delivery on time
due to a mechanical malfunction.

12 我們三天內會送達。

We will make the delivery within three days.

13 這批貨 最快要下禮拜 才會到。

This batch of products will be delivered next week.

14 我們可以分批交貨嗎？

May we deliver in batches?

141 客戶詢問交貨時間？

1 你預定 何時交貨 ？
When do you plan to make the delivery?

2 產品 進度如何 ？
What is the current production schedule?

3 你們什麼時候可以出貨？
What time can you make the delivery?

4 你自己說一個交貨期限給我。
Just give me a deadline for your delivery.

5 你們已經 出貨了嗎 ？
Have you made the delivery yet?

6 趕得上 交貨截止日吧？
Can you meet the delivery deadline?

7 為什麼一再延期？
Why has the delivery been postponed again and again?

8 貨 還要多久 才能送到？
How long will it take you to make the delivery?

9 星期五前可以交貨嗎？
Could the delivery be made before Friday?

10 不準時交貨，我就 退貨 。
I will reject the delivery if it isn't on time.

11 可以馬上出貨給我嗎？
Can you make a delivery for me right now?

12 你們現在完成多少了？
How much have you completed?

13 我一定要在月底前收到東西。
I have to receive the products by the end of this month.

14 你們現在 有庫存嗎 ？
Do you have any stocks available now?

15 難道不能 加班幫我趕 一下？
Is it possible for you to work overtime for me?

142 品質保證。

1 我辦事，您放心。

Don't worry about what I'm handling.

2 我們在業界是 有口碑 的。

We have a good reputation in this industry.

3 別間公司絕對做不出這種品質。

Other companies could never match our quality.

4 我們的產品絕對 不輸其他同業 。

Our products are at least as good as those of other companies in the industry.

5 貨品保證 毫無瑕疵 。

We guarantee that there's no fault in the goods.

6 我們公司的產品您可以放心。

You can rest assured about our company's products.

7 我們絕 不賣假貨 。

We never sell fake products.

8 品質絕對與您當初看的樣品一樣。

The quality is absolutely the same as the sample you saw.

9 我們公司提供 一年保固 。

Our company provides a one-year warranty.

10 本公司產品保證 原裝進口 。

Our company's product is guaranteed to be the original import.

11 我們有提供 免費維修 服務。

We provide free maintenance service.

12 我們廠內有嚴格的商品控管。

We have a strict process of quality control in our factory.

13 我們不可能自己 砸自己的招牌 。

We'd never ruin our own reputation.

14 如果有差錯，我不收半毛錢。

If there are any mistakes then I will not take a dime from you.

142 詢問客戶滿意度？

❶ 您用得 滿意嗎 ？
Are you satisfied with its performance?

❷ 請問您覺得 哪裡需要改進 ？
Where do you think it needs improvement?

❸ 我們有沒有需要修正的地方？
Is there anything we need to correct?

❹ 您滿意這次的產品嗎？
Are you satisfied with the merchandise this time?

❺ 我們的工作效率您滿意嗎？
Are you satisfied with our work efficiency?

❻ 您覺得我們公司的 配合度 如何？
How do you feel about our company's
coordination?

❼ 您滿意我們提供的服務嗎？
Are you satisfied with the service we've provided?

❽ 我們日後還 有合作機會嗎 ？
Will there be any other chances for us to cooperate
in the future?

❾ 這次合作您還滿意嗎？
Are you satisfied with our cooperation?

❿ 已經交貨的商品您覺得如何？
What do you think about the delivered product?

⓫ 您覺得 成效如何 ？
What do you think of the result?

⓬ 您驗收後覺得如何呢？
How do you feel after checking on the delivery?

⓭ 多謝您的誇讚，我們會繼續努力。
Thanks for your praise; we will keep trying our best.

⓮ 您還 會繼續使用 本產品嗎？
Will you keep on using this merchandise?

143 名牌…。

❶ 我喜歡買名牌。
I love buying name brands.

❷ 我存錢就是 為了買名牌 。
I save up for name brands.

❸ 我相信名牌的品質。
I trust the quality of name brands.

❹ 我喜歡名牌的設計。
I like the design of name brands.

❺ 我最愛 LV。
LV is my favorite.

❻ 名牌包包 永不退流行 。
Name-brand bags will never go out of fashion.

❼ 名牌服飾配件的顏色特別鮮豔。
The colors of name-brand accessories are
particularly bright.

❽ 30 歲時我買了第一個 Gucci 包。
I bought my first Gucci bag at age thirty.

❾ 我 從不用 名牌。
I've never had a name-brand item before.

❿ 我會 分期付款 買名牌。
I pay for name-brand items in installments.

⓫ 名牌讓很多人變得比較有自信。
Name-brand items make many people more confident.

⓬ 聽說 亞洲人最愛 用名牌。
It's said that Asians are name brands' top customers.

⓭ 二手名牌 的銷路也不差。
The secondhand name-brand item market is active as well.

⓮ 名牌在歐洲價格比較便宜。
The prices of name-brand items are lower in Europe.

⓯ 有些名牌仿冒品看起來 幾可亂真 。
Some name brand imitations look just like the real thing.

143 你覺得名牌…？

❶ 哇！LV的 新款 包包？
Wow! Is that the new LV bag?

❷ 你喜歡用名牌嗎？
Are you fond of name brands?

❸ 你常買名牌嗎？
Do you buy name-brand items often?

❹ 你有LV的包包嗎？
Do you have any LV bags?

❺ 為什麼有人喜歡 追求名牌 ？
Why do some people like to pursue name brands?

❻ 你 捨得花大錢 買名牌嗎？
Are you willing to pay an arm and a leg for name-brand items?

❼ 這雙鞋子是 哪個牌子 的？設計真獨特。
Which brand is this pair of shoes? Its design is unique.

❽ 名牌真的比較 好用嗎 ？
Are those name-brand items really more practical?

❾ 你會分期付款買名牌嗎？
Do you pay for name-brand items in installments?

❿ 你能分辨出真假名牌嗎？
Can you tell the difference between the real and the fake name-brand items?

⓫ 這是 真品 還是 仿冒品 ？
Is it real or an imitation?

⓬ 你會買二手名牌嗎？
Do you buy secondhand name-brand items?

⓭ 你喜歡 全身名牌 的感覺嗎？
Do you like the feeling of being decked out in name-brand items from head to toe?

144 美容保養…。

❶ 沒有醜女人，只有懶女人。
There are no ugly women, only lazy ones.

❷ 台灣的女生超愛用面膜。
Girls in Taiwan love beauty masks.

❸ 皮膚的清潔工作最重要。
Cleanliness is the most important thing for skin care.

❹ 很多人喜歡天然的保養品。
Many people are fond of natural skin care products.

❺ 擦乳液可以保護皮膚。
Lotion will help protect your skin.

❻ 夏天出門一定要擦防曬。
You must wear sunscreen when you're out during the summer.

❼ 聽說按摩臉部會改善肌肉鬆弛。
It's said that massaging your face will improve flabby muscles.

❽ 一到夏天美白產品就熱賣。
Skin whitening products are popular in summer.

❾ 去角質會讓皮膚更細緻。
Exfoliating will give skin a fine texture.

❿ 很多女生認為皮膚白就是漂亮。
Some girls equate beauty with fair skin.

⓫ 皮膚脫皮，就是太乾燥了。
If your skin flakes off, it's too dry.

⓬ 很多人做了拉皮手術。
Many people get facelifts.

⓭ 多吃水果蔬菜是最簡單的美容方法。
Eating more fruits and vegetables is the simplest way to beauty.

⓮ 女生都願意在美容產品上花大錢。
All girls are happy to spend fortunes on beauty products.

144 你覺得美容保養…？

❶ 你用名牌保養品嗎？
Do you use name-brand skin care products?

❷ 你 擔心變老 嗎？
Are you afraid of getting old?

❸ 你有做什麼 特別的保養 嗎？
Do you have any particular skin maintenance method?

❹ 你常注意美容資訊嗎？
Do you pay much attention to beauty news?

❺ 你每個月 花多少錢 買保養品？
How much do you pay for beauty products each month?

❻ 你的臉色暗沉嗎？
Do you have a dull complexion?

❼ 你相信面膜的功效嗎？
Do you trust those beauty masks?

❽ 你也認為 皮膚白就是漂亮 嗎？
Do you think that fair skin equals beauty?

❾ 你有毛孔粗大的問題嗎？
Are you troubled by large pores?

❿ 皮膚太乾燥怎麼辦？
What if your skin is too dry?

⓫ 出現小細紋該怎麼辦？
What should I do when fine lines appear?

⓬ 如何防止臉部肌肉鬆弛？
How can I prevent flabby facial muscles?

⓭ 怎樣讓肌膚 白回來 ？
How can I get my skin white again?

⓮ 如何 青春永駐 ？
How can I stay young?

⓯ 出現 魚尾紋 了，怎麼辦？
What am I going to do about my crow's feet?

145 減肥…。

❶ 減肥彷彿成了 全民運動 。
It seems that weight loss has become a civic movement.

❷ 減肥的方法太多了。
There are all kinds of ways to lose weight.

❸ 身體一胖穿衣服就 不好看 。
Once you gain weight, your clothes don't look as good on you.

❹ 一星期瘦 0.5 公斤最理想。
It'd be perfect if you could lose half a kilo per week.

❺ 減肥成功後，千萬 不要再復胖 。
Once you get rid of the fat, be sure it doesn't come back.

❻ 醫院現在也有推出專門的減重班。
Even hospitals are promoting weight-loss programs now.

❼ 減肥藥可 不能亂吃 。
Don't just take any diet pills.

❽ 台灣有很多減肥 減出問題 的案例。
There are many weight-loss issues in Taiwan.

❾ 我還是覺得自己可以 再瘦一點 。
I still think there's room for me to lose a little weight.

❿ 我一定可以 減肥成功 。
I'm definitely going to cut down my weight to the ideal standard.

⓫ 很多減肥廣告都 誇大不實 。
Many ads about weight loss are fake.

⓬ 太瘦並不健康。
It's not good to be too thin.

⓭ 肥胖是不健康的前兆。
Obesity is a sign of unhealthiness.

⓮ 減肥要有意志力才能成功。
It takes willpower to lose weight.

145 你覺得減肥…?

1 最近 發福 了嗎?
Have you put on some weight lately?

2 斷食減肥 法會不會很辛苦?
Is cutting down on your diet a burden?

3 每個台灣人都覺得自己需要減肥嗎?
Do Taiwanese people all feel like they need to lose weight?

4 秤秤看你現在多重。
Check how much you weigh now.

5 電視 購物頻道 上的減肥藥真的有效嗎?
Are those weight-loss medicines on the TV shopping channel effective?

6 究竟有多少方法可以減肥啊?
How many ways on earth are there to lose weight?

7 你成功瘦了幾公斤?
How many kilograms have you lost?

8 減肥可 別傷了健康 。
Don't harm your health while losing weight.

9 減肥後是不是很 容易復胖 ?
Is it easy to gain weight again after losing weight?

10 台灣似乎有為數不少關於減肥的書。
Seems there're quite a few books about weight loss in Taiwan.

11 怎樣的人容易變胖?
What kind of person tends to gain weight?

12 快樂就好,幹麼這麼在意 身材?
What's all the fuss about your figure so long as you can choose to be happy?

13 你又不胖 ,幹麼減肥?
Lose weight? Why bother! You're not fat.

146 整型… 。

❶ 韓國有很多 人工美女 。
South Korea has many man-made beauties.

❷ 我還是 不敢嘗試 整型。
I still don't dare to give plastic surgery a try.

❸ 很多人整型後變得有自信。
Many people become more confident after having plastic surgery.

❹ 我老了一定會去拉皮。
I'm going to tighten my skin when I get older.

❺ 整型 失敗的例子 其實不少。
Actually, there are many failed examples of plastic surgery.

❻ 整型是變美最快的方法。
Plastic surgery is the fastest way to become beautiful.

❼ 現在的整型手術可以 做得很自然 。
Plastic surgery nowadays can be done very naturally.

❽ 其實有些整型手術費用不高。
Actually, some plastic surgery operations are not that expensive.

❾ 很多人 割雙眼皮 。
Many people have plastic surgery to get double-fold eyelids.

❿ 很多學生 利用暑假 整型。
Many students get plastic surgery during summer vacation.

⓫ 整型手術讓許多人 美夢成真 。
Plastic surgery makes many people's dreams come true.

⓬ 隆鼻的人也不少。
There are many people who have had nose jobs.

⓭ 整型手術幾個小時就能完成。
Plastic surgery can be done in a couple of hours.

⓮ 抽脂 是熱門的整型項目。
Liposuction is the most popular form of plastic surgery.

146 你覺得整型…?

❶ 你 做過整型 手術嗎?
Have you ever had plastic surgery?

❷ 你會嘗試整型嗎?
Would you give plastic surgery a try?

❸ 你贊成整型嗎?
Do you agree with plastic surgery?

❹ 你 最想改變 哪一個部位?
Which part of your body would you like to change most?

❺ 你想 豐胸 嗎?
Would you like to have breast implants?

❻ 你想割雙眼皮嗎?
Would you like to have double-fold eyelids?

❼ 你想 隆鼻 嗎?
Would you like to have a nose job?

❽ 整型會讓你更有自信嗎?
Will plastic surgery make you more confident?

❾ 你覺得整型有危險嗎?
Do you think there's any danger to plastic surgery?

❿ 你擔心整型可能會有 後遺症 嗎?
Do you worry about the possible side effects of plastic surgery?

⓫ 整型失敗你會怎麼樣?
What would you do if the plastic surgery failed?

⓬ 家人贊成 你整型嗎?
Does your family agree with you having plastic surgery?

⓭ 你不能接受自己既有的樣子嗎?
Can't you accept the way you look right now?

⓮ 你有朋友動過整型手術嗎?
Do you have any friends who have had plastic surgery?

⓯ 整型的 費用很高嗎 ?
Is the price of plastic surgery high?

147 八卦…。

❶ 很多人愛看 八卦新聞。
Many people like to read gossip columns.

❷ 很多人愛聊八卦。
Many people like to gossip.

❸ 八卦風近幾年非常盛行。
Gossip has grown very popular over the past few years.

❹ 電視新聞也越來越八卦。
There has been more and more gossip on the TV news.

❺ 蘋果日報是台灣第一份 八卦報紙 。
The Apple Daily was the first gossip newspaper in Taiwan.

❻ 藝人的八卦往往引起熱烈討論。
The gossip on entertainers often gives rise to enthusiastic discussion.

❼ 同一件八卦，不同媒體有不同的報導。
Different media have different reports on the same gossip.

❽ 名人的緋聞 也是大家注意的焦點。
The love affairs of celebrities are also focuses of interest.

❾ 狗仔隊 最愛偷拍名人隱私。
Paparazzi love to take sneak shots at celebrities' privacy.

❿ 很多八卦新聞 都是鬼扯 。
Much gossip is simply made up.

⓫ 醜聞見光讓很多人身敗名裂。
Public scandals cause many people to lose their good standing and reputation.

⓬ 狗仔隊真是 唯恐天下不亂 。
It is the paparazzi's pleasure to see a chaotic world.

⓭ 八卦報導侵犯了許多人的 隱私 。
Gossip reports really invade many people's privacy.

147 你覺得八卦…？

❶ 你喜歡看八卦報導嗎？
Do you like to read the gossip news?

❷ 這一期壹週刊的 封面人物 是誰？
Who is on the cover of this issue of Next magazine?

❸ 你相信八卦雜誌所寫的嗎？
Do you believe the articles in gossip magazines?

❹ 最近最熱門的八卦是什麼？
What has been the most popular gossip recently?

❺ 誰是這次 緋聞的男主角 ？
Who is the leading man in this love affair?

❻ 最熱門的八卦主角是誰？
Who is the hottest gossip topic?

❼ 為什麼那麼多人愛看八卦新聞？
Why are there so many people who love to read gossip?

❽ 最近 最勁爆 的新聞是什麼？
What is the most explosive sexy news these days?

❾ 難道沒有別的東西可以報導嗎？
Isn't there anything else to report?

❿ 你對八卦新聞有什麼想法？
What do you think about gossip columns?

⓫ 你同情那些被 放大檢視 的公眾人物嗎？
Do you sympathize with these public figures under
scrutiny?

⓬ 你覺得有人在乎 真相 嗎？
Do you think there is anyone who cares about the
truth?

⓭ 你覺得公眾人物應該保有自己的隱私嗎？
Do you think that public figures should have their
privacy protected?

⓮ 你覺得八卦報導是 社會的亂源 嗎？
Do you think gossip news is the origin of social chaos?

148 捷運…。

❶ 台北的捷運很方便。
The MRT system in Taipei is really convenient.

❷ 上下班時間捷運十分 擁擠 。
It's very crowded during rush hour.

❸ 搭捷運上班的人很多。
There are many people who take the MRT to work.

❹ 捷運改變了我們的生活。
The MRT system has changed our lives.

❺ 捷運後 轉乘公車半價 優待。
There's a 50% discount on bus fare if you transfer from the MRT.

❻ 建造捷運花了很長的時間。
It took a long time to build the MRT.

❼ 很多人搭捷運後轉乘公車。
Many people transfer to buses after taking the MRT.

❽ 幾乎大家都 用悠遊卡 搭捷運。
Almost everyone uses EasyCards to take the MRT.

❾ 台北捷運偶爾 24 小時營業。
The Taipei MRT system is occasionally open for twenty-four hours.

❿ 假日時，可以 帶腳踏車 搭捷運。
You can take your bike on the MRT during holidays.

⓫ 捷運站的 標示混亂 ，讓人搞不清楚。
The signs in the MRT stations are confusing.

⓬ 台北捷運以 顏色區分 路線。
The Taipei MRT lines are distinguished by color.

⓭ 台北車站是主要的捷運 交會站 。
Taipei Main Station is the main transfer station.

⓮ 捷運末班車大概是晚上十二點。
The last train boards at about twelve pm.

148 你覺得捷運…？

1 你覺得搭捷運比公車方便嗎？
Do you think the MRT system is more convenient than the bus?

2 你家附近有 捷運站嗎？
Is there an MRT station near your place?

3 悠遊卡搭捷運有優惠嗎？
Is there a discount for taking the MRT with an EasyCard?

4 晚上搭乘捷運 安全嗎 ？
Is it safe to take the MRT at night?

5 捷運 首班車 是幾點？
What time is the first train of the MRT?

6 你覺得捷運的票價 太貴嗎 ？
Do you think the MRT fare is too expensive?

7 紙鈔能購買捷運車票嗎？
Can I buy an MRT ticket with bills?

8 搭乘捷運要 如何買票 ？
How do I buy a ticket to take the MRT?

9 你覺得台北捷運舒適嗎？
Do you think the Taipei MRT is comfortable?

10 你覺得捷運的路線標示清楚嗎？
Do you think the line sign is clear enough?

11 悠遊卡的錢不夠了，要 怎麼加值 呢？
How do I add money to my EasyCard when there's not enough stored on it?

12 每一種公車都接受悠遊卡嗎？
Does every bus take EasyCard?

13 捷運周邊有 熱門景點 或餐廳嗎？
Are there any hot spots or restaurants around the MRT?

14 目前 只有台北市 有捷運嗎？
Is Taipei the only city that has an MRT system at the moment?

149 天氣…。

❶ 今天天氣真好！
What a wonderful day today!

❷ 今天天氣 總算放晴 了。
It's finally clearing up today.

❸ 我喜歡涼爽的天氣。
I like cool weather.

❹ 最近 早晚溫差大 。
There's been a big difference in temperature between day and night recently.

❺ 今年夏天特別熱。
It's been particularly hot this summer.

❻ 氣象預報經常 不準 。
The weather forecast is often inaccurate.

❼ 梅雨季節 即將開始。
The rainy season is about to begin.

❽ 昨天的 最低溫 在淡水。
The coldest temperatures yesterday were in Danshui.

❾ 七、八月最常出現颱風。
Typhoons occur most frequently between July and August.

❿ 最近常有 豪雨特報 。
There have been many heavy-rain alerts lately.

⓫ 聽說這星期都會下雨。
I heard that it's going to rain for the whole week.

⓬ 氣象預報說週末有機會下雪。
The weather forecast says that there's a good chance it will snow this weekend.

⓭ 今天 氣溫高達 攝氏 40 度。
The temperature reached forty degrees Celsius today.

149 你覺得天氣…？

1 今天 天氣如何 ？
How's the weather today?

2 最近 常下雨嗎 ？
Has it rained often lately?

3 最近早晚溫差大嗎？
Is there a big difference in temperature between day and night?

4 你每天看 氣象預報 嗎？
Do you watch the weather forecast every day?

5 有颱風 嗎？
Is there a typhoon?

6 今天的氣象報告怎麼說？
What does the weather report say?

7 週末的天氣 適合去爬山 嗎？
Will the weather be good for us to go mountain climbing this weekend?

8 已經進入了梅雨季節了嗎？
Is it already the rainy season?

9 有機 會下雪嗎 ？
Is there a possibility that we'll get snow?

10 上海的天氣和台灣一樣嗎？
Is it the same weather in Shanghai as it is here in Taiwan?

11 你習慣台灣的氣候嗎？
Are you used to the weather in Taiwan?

12 天氣什麼時候放晴？
When will it clear up?

13 這裡的冬天經常下雪嗎？
Does it snow often here in the wintertime?

14 明天的 降雨機率 是多少？
What's the chance of rain tomorrow?

150 樂透…。

1 我從沒買過樂透。
I've never played the lottery.

2 我每星期買樂透。
I play the lottery every week.

3 買樂透可以 自己選號 。
You can pick your own lottery numbers.

4 也可以由電腦選號。
Or you can choose numbers with a computer.

5 樂透彩可以增加政府的收入。
The lottery can increase the government's revenue.

6 中了樂透我一定馬上辭職。
I'll quit once I hit the jackpot.

7 我每期 都槓龜 。
I miss the jackpot every time.

8 樂透彩造就很多 百萬富翁 。
The lottery has made many multimillionaires.

9 一張樂透彩五十元。
The cost of each ticket is fifty NT.

10 我 中過兩次 樂透。
I've won the lottery twice.

11 如果這次沒人中獎，獎金就累積到下次。
If no one hits the jackpot, then it carries over to next time.

12 樂透彩是合法的。
The lottery is legal.

13 這一期的頭彩獎金已經 累計到 十億元。
This time the jackpot is up to one billion NT.

14 有人告訴我這組號碼 中獎機率高 。
Someone told me this combination is sure to win.

15 這間彩券行曾經 開出過頭獎 。
Someone hit the jackpot from this vendor before.

150 你覺得樂透…？

❶ 哪裡可以買 到樂透？
   Where can I get a lottery ticket?

❷ 你買過樂透嗎？
   Have you bought any lottery tickets?

❸ 你自己選號嗎？
   Do you pick the numbers yourself?

❹ 你用 電腦選號 嗎？
   Do you let the computer pick the numbers for you?

❺ 你一次買幾張樂透彩券？
   How many tickets do you get at a time?

❻ 你每星期買樂透嗎？
   Do you put money into the lottery every week?

❼ 樂透 什麼時候開獎 ？
   When are they going to run the lottery?

❽ 樂透的獎金是多少？
   How much is the prize of the lottery?

❾ 樂透是 合法活動 嗎？
   Is the lottery a legal activity?

❿ 樂透之外，還有其他的彩券嗎？
   Are there any other kinds of raffles besides the lottery?

⓫ 樂透要 如何對獎 ？
   How do I check to see if I've won?

⓬ 樂透一張多少錢？
   How much is it for one lottery ticket?

⓭ 台灣人熱衷 樂透嗎？
   Are Taiwanese people into the lottery?

⓮ 有沒有 明牌 可以告訴我？
   Is there a sign from God that can tell me the
   winning numbers?

⓯ 你中過樂透獎嗎？
   Have you ever won the lottery?

151 旅遊…。

❶ 我喜歡自助旅行。
 I like to travel on my own.

❷ 跟團比較方便。
 It's more convenient to go with a group.

❸ 我通常參加旅行團。
 I usually go with travel groups.

❹ 我 每年出國 旅遊一次。
 I go abroad for touring every year.

❺ 出國旅遊 安全最重要 。
 Safety is the top concern when going abroad.

❻ 出國前最好 先訂好旅館 。
 You'd better take care of the hotel reservation
 before leaving the country.

❼ 自助旅行未必比較便宜。
 Traveling independently does not necessarily cost
 less.

❽ 出國前最好先收集一些旅遊資訊。
 You'd better gather together some travel
 information before going abroad.

❾ 很多人 利用年節 出國旅遊。
 Many people go abroad during the New Year's
 holiday.

❿ 旅遊品質是 一分錢一分貨 。
 When you travel, you get what you pay for.

⓫ 國內旅遊的費用並不便宜。
 The cost of domestic tourism isn't cheap at all.

⓬ 我喜歡精緻旅遊，不喜歡 走馬看花 。
 I prefer having a nice trip to giving only a passing
 glance at things.

151 你覺得旅遊…?

1 你喜歡旅遊嗎？
Do you like to travel?

2 你 去過哪幾個 國家？
Which countries have you been to?

3 你最喜歡哪個地方？
What's your top choice?

4 你今年有旅遊計畫嗎？
Have you got any travel plans for this year?

5 你 最想去哪一個 國家旅遊？
Which country is your top choice?

6 你多久安排一趟出國旅遊？
How often do you arrange trips abroad?

7 這趟旅遊你 花了多少錢 ？
How much did you pay for this trip?

8 你會避開 旅遊旺季 嗎？
Do you avoid the peak travel season?

9 這次你的旅遊預算是多少？
What's your budget for this trip?

10 你喜歡 跟團 還是 自助旅行 ？
Do you prefer going with a group or going by yourself?

11 你喜歡國內旅遊還是國外旅遊？
Do you prefer domestic travel or foreign tours?

12 這次旅遊你打算 去多久 ？
For how long do you plan to go this time?

13 國內旅遊 會比較便宜嗎？
Will a domestic tour be cheaper?

14 自助旅行是不是很危險？
Is it dangerous to travel on one's own?

15 台灣每年很多人出國旅遊嗎？
Do a lot of Taiwanese people travel abroad every year?

152 健康….。

1 我最近睡得很安穩。
Lately I've been sleeping soundly.

2 病況 算是控制住了。
I have the condition under control for now.

3 我盡量讓自己的生活變得規律。
I'm trying to keep more regular hours.

4 我還是經常頭痛。
I still get headaches constantly.

5 我今天的 精神很好 。
I'm full of vitality today.

6 肥胖是不健康的前兆。
Obesity is a sign of unhealthiness.

7 年紀大了 不能熬夜。
Avoid staying up late once you reach a certain age.

8 每天五種蔬果身體會更健康。
Eating five kinds of fruits and vegetables every day
makes you healthy.

9 失眠 在台灣已經成為很多人的問題。
Insomnia has become a problem for many people
in Taiwan.

10 最近經常 腰酸背痛 。
I've been getting pains in my waist and back for
some time.

11 各種污染是讓人不健康的主因。
All this pollution is a major cause of unhealthiness.

12 人過三十身體差很多。
You can't keep the same shape once you pass thirty.

13 癌症算是現代人的 文明病 。
Cancer's a disease of modern civilization.

14 健康是人生 最大的財富 。
Health is the greatest wealth in life.

152 你覺得健康⋯?

❶ 最近好嗎？
How have you been lately?

❷ 最近精神好點了嗎？
Have you been more energetic?

❸ 病情 好點了嗎 ？
Are you getting any better?

❹ 你還是經常熬夜嗎？
Do you still stay up late often?

❺ 你的 生活規律 嗎？
Do you keep regular hours?

❻ 你有經常在做運動嗎？
Do you exercise regularly?

❼ 你有定期做 健康檢查 嗎？
Do you get health examinations regularly?

❽ 有 去看醫生 嗎？
Have you gone to the doctor?

❾ 你去看病醫生怎麼說？
What did the doctor say?

❿ 最近睡得好嗎？
Have you been sleeping well lately?

⓫ 你有覺得 哪裡不舒服 嗎？
Is there anywhere on your body that feels
uncomfortable?

⓬ 要不要 我陪你去 看醫生？
Do you want me to go to the doctor with you?

⓭ 你以前身體會有這種感覺嗎？
Have you felt like this before?

⓮ 現代人 罹患癌症 的人愈來愈多？
Are there more and more people getting cancer in
modern times?

333

153 政治…。

❶ 我 無黨無派 。
I have no political affiliation.

❷ 我沒有加入任何政黨。
I haven't joined any political party.

❸ 許多人 熱衷政治 。
Many people are passionate about politics.

❹ 現在的年輕人越來越不關心政治。
Young people nowadays show more and more indifference to politics.

❺ 有些人對政治 漠不關心 。
Some people are apathetic about politics.

❻ 許多政治人物令人失望。
Many politicians disappoint people.

❼ 每一個政黨都有各自的支持者。
Each party has its own supporters.

❽ 我支持執政黨。
I support the ruling party.

❾ 政治和黑金 常常扯上關係。
Politics is often linked to corruption.

❿ 政局會影響經濟。
The political situation will affect the economy.

⓫ 台灣每四年舉行一次總統大選。
A presidential election is held in Taiwan once every four years.

⓬ 在野黨和執政黨總是 對立 。
The opposition party is always against the ruling party.

⓭ 許多政治人物 愛作秀 。
Many politicians love to show off.

⓮ 真正 替人民做事 的政治人物實在不多。
There are not many politicians who really serve the people.

153 你覺得政治…?

❶ 你熱衷政治嗎?
Are you passionate about politics?

❷ 你 支持哪一個 政黨?
Which political party do you support?

❸ 你支持 執政黨 還是 在野黨 ?
Do you support the ruling party or the opposition party?

❹ 你對政治完全沒興趣嗎?
Are you not interested in politics at all?

❺ 每次選舉你都前往投票嗎?
Do you vote in every election?

❻ 你今年 有投票嗎 ?
Did you vote this year?

❼ 你曾 被賄選 嗎?
Have you ever sold your vote?

❽ 你贊成統一還是獨立?
Do you support either unification or independence?

❾ 你相信政治人物的話嗎?
Do you believe what politicians say?

❿ 你覺得民意代表真的 為民喉舌 嗎?
Do you think that the public representatives really speak for the people?

⓫ 你最欣賞的政治人物是誰?
Who is your favorite politician?

⓬ 你關心 立法問題 嗎?
Are you concerned about legislative issues?

⓭ 你常看 call-in 節目嗎?
Do you often watch those call-in shows?

⓮ 你曾參與 示威遊行 嗎?
Have you participated in a protest march?

154 治安…。

1 今天我接到一通 詐騙電話 。
I received a fraudulent phone call today.

2 治安越來越差了。
Public security is getting worse and worse.

3 詐騙案件越來越多。
Fraud is becoming more and more frequent.

4 應召場所 到處充斥。
Prostitution is everywhere.

5 超商在晚上經常被搶。
Convenience stores usually get robbed at night.

6 現在的歹徒是 愈來愈囂張 了。
These days criminals are getting more and more insolent.

7 現在的歹徒連警察也敢殺。
Criminals nowadays even dare to kill police officers.

8 手機和網路讓犯罪變得更容易。
Mobile phones and the Internet make it easier to commit crimes.

9 很多壞人都 逍遙法外 。
Many lowlifes stay out of the law's reach.

10 綁票現在是司空見慣。
Nowadays kidnapping is a common occurrence.

11 輟學 的青少年造成不少治安問題。
Juveniles who drop out of school cause many of the problems in public security.

12 晚上最好不要 在外面逗留 。
It's better not to stay outside at night.

13 現代人要學會 自我保護 。
Modern people have to learn to protect themselves.

154 你覺得治安…？

❶ 你覺得社會治安好嗎？
Do you think public security is good or not?

❷ 為什麼治安越來越差？
Why is public security getting worse and worse?

❸ 你家 有裝保全 嗎？
Do you have a security system in your home?

❹ 你覺得警察能保護人民嗎？
Do you think the police can protect the people?

❺ 你這麼晚回家安全嗎？
Is it safe for you to return home so late?

❻ 夜晚你 敢一個人出門 嗎？
Do you dare to go out alone at night?

❼ 你家附近的治安好嗎？
Is the public security around your neighborhood good?

❽ 報警 有用嗎？
Is making a report to the police any use?

❾ 你接過詐騙集團的電話嗎？
Have you ever received a phone call from scammers?

❿ 你 曾經受騙 匯款給詐騙集團嗎？
Were you ever tricked into remitting money to swindlers?

⓫ 你家附近常有警察 巡邏 嗎？
Do the police often patrol your neighborhood?

⓬ 聽說又發生 銀行搶案 ？
I heard that another bank was robbed today.

⓭ 你認為警察 能破案嗎 ？
Do you think the police can solve crimes?

⓮ 今天發生警匪槍戰嗎？
Were there any shootouts between the criminals and police today?

155 貧與富…。

❶ 有錢人一餐可以花上幾萬元。
The rich can spend tens of thousands on a meal.

❷ 現在社會 笑貧不笑娼 。
Society nowadays laughs at the poor, not the streetwalker.

❸ 有些人連小孩的營養午餐費都繳不出來。
Some people can't even pay their children's lunch money.

❹ 納稅人都是辛苦的 薪水階級 。
The taxpayers make up the hard-working salaried class.

❺ 社會上 貧富差距 越來越大。
The gap between the poor and the rich is getting wider and wider in our society.

❻ 窮人家 的孩子沒機會受到更好的教育。
Children of the poor don't have the opportunity to receive a better education.

❼ 很多人因為活不下去而自殺。
Many people have committed suicide because they couldn't handle their lives.

❽ 很多人 三餐不繼 。
Many people live in want.

❾ 有些窮人因媒體報導而獲得幫助。
Some poor people get help because of media reports.

❿ 物價越來越高 ，等於薪水越來越薄。
Rising commodity prices equal smaller salaries.

⓫ 很多人沒有房子可住。
Many people don't have a house to live in.

⓬ 我沒有錢，但我很快樂。
I don't have money, but I'm happy.

155 你覺得貧與富…？

❶ 台灣的貧富差距越來越大了嗎？
Is the gap between rich and poor widening?

❷ 羨慕有錢人 嗎？
Do you envy the rich?

❸ 為什麼有些人那麼有錢？
Why are some people so rich?

❹ 為什麼有那麼多 流浪漢 ？
Why are there so many homeless people?

❺ 台灣有完善的 社會福利 制度嗎？
Does Taiwan have a well-developed social welfare system?

❻ 你 定期捐款 給慈善團體嗎？
Do you regularly donate to charity?

❼ 你覺得政府應該多照顧窮人嗎？
Do you think that the government should take better care of the poor?

❽ 你覺得要對富人課更重的稅嗎？
Do you think that it is necessary to levy higher taxes on the rich?

❾ 這是一個 金錢決定一切 的年代嗎？
Is this the era of "money talks?"

❿ 窮人真的是因為不夠努力嗎？
Is it true that the poor don't work hard enough?

⓫ 你覺得你的 生活富裕嗎 ？
Do you feel like your life is rich?

⓬ 你會捐錢給路邊的乞丐嗎？
Do you give change to beggars on the roadside?

⓭ 有錢人一定 比窮人快樂 嗎？
Are the rich definitely happier than the poor?

156 青少年問題…。

1 家庭是青少年問題的起因。
The family is the origin of the juvenile problem.

2 現在的青少年都 太早熟 了。
Youth today mature too early.

3 社會應該幫助 中輟生 重返校園。
Society should help dropout students return to school.

4 教條式的規範青少年很難接受。
Young people do not take well to dogmatic discipline.

5 我不知道如何和我的孩子溝通。
I don't know how to communicate with my children.

6 很多青少年都有 翹家 的經驗。
Many youths have had the experience of running away from home.

7 現在的青少年要面對的問題比過去更多。
Youth nowadays are facing far more problems than before.

8 部分青少年對毒品沒有抵抗力。
Some young people don't have the strength to avoid drugs.

9 現在的青少年簡直是 目無尊長 。
Young people nowadays are simply rude.

10 青少年需要家長與老師更多關心。
Youth need more care from parents and teachers.

11 青少年對性有許多 錯誤的觀念 。
There are many mistaken ideas that juveniles have about sex.

12 青少年時期朋友的影響力很大。
The friends of one's youth are very influential.

13 很多少女靠 援交 賺生活費。
Many young girls make a living by prostitution.

14 不健全的家庭 容易教育出問題青年。
Unhealthy families often produce troubled youths.

156 你覺得青少年問題…？

❶ 現在的年輕人 出了什麼問題 ？
What is the problem with young people nowadays?

❷ 現在的年輕人為什麼動不動就自殺？
Why do more young people nowadays commit suicide?

❸ 為什麼青少年問題越來越嚴重？
Why is the youth problem getting more and more serious?

❹ 不知道青少年為什麼 愛飆車 。
We really don't know why young people love joyriding.

❺ 真不知道現在的青少年 在想什麼 。
I really don't know what teenagers today are thinking.

❻ 現在的青少年壓力太大了嗎？
Are young people nowadays under too much pressure?

❼ 要如何加強青少年的 性教育 ？
How can sexual education for the youth be strengthened?

❽ 為什麼小孩有心事都不對我說？
Why do my kids not want to tell me what is on their minds?

❾ 你能和你的孩子溝通嗎？
Can you communicate with your child?

❿ 為什麼青少年會 染上毒癮 ？
Why do teenagers become addicted to drugs?

⓫ 我不知道我的孩子究竟在想什麼。
I don't know what my child is thinking at all.

⓬ 怎麼樣才能讓孩子跟我溝通？
How can I get my kids to communicate with me?

⓭ 為什麼青少年嚮往 加入幫派 ？
Why do juveniles look forward to joining a gang?

⓮ 為什麼那麼多青少年 徹夜不歸 ？
Why are there so many young people who don't return home at night?

157 上班族…。

❶ 70％的人都是上班族。
About 70% of people belong to the commuter class.

❷ 領薪 是上班族最期待的。
Payday is the most highly anticipated day for working people.

❸ 加班是上班族的夢魘。
Working overtime is the nightmare of the commuter class.

❹ 跳槽 是上班族的定律。
Switching companies is the law of the commuter class.

❺ 有些上班族也有 業績壓力 。
Some working people have to deal with the stress of performance expectations.

❻ 我大學畢業後就成為上班族。
I became part of the commuter class after I graduated from college.

❼ 上班族必須 按時上下班 。
A member of the commuter class must be punctual at work.

❽ 上班族 過勞死 的問題時有耳聞。
The problem of karoshi, or death from overwork, has been heard of among the commuter class from time to time.

❾ 商業午餐是針對上班族設計的。
Commercial lunch menus are designed for the commuter class.

❿ 週休二日 是上班族的福音。
The weekend is the blessing of the commuter class.

⓫ 上班族的職業病也不少。
Commuters also have their share of occupational illnesses.

⓬ 上班族必須忍受 擁擠的捷運 。
The commuter class has to put up with the crowded MRT.

157 你覺得上班族…?

1 畢業後你希望當一個上班族嗎？
Do you want to be part of the commuter class after graduating from school?

2 你是個快樂的上班族嗎？
Are you a contented member of the commuter class?

3 你是個愛聊八卦的上班族嗎？
Are you a commuter who likes to gossip?

4 你 擔心裁員 減薪嗎？
Do you worry about layoffs and pay cuts?

5 你有上班族的 職業病 嗎？
Do you have an occupational disease common among the commuter class?

6 你成為上班族多久了？
How long have you been a member of the commuter class?

7 如果可以選擇，你寧願不上班嗎？
Would you rather not go to work if you could choose not to?

8 你擔心自己過勞嗎？
Do you worry about being overworked?

9 你做好 退休規畫 了嗎？
Have you already made your retirement plan?

10 你擔心自己喪失競爭力嗎？
Do you worry about losing your competitiveness?

11 你覺得職場上 男女平等 嗎？
Do you think that gender equality exists in the workforce?

12 你擔心長江 後浪推前浪 嗎？
Do you worry about being outdone by younger generations?

13 你有 職業倦怠 嗎？
Do you feel tired of your job?

158 失業…。

❶ 失業率越來越高。
The unemployment rate is getting higher and higher.

❷ 許多公司 進行縮編 ，精簡人力。
Many companies are in the process of laying off and downsizing.

❸ 很多人一直找不到工作。
Many people can't find a job at all.

❹ 父母親失業，很多家庭陷入 經濟危機 。
Many families fall into economic crisis due to the parents being out of work.

❺ 中年失業 令人同情。
Middle-aged unemployment is a pitiable situation.

❻ 失業經常是自殺的原因之一。
Unemployment is often one of the reasons for suicide.

❼ 工廠外移 到大陸，許多員工被裁員。
Many employees are laid off due to factories having moved to mainland China.

❽ 公司 惡性倒閉 ，員工都沒領到薪水。
Employees haven't received their salaries due to vicious company shutdowns.

❾ 失業會造成嚴重的社會問題。
Unemployment will cause serious social problems.

❿ 政府舉辦了 失業勞工 訓練課程。
The government has a training program for unemployed laborers.

⓫ 我每個月領 失業救濟金 。
I receive an unemployment relief check every month.

⓬ 公司發給我三個月的遣散費。
My company compensated me for my dismissal with three months' pay.

158 你覺得失業…？

❶ 你為什麼失業？
Why are you unemployed?

❷ 你 失業多久 了？
How long have you been unemployed?

❸ 你被老闆 炒魷魚 了？
Did you get fired by your boss?

❹ 你有領到失業救濟金嗎？
Have you claimed any unemployment relief funds?

❺ 台灣的 失業率高 嗎？
Is the unemployment rate high in Taiwan?

❻ 國外的失業率比台灣高嗎？
Are the unemployment rates of foreign countries higher than Taiwan's?

❼ 你有 找工作 嗎？
Have you looked for a job?

❽ 你有領到 遣散費 嗎？
Did you get compensated for your dismissal?

❾ 政府有實際措施解決失業問題嗎？
Are there any practical methods that the government has proposed to solve the unemployment problem?

❿ 失業了沒收入你怎麼辦？
What will you do if you're unemployed and without any income?

⓫ 政府對失業勞工有任何 補助 嗎？
Are there any subsidies the government gives to the unemployed?

⓬ 家庭生活 還過得去嗎 ？
Is your family life tolerable?

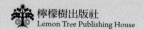
檸檬樹出版社
Lemon Tree Publishing House

小冊系列 E02

實用英語會話大全【mini book】：
靈活運用英語必備的4,500句會話（附 透明書套＋檢測學習遮色片）

初版 1 刷　2015 年 2 月 6 日

作者	王琪
英語審訂	郝凱楊（NICHOLAS B. HAWKINS）
封面設計‧版型設計	陳文德‧洪素貞
責任編輯	蔡依婷
協力編輯	黃冠禎

發行人	江媛珍
社長‧總編輯	何聖心
出版者	檸檬樹國際書版有限公司 檸檬樹出版社
	E-mail：lemontree@booknews.com.tw
	地址：新北市235中和區中安街80號3樓
	電話‧傳真：02-29271121‧02-29272336
會計‧客服	方靖淳
法律顧問	第一國際法律事務所 余淑杏律師
	北辰著作權事務所 蕭雄淋律師

全球總經銷‧印務代理	知遠文化事業有限公司
網路書城	http://www.booknews.com.tw 博訊書網
	電話：02-26648800　傳真：02-26648801
	地址：新北市222深坑區北深路三段155巷25號5樓

港澳地區經銷	和平圖書有限公司
	電話：852-28046687　傳真：850-28046409
	地址：香港柴灣嘉業街12號百樂門大廈17樓

定價	台幣280元／港幣93元
劃撥帳號	戶名：19726702‧檸檬樹國際書版有限公司
	‧單次購書金額未達300元，請另付40元郵資
	‧信用卡‧劃撥購書需7-10個工作天

實用英語會話大全 mini book / 王琪作.
-- 初版. -- 新北市：檸檬樹, 2015.02
面；　公分. -- (小冊系列；E02)
ISBN 978-986-6703-88-1（平裝）

1.英語 2.會話

805.188　　　　　　　　　　103020541

檸檬樹出版

檸檬樹出版